ALSO BY EDWARD BLOOR—

TANGERINE

CRUSADER

STORY TIME

LONDON CALLING

TAKEN

A PLAGUE YEAR

SUMMER OF SMOKE

CANDLEMAS EVE

CENTENNIAL

FIRESIDE CHATS

MEMORY

LANE

Chapbook Press

Schuler Books
2660 28th Street SE
Grand Rapids, MI 49512
(616) 942-7330
www.schulerbooks.com

www.edwardbloor.net

Memory Lane

ISBN 13: 9781966196495

Library of Congress Control Number: 2025922586

Printed in the United States by Chapbook Press.

For Pam, Amanda, and Spencer—

the first circle

Memory Lane

Vacation Destination

Ronkonkoma, New York

Guests

Chapter 1

Most stories begin with the arrival of something that doesn't belong; something that upsets the status quo. For me, that something was the paperboy.

First of all, we don't get a paper. Most of our neighbors don't, either. And if they do, it arrives in a speeding van, just before dawn, with a phantom driver at the wheel. It does not arrive in the basket of a shiny red bike, at midmorning, with a cute boy at the handlebars. I'll bet there hadn't been a paperboy riding through the neighborhood in thirty years. Yet there he was, at 9:30 on a Sunday morning, capturing my attention; not belonging; upsetting the status quo.

So I'll begin with him.

I was outside waiting to drive to church with my grandparents, the perpetually late John and Margaret Abel. They were still inside, probably because of a lost set of car keys, or a lost pair of glasses, but the possibilities were almost limitless.

I was staring absently at their house. It's a large two-story Cape Cod, covered with dark gray and white shingles that mildew whenever it rains. This always prompts my grandmother to climb up on a stepladder with a stiff brush and a bucket of Mr. Clean.

As I waited, I slowly became aware of a sound—a rhythmic, soft, slapping sound. I turned and looked east down

Blacksmith Road and, in the distance, I saw the thing that didn't belong.

A paperboy.

He was heading my way in a slow, deliberate, criss-crossing pattern, maneuvering a bright red bike that I would soon learn was a 1955 Schwinn Racer. It had a big wire basket in front from which the boy was pulling out newspapers and tossing them onto each lawn.

I stepped down to the edge of the driveway and focused in on his face, quickly realizing that I knew him. Douglas Zorn. He had gone to Jonas Salk Middle School a few years ahead of me.

That got me more interested. (I should mention here that, like my mother, I am a bit taller than average. Unlike my mother, I'd rather not be, so I compressed my spine, lowered my head, and waited for him.) By the time Douglas Zorn finally noticed me, I had managed a surprised, *What are you doing here?* grin. He hurled one more paper onto a neighbor's lawn and pulled to a stop in front of me.

He was quite tall, so I relaxed. He wasn't grinning, though, and he got immediately to the point. "Hi, Alice. I was really sorry to hear about your mother."

My smile faded away. "Thank you."

"She was real nice."

I muttered, "Yeah."

"She used to walk me down to speech therapy at Gardiners

Avenue Elementary." He added, somewhat doubtfully, "I guess I had a lisp. Mrs. Lynch was a real nice lady."

"Yeah." I changed the subject. "So what are you doing now?"

It took a moment for Douglas to stop frowning. He finally said, "I'm at Division High." I must have looked puzzled. We exchanged blank stares for a moment; then he pointed at the bicycle basket. "Oh. Do you mean *right* now?"

"Yeah."

"Sorry. I'm, uh, working. I'm delivering fliers for Memory Lane." He held up an advertisement that was fashioned to look like a newspaper.

(I should point out that I already knew about Memory Lane. My mom had scoped it out for my grandparents' fiftieth wedding anniversary, but I played dumb to keep Douglas talking.) I asked, "Memory Lane, huh? What's that?"

He pointed at the brochure and told me, with genuine enthusiasm, "It's a vacation destination, a new kind of theme park! Really, a totally new concept. Like nothing you've ever heard of before. "

"Uh huh."

"They've got three in the Midwest, but this is the first one in the East."

And although I knew the answer to the next question, too, I prompted him with undetectable stupidity. "Oh? Where is it?"

"It's out near the airport, in Ronkonkoma." Douglas's

enthusiasm bubbled over again. "It's awesome! They, like, completely immerse you in a time period. They completely change your reality."

A change of reality sounded good to me. I took a flier, folded it up, and stuck it in my dress pocket. I asked Douglas, "So, what do you do there?"

"Different stuff. Today I'm doing field marketing, dropping off fliers about our soft opening. They've targeted your neighborhood as a place where people would remember the 1950s, right?"

I looked back at my grandparents' house. "Yes. That's right."

"So they have me on a 1955 Schwinn Racer. And I talk to people about stuff from that era—all the stuff that was hot back then, you know? Like Marilyn Monroe. And Elvis."

"Uh huh."

"And I'm meeting the family who'll be starring in our new marketing campaign. That should be exciting—" Douglas suddenly caught himself, like he was ashamed. "Not that you're thinking about vacation parks, I know."

I nodded somberly. He started to back away. I didn't want him to go, so I asked, "How did you get the job?"

Douglas stopped pedaling. "My sister. She's a hotshot with the company. She's making the big bucks. She started at the original park, outside of St. Louis. Just doing stuff like I'm doing now. Anything and everything, you know? And now she's back here, opening up this new park."

"That's great."

It seemed to me, for a split second, that Douglas's eyes traveled up and down the length of my body, like he was checking me out. But then his eyes darted behind me, very quickly, like he had seen something move. Something disturbing.

I turned and followed his gaze toward the garage. My grandfather was standing there. And he had the strangest look on his face—half bewildered, half angry. (I was used to the bewildered part, but why was he angry?) He had a set of car keys dangling in his left hand. His right hand was raised up and pointing threateningly at Douglas. He warned him, "You clear out! Do you hear me? Clear out of here!"

Douglas's head snapped up and away, recoiling from the raspy old voice. He backpedaled a few more feet. He shot a quick glance at me, as if to ask, *What did I do?* The best I could manage was a puzzled shrug. Douglas pushed down on the pedal and rolled forward, heading south on Potters Road. My grandfather then stomped into the house, presumably to tell my grandmother that he had found the missing keys. Or that he had scared off a paperboy.

Bizarre.

Some days, my grandfather is just fine. He asks me how I am, how school is, and so on. Some days, he is not fine, and he stares at me like he just did at Douglas Zorn. Like I am an intruder on his property. Some days, my grandmother is fine, too, and she speaks to me kindly. But mostly she is off in her own world, either sitting in front of a blaring TV watching soap operas or cleaning those white shingles. (My Mom had a secret name for her, a name that I was never, ever, to use in front of anyone. She called her *Mrs. Clean.*)

I continued to watch Douglas throw newspapers on lawns, without incident. But then he reached the McCains' house—a run-down, overgrown, eyesore of a place. I had known about the McCains long before I had moved in here. Everyone in the neighborhood, including my grandparents, shunned them.

Even my mom shunned them, but for her own reason. She particularly despised Dennis McCain. He had once accused her of pushing him at Jonas Salk Middle, but that's another story. She called Dennis 'a coat holder,' meaning he tried to instigate fights for his cousin Matt and then stand there holding his coat. What a creep.

The McCains had a large, dysfunctional family. There were always several dilapidated cars in the driveway and several unpleasant-looking people hanging out on the lawn, including the two I was watching—Dennis and Matt.

While Dennis was more of a snake, lying and manipulative, Matt was openly aggressive and violent. My mom said Matt had a psychiatric condition called Conduct Disorder. I'm sure she was right. Kids all over Levittown knew him, or knew of him, and kept far away.

Unfortunately, that wasn't an option for Douglas Zorn who had just thrown a newspaper at him. From my vantage point, I could see events unfolding very clearly. Matt McCain—light-haired and muscular, about seventeen years old—was holding a newspaper under Douglas's chin like a knife blade, while Dennis—darker-haired and more rodent-like—was holding the handlebars of the bike, preventing it from moving. Douglas, clearly frightened, seemed to be nodding and agreeing to something.

Suddenly, I heard my grandparents' car start up behind me. They drove a big, white Cadillac Deville. (Actually, only my grandmother drove it. My grandfather was less and less capable of doing anything complicated.) I walked over to the car, pulled open the rear door, and climbed in. I said, "I think there's some trouble at the McCains."

Neither of my grandparents seemed to hear me, which was pretty common. My grandmother put the clunky old car into gear and turned right on Potters Road. Through the front window, I could see that Matt and Dennis McCain were still messing with Douglas, but our big car just kept rolling past them. I watched my grandmother's eyes in the mirror. She never even gave them a glance.

I did, though. And I thought immediately of my mom. She would have stopped the car and stopped the bullying, no question, no matter how big or how psycho the bullies were.

My mom was fearless like that. I thought of one of Mom's

favorite quotes. It's from Dear Abby, who, I would soon learn, started publishing quotes in 1956: "The best index to a person's character is (1) how he treats people who can't do him any good, and (2) how he treats people who can't fight back." That was the best index to the McCains' character, all right.

We drove in silence down Jerusalem Avenue toward the Hempstead Turnpike, soon passing the Dalton Funeral Home. I remembered sitting and waiting in that parking lot while a man in a black suit attached *Funeral* flags to all the cars. I remembered cars starting their engines and lining up, like for a small-town parade. I remembered the hearse pulling out slowly, stopping all traffic. And I remembered the last car that made it through. It had a yellow bumper sticker that said: *A drunk driver killed my child, and I'm MADD.*

A few minutes later, we pulled into the parking lot at St. Bernard's Catholic Church. A white Hyundai SUV was already idling there with my aunt, uncle, and cousins inside. I suppressed an urge to look away. That's what Mom and I did whenever we caught sight of them—on the road, in a parking lot, wherever. We avoided them. They were just too weird.

But now these same people, the Blanchards, were the only family I had left—along with the old, stone-faced, silent couple in the front seat. Did Mom ever think this moment would come when I would have to accept these people as my family? I doubt it. Yet here I was, with no choice but to move in with them.

I climbed out of the car and walked over to the SUV. Uncle Jim had the window rolled down, and I could hear him muttering an advertising jingle, "Best of all, it's a Cadillac." Uncle Jim is from Chicago. He's a rabid Notre Dame football fan. Lately (this is according to my mom), his football watching and beer drinking have caught up with him. He has a gut, and the capillaries in his cheeks and nose have burst, giving him a permanently wind-burned look.

My cousin Patrick stirred behind him in the back seat. Patrick is two years older than me. He is a big guy—stocky, and ruddy, and round. He looks like Uncle Jim in younger days.

My cousin TJ, Thomas James, was sitting across the car from Patrick. He closed up a notebook and smiled at me. TJ is a year younger than me. He is, as they say, 'all Aunt Betty,' thin and slight, with clear white skin, beautiful blue eyes, and blonde hair. He is so ridiculously good-looking that people assume he is a model.

Mom had another favorite quote: "You can choose your friends, but not your family." Well, I couldn't even do that. My dad's half of the family was all gone. Every one of them. Anybody I had left to choose was sitting right here in this parking lot.

After some muttered hellos, we shuffled inside and took our places in the front of the church. This was a ritual that my grandparents had repeated for fifty years, sitting up in the first pew. I was not comfortable with that at all. Mom and I didn't really go to mass, so it was awkward whenever I had to make the responses. Sometimes I faked it, moving my lips and muttering. Today, I didn't even bother. The priest had such a heavy Spanish accent that the mass could have been in Latin for all I knew. I literally did not understand a word. Instead, I let myself drift off into my own thoughts, into my own memories.

My memories are very important to me now. They are, basically, all I have left of my parents. The first memory I had that morning was about my mother. Here it is: Mom had driven me to Jonas Salk Middle School, as usual, on the last day of her life. While inching ahead in the drop-off circle, she explained that she had to drive to the School Board office at 9:00 am. They were deciding whether a boy named Roger would be allowed to return to school or would be expelled. The last words she said to me were, "Is pizza okay for dinner?"

I answered, "Sure."

After that, she leaned over and placed a light kiss on my cheek. I never saw her again. Not alive anyway.

Her death had made me a full orphan. I had been a half-orphan before that, since the age of three. That's when my father died.

I have a faint memory of him carrying me around on his shoulders. I remember having to duck under an archway. I think it was in our old apartment. But I also have a photo of the two of us under an archway, and my mother told me he used to carry me around like that, so I don't know if that memory is real.

I do have a strong, real memory of him, though. Here it is: He is standing in front of a switch in our old kitchen, preparing to turn off the lights. Mom rounds the corner carrying a chocolate birthday cake with glowing yellow candles and sets it in front of me. I know that is a real memory. It's too good to be made up.

After the mass ended, my grandparents headed straight to their car, and Uncle Jim and Patrick headed to theirs. For some reason, Aunt Betty and TJ got in line to speak to the priest. (In Spanish?) I didn't know what to do, so I just stood around, staring blankly at the parking lot. That's when I had a final, very troubling memory from long ago—ten years, at least. Here it is: Mom and I were standing right there, in the church parking lot, on one of our rare visits. Aunt Betty and Patrick were standing next to us. Aunt Betty and Mom were *screaming* at each other. Really screaming. But I couldn't remember their words. What were they so upset about? They had always spoken to each other coolly—on the phone, in public, at family gatherings. So why, in this one scene, were they in each other's faces, spewing words that my three-year-old self had never heard before, and could not understand?

This memory was interrupted, suddenly, by my cousin TJ. He came up next to me holding up the church announcements.

He said, "Look at the names of the people who died this month. They're all like *Walter This* and *Esther That*. Who names their kid Walter, or Esther?"

I shook my head to clear my thoughts. I finally replied, "What?"

"Who names their kids that?"

"What?"

"Walter and Esther."

"I don't know. Old people? Dead people?"

"Yeah." TJ crinkled his perfect nose. "Here's an Ethel. And an Ernest. Who would do that to a child?"

I shook my head. "Well, I have to tell you, Alice isn't much better."

"Oh it is," he assured me. "It's much better."

"No. I researched it. It's really old."

TJ repeated curiously, "You researched it?"

"Yes. My name peaked in popularity in 1880, at number eight. Then it began a steady slide. It dropped into the one hundreds in the 1950s, the two hundreds in the 1960s, the three hundreds in the 1980s. You get the picture."

TJ nodded thoughtfully. "Yeah. Names do come and go, like fashions. They say, 'What's in a name?' but, you know, they really do matter. There *is* such a thing as a Patrick, and my brother happens to be one. Just as there is such a thing as an Ashley, a George, a Sofia. Some people get seriously *misnamed*, and it is seriously traumatic for them. You can be a

Madison trapped in a Mary Lou's body, like one of those poor transsexual guys you see on Oprah. Instead of a sex change, though, you need a name change."

I suggested, "Maybe everyone should have a baby name, for ten or twelve years, and then get a grown-up name."

TJ nodded. "That's a good idea. Now how about you? Who were you named after?"

"My father. Sort of. He was Alex. Or Al."

"And I'm named for mine. Thomas. Not that he even uses it."

"What about Patrick?"

TJ explained, "He's named for our grandfather. He died when Dad was in college."

"I did not know that."

"He had some kind of cancer."

Aunt Betty finally joined us. She whispered, "Father Dunne took special classes to learn Spanish. You'd think these Spanish priests would bother to learn English."

I should explain here that Father Dunne is my grandmother's brother, 'the priest in the family.' He drives over from New Jersey to perform family weddings, baptisms, funerals. (Except for my parents' wedding. That was performed by a hotel manager in Atlantic City, something Mom used to bring up whenever she got mad at the church.)

I asked Aunt Betty, "Would it be all right if I rode back with you?"

We both looked at my grandparents' car. They were sitting inside with the motor running. Aunt Betty waved at my grandmother, pointed at me, and then at her Hyundai. My grandmother must have understood because she put her car in gear and pulled out, leaving me behind.

TJ and I joined the sleeping Patrick in the back. As she was climbing in, Aunt Betty leaned over the front seat and handed me a folded-up piece of paper. "Here, Alice. I found this last night in a magazine. This might be a good time for you to look at it." It was a glossy page with the title: *The Five Stages of Grief, from Elizabeth Kubler-Ross*. She just stared, waiting for me to read it, so I scanned it quickly.

The five stages of grief were: *denial, anger, bargaining, depression*, and *acceptance*. There were little explanations following each one, and here they are: *denial*—refusing to believe it is happening; *anger*—venting at the deceased or others; *bargaining*—trying to get something out of the situation; *depression*—giving up, crying; *acceptance*—Okay. This has happened. Let's move on.

I thought, *No. I'm not feeling any of these. Not really*. She seemed to be waiting for some reaction, though, so I looked up and said, "Thanks, Aunt Betty. I'll read this more carefully later."

Aunt Betty smiled sadly and turned to the front. She buckled her seatbelt, said, "Okay, Jim," and we pulled out into the light morning traffic.

I stared out the side window at my world. Every place we passed had a memory for me—the Pathmark where my father had worked; the Lord and Taylor Outlet where Mom and I had shopped; the apartment complex where I was born.

Soon, we stopped at a light across from a bar named Fighting Father Duffy's. Aunt Betty pointed to it. "Grandpop used to drink right over there. Father Dunne, too."

I said, "Really? A priest can go to a bar and drink?"

Aunt Betty shrugged. "Maybe he thought it was okay because the bar was named after a priest."

Uncle Jim suggested, "Maybe he just had a Coke."

"Maybe."

"It's the pause that refreshes."

Aunt Betty crinkled her nose. "What?"

"Coke. That was one of their ad slogans. Like: *It's the real thing*. And *Things go better with Coke*."

"Oh, yeah."

We rolled past Levittown cape houses with their crayon colors: powder blue, canary yellow, cinnamon brown, battleship gray. Finally, we were back on Potters Road and passing the squalor of the McCains' place. Matt and Dennis were still standing on the front lawn, still staring at the cars going by, still looking for trouble. What a pair of losers.

After he parked in the driveway, Uncle Jim hopped down, reached under the seat, and pulled out a Nerf football. As Patrick and TJ straggled out, he called to them. "Come on, guys. Let's toss this around for a few minutes. Let's work up an appetite for lunch."

Aunt Betty frowned. "You shouldn't over-exert, Jim. Not with your blood pressure."

Patrick looked stealthily down the street, toward the McCains. He didn't even answer his dad; he just walked inside. TJ at least said, "Not now, Dad. Maybe later."

The McCains sauntered out to the curb and leered at us. Matt McCain yelled over, "Hey! Can we play?"

Uncle Jim actually answered them, in a friendly way, like they were normal people. "I guess not. Maybe next time, guys."

Once inside. Aunt Betty and Uncle Jim turned into the kitchen. Aunt Betty announced, "We need to check Jim's blood pressure, Mom. I don't like how red he looks. Can we use Grandpop's cuff?"

Patrick, TJ, and I sat in the living room. They immediately fell into their usual routine, mocking each other back and forth. TJ pulled his blonde hair out to the sides and asked me, "Should I go blonder for public school, Alice? You know? Like surfer dude, with highlights?"

To which Patrick added, "Surfer dude, with I-like-guys-lights?"

TJ ignored him and pushed his hair straight up. "Or should I sweep into school wearing a truly bold statement? A Mohawk?"

To which Patrick added, "A ho-mo-hawk?"

TJ acted as if Patrick was not there, but I wasn't so inclined. I had already heard enough. I asked him, "Patrick, do you rehearse these things ahead of time?"

He looked at me dumbly. "What?"

TJ answered for him. "No. He just repeats, endlessly, like a bad burrito."

I shook my head, thinking, *This is my new family? Please, Mom, no. This is who you left me with? These two silly boys, locked in this silly banter? Silly, stupid, all the time?*

I could hear Aunt Betty's voice rise in the next room. She was talking breathlessly about Memory Lane, and that puzzled me. I looked from Patrick to TJ. "Isn't Memory Lane a really expensive place?"

TJ's eyes brightened. "Not to us!"

"Why?"

Patrick said, "Our grandmother died."

Patrick didn't elaborate, so TJ did. "The grandmother we never met; the one married to the cancer guy. She was in some nursing home in Illinois for, like, twenty years. She died last week and left money to Dad, and Dad seems to want to get rid of it, so Memory Lane is on."

"It's on? What does that mean? We're going there?"

TJ nodded.

"That's news to me. When would we go?"

TJ gestured toward the kitchen. "Mamà (He pronounced it

ma-mahh) brought a calendar with her today. It's one of those creepy St. Bernard's Parish calendars with names of, like, five saints on every day."

"Let's try that question again, TJ: When would we go?"

"Well, on their golden anniversary, of course! November the somethingth."

I clarified that. "November the 24th, 1957."

TJ smiled. "I *knew* you knew."

After a few more minutes, during which the three of us sat doing absolutely nothing, which seemed to be just fine with them, I took the initiative. "Do you guys want to hang out upstairs?"

TJ smiled brightly, showing symmetrical dimples. Patrick shrugged his large, rounded shoulders. Then they followed me up to my Mom's old room.

When I moved in here last month, my grandmother told me, "You can take your pick of the rooms upstairs. Betty's is bigger, but you can take Donna's if you want." What kind of choice was that? Of course I wanted Donna's room. And I set it up like my room back on Haven Lane, placing my bed, dresser, and computer desk in the exact same spots.

TJ sat on the bed, near the bottom, and started to bounce slightly. Patrick staked out a spot next to the window and peered out at the street. He said, "I remember when I was in fourth grade. Matt McCain was still in fifth. He'd been held back. He finally got kicked out of school that year."

I asked, "For what?"

"For being a freaking psycho!"

"Yeah? What did he do?"

"He did all kinds of stuff, every day. Like, every hour of every day. The whole school was scared of him. The teachers, too."

TJ bounced faster. "Tell us something specific."

"Let's see. He used to sneak up behind the fifth-grade girls and molest them. Is that specific enough?"

"No!" TJ answered. "Give us details. He would molest them how?"

Patrick squinted at him. "What?"

"I mean, are we talking about actual forcible rape here? Bodice ripping and all that?"

"Don't get so excited, T-Gay. He did this stuff to girls."

"What did he do to them?"

"What do you care?"

I broke in, "Come on, Patrick. You just said he's a psychotic girl molester. What exactly did he do?"

"He grabbed Kellie Russo from behind, I remember that. He felt her up, and then let her go. She turned around and tried to slap his face, but he blocked her hand. Then he slapped *her*, real hard, and she fell down on the asphalt. It was a pretty wild scene. Everybody came running over, teachers and all."

TJ stopped bouncing.

I asked, "Well, what did the principal do?"

"The principal? Our principal back then was McWhorter."

"Oh no!"

"Yeah. Totally useless. He didn't do anything. But Kellie Russo's parents did. They got McCain kicked out. He got put in a special class for psychos."

"An EMH class?"

"Huh? What's that?"

"Emotionally Mentally Handicapped. It's not for psychos, though. It's for kids who don't do well in the mainstream."

"Well, I guess that would be Matt McCain. He didn't do well around mainstream humans. By the time I got to middle school, he had already been expelled from there, too."

TJ asked, "Who did he feel up there?"

"Nobody. He was in PE, playing baseball, and he got hit with a pitch. Totally by accident. He charged the pitcher's mound and busted the kid across the mouth with a metal bat. He broke, like, twelve of the kid's teeth. I don't know where he went after that."

I said, "I do. Mom told me about that baseball bat incident. He got sent to The Gateway. It's a school for kids with real problems. You get a lot of special attention there. I remember Mom saying, 'The McCains are getting their tax dollars worth.'"

"What's that mean?"

"It means they're not as dumb as they act. They know how to work the system. They know how to get what they want."

TJ suddenly looked up and asked me, "Miss Alice, is that a French braid you're wearing?"

My hand shot up to the crisscross ropes of hair. "Yes."

"It's looking a bit ratty."

"Yes. I know."

"Did you do it yourself?"

"Yes."

"Where did you learn how?"

"My mom."

He answered sadly, "Oh," but he perked up immediately. "I do my mom's sometimes; though her hair's not really long enough. We did a home school project on braids: French braids, Dutch braids, French twists."

Patrick grumbled, "That's what you did in home school?" TJ ignored him.

I admitted, "I really have to undo mine tonight. It is kind of dirty."

TJ hopped up. "I could help you."

"You could?"

"They're easier to undo than to do."

"True. Okay."

Patrick glanced furtively out the window. He finally asked, "Is Matt McCain out there all the time?"

"Quite a bit."

Patrick grimaced. "How do you stand it?"

"I just ignore him. And he ignores me. Except for the odd

obscenity."

"Yeah? Lucky you."

"My mom told me that Matt McCain needs medication for a psychological disorder."

Patrick frowned. "What medication? Do they have stop-being-a-psycho pills?"

"Yes, they do. There are meds that would help him. My mom wanted to tell his mom about some medications, and some therapists, but the administrators wouldn't let her."

"Why not?"

"Lawsuits! School administrators blame everything on lawsuits. No teacher can say the obvious thing to a psycho kid's parents. Definitely not if your administrators are Burnam and McWhorter."

Patrick muttered, "McWhorter's such a wuss. McWusser."

TJ asked, "So what do Matt McCain's parents think? That he's normal, and everyone else is crazy?"

"Who knows?"

TJ suggested, "Maybe they think he'll grow out of it, like I grew out of my asthma attacks."

"Maybe. Anyway, the one my mom really hated, although she would never actually use that word, is Dennis McCain. She said there's no medical reason for him to be a jerk, he just is one. She also hated his father and grandfather."

Patrick seemed surprised. "Hated them? Why?"

"They came and attacked her one day at school."

Patrick's jaw fell. "What? They hit her?"

"No, but just about. They hit her with words, threatening words. That happens to teachers a lot; they just don't talk about it. But this one day, I was sitting in the office waiting for her to drive me home, and I saw the whole thing."

TJ pointed me to the spot on the bed where he'd been sitting. He started to work unbraiding my hair as I explained to them, "I need to back up a little, though. I already knew that my mom was having trouble with some eighth-grade boys when she was on bus duty. The teacher who had duty before her let some kids into the school before the first bell, which was against the rules. My mom wouldn't break the rules. But these boys decided they were going to push past her and go in anyway. Well, my mom grabbed the first one, Dennis McCain, and pushed him back outside.

"The next day, I was sitting in the office and this little wiry guy with black hair and this big old guy with white hair came storming in. They started yelling at the kids behind the desk, 'Get the principal out here!'

"The office kids got real scared; nobody knew what to do. I saw Mr. McWhorter stick his head out of his door and then pop it right back in, like a turtle."

"Mr. McWusser," Patrick repeated. "Everybody knows that McWhorter's a wuss."

"Finally, someone called Mrs. Burnam, and she walked into the office. She introduced herself to these two guys, and the little one started screaming right away that some teacher had pushed his kid, and he wanted her fired. I couldn't believe what I heard next. The little guy pulled a scrap of paper out of his pocket and read off 'Lynch! Who's this Mrs. Lynch? Get her in here.'

"So, did Mrs. Burnam put them in their place? No. She raised up her walkie-talkie and called my mom and told her to come to the office right away.

"Mrs. Burnam asked the two, 'Do you want to sit in my office?' But the little guy snarled, 'No. We'll wait right here. Get her in here.'

"Now, at this point, a good principal would be calling in the resource officer, or just calling the police, but Mrs. Burnam was still sucking up to them. While we all waited, the older guy spoke up. 'I'm Captain Ed McCain, Dennis's grandfather. This is my son. I lost my other son on nine-eleven, at the World Trade Center, in the line of duty.'

"My mom walked in just then, and the little guy rounded on her, holding up his scrap of paper. 'Are you Lynch?'"

I paused there, shuddering at the memory; reliving my revulsion for those men. But then I continued evenly, "Mom leaned back like she had been slapped. She answered, 'I am Mrs. Lynch. What's going on here?'

"He stepped forward and stuck his index finger in her face. At that point, I'd have had him arrested, but Mrs. Burnam just stood there. He shouted, 'I'll tell you what's goin' on! You grabbed the wrong kid. And that's the last kid you're going to grab. You're through.'

"Mom looked at Mrs. Burnam and got no response. She finally stammered, 'What are you talking about? Mrs. Burnam? Can you get involved here?'

"The old guy intoned, like it was some great revelation, 'The boy you grabbed happens to be the nephew of a fallen New York City firefighter.'

"Mom tried one more time. 'Mrs. Burnam, are you going to take charge of this situation or not?'

"Mrs. Burnam answered just above a whisper, 'You gentlemen are welcome to fill out an incident report with Mr. McWhorter. Describe exactly what happened, and the district will investigate.'

"The McCains shook their heads as one. The smaller one spoke. 'No, no, no. This is our 'report' right here. What we just told you. Now you take care of it.'

"He started for the door. His father did, too, adding, 'If I want to get something *investigated*, I'll call the mayor of New York. Have you heard of him? He happens to be a friend of mine.'

"The son pointed again at Mom. 'Nobody touches my kid. End of story.'

"They both stomped out, looking very pleased with themselves. Mom was in tears by then, in front of the office staff; in front of students; in front of me. She finally managed to ask the useless Mrs. Burnam, 'Can you tell me what just happened here?'

"Mrs. Burnam muttered, 'Mr. McCain claims you pushed his son Dennis.'

"She answered, 'I pulled him back out of the building. After he pushed past me yesterday morning.'

"Mrs. Burnam asked her, 'Did you write that incident up?'

"Mom said, 'I certainly did. Didn't you read the referral?' The principal puckered her lips. Mom added, 'Obviously not, or you wouldn't have just stood there saying nothing, I would hope.'

"Mrs. Burnam turned and called, 'Mr. McWhorter!' His head stuck out again immediately, like he had been cowering in there the whole time. 'Get me Mrs. Lynch's referral about the McCain boy.'

"As he disappeared again, I ran to Mom and hugged her tight around the waist. I could feel her heart pounding. Then Mrs. Burnam walked up to us, reading the referral and saying, 'All right. I wish I had known about this earlier, Mr. McWhorter. I will now be prepared should they come back. In the mean time, Mrs. Lynch, I think it best that you be excused from bus duty.'

"Mom didn't reply. She and I turned and walked out arm in arm. She was really shaken up for the rest of that night. But she *did* show up for work in the morning, and she did do her bus duty. And that little rat Dennis McCain did not try to push past her again."

Patrick asked, "Did his father and grandfather ever come back?"

"No. Of course not. They had already done what they set out to do—to mistreat somebody who could not fight back."

Patrick shook his large head. "It sucks that your mom had to put up with that. I could never be a teacher. I wouldn't even want to be a teacher's kid."

"No? Why?"

"Other kids would pick on you."

I told him, "No one ever picked on me."

He seemed surprised to hear that. Just then, our grandmother called up the stairway, "Come on, you three! Dinner's ready."

TJ whispered, "It's technically brunch, but whatever."

We trooped down to the kitchen and took seats around the table. Seven places had been set with plates, napkins, utensils, and glasses of tap water. My Uncle Jim already had a bottle of Budweiser going. When my grandfather entered through the kitchen door and saw the beer bottle, he went and got one, too.

Sunday dinner consisted of roast beef, gravy, mashed potatoes, and peas. We had eaten that same combination at my grandparents' house for as long as I could remember. Now that I actually lived with them, I knew that this menu was not exclusively for Sundays. It could be served any night of the week, and it often was. The only alternate menus were fried chicken, mashed potatoes, and peas and—on Fridays—fish sticks, mashed potatoes, and peas.

Out of pure habit, I suppose, Patrick loaded one pea onto the end of his fork and aimed it at TJ. Aunt Betty slapped at his wrist, dislodging the pea from its perch. "There will be none of that today, Patrick. We have a special surprise for Grandmom and Grandpop. We need to talk about that now because *part* of the surprise is happening right after we eat."

My grandmother responded sternly, "We need to thank God first, I think." She bowed her head and appeared to pray. The rest of us did the same, but I bet only Aunt Betty really prayed.

Before Aunt Betty could resume speaking, though, my grandmother held up her hand. "Let me say something first, Betty. It's important. Your grandfather and I have been promising for years that, when the time comes, we'd leave this house to you and Donna." She looked to my grandfather and back. "Well, we've decided that the time has come. Your grandfather needs more care than I can provide, so it's time we moved into the Assisted Living Facility. We'll have our own apartment there, and we'll have twenty-four hour medical care available at the push of a button.

"Betty, this house is bigger than yours. It's big enough for Patrick and TJ to each have a bedroom, with one left over for Alice." She looked at me. "Alice, since your mother has passed away, her half of the house, of course, will go to you."

I thought Aunt Betty would be astounded at this news and start to cry hysterically. I've seen her melt down over far less than this. Instead, she winked at me. She had already known! That's why she was okay with paying for Memory Lane. She was getting a free house (or half a house).

After a respectful pause, Aunt Betty replied, "Thanks, Mom. Thanks, Pop. We really appreciate that, and we look forward to visiting you in your new place. I know it will be great." She eyeballed Uncle Jim until he put his beer down. "You are doing something wonderful for us, so we want to do something wonderful for you. You both know what November 24th is, I am sure."

My grandfather replied (I think he was kidding), "Is Notre Dame playing that day, Jim? Are they playing Boston College?"

"Nah. That's November 16th, Pop. November 24th is your day. It's all about you."

Aunt Betty chided my grandfather gently. "You know what day that is. The greatest day of your lives! Your wedding anniversary." She looked back and forth between her two parents. "You made it to the *fiftieth*, the golden anniversary. How many people can say that?"

Neither grandparent had an answer to that question, so she went on. "Donna and I started talking about this three months ago, but what we had in mind seemed just too expensive. Now,

Jim and I have come into some money, and here's what we want to do with it. Jim, do you want to tell them?"

"No. You go ahead."

"We want to take you to a special vacation destination. We want to reenact the week of your wedding, with everything exactly as it was back then."

My grandfather spoke again. "What? Are you sticking us in a time machine, Betty?"

She smiled mischievously. "In a way, Pop. And we're jumping in there with you. It's hard for me to explain, so that's why we invited someone to come here at one o'clock. Her name is Teresa Zorn, and she is really wonderful at describing how Memory Lane works."

My ears perked up when I heard the name Zorn. Was this the sister Douglas had told me about? It had to be. I had thought about Douglas a lot since that day on the driveway. A lot. Now I could find out if he had escaped uninjured from the McCains.

Sunday dinner ended on that upbeat note. Grandmom, Aunt Betty, and I started to clean up. Aunt Betty called after Uncle Jim, "We'll need seating for eight people in the living room, Jim."

My uncle picked up two kitchen chairs and carried them with him; then he returned for two more. By the time we entered the room, my grandfather was sitting on one end of the long couch with Uncle Jim on the other. Each had a Budweiser in hand. Aunt Betty sat in the armchair next to her husband, facing the front. She pointed to the middle of the couch for my grandmother to sit. "That'll be perfect for you and Pop. You can spread out brochures on the coffee table."

Three of the kitchen chairs were arranged in an arc leading to the front door. Patrick and TJ were seated on two of them, so I took the empty chair next to TJ. Then we all stared at the last chair and waited.

I heard an engine sound on the driveway. So did Aunt Betty because she hopped up, hurried to the door, and slipped outside. We all listened to her muffled, sing-songy greeting. "Hi! How are you?"

"Fine! How are you?"

"You found us okay?"

"Yes, of course. I know the area very well."

"Well, come in! Come in!"

Aunt Betty stepped back inside followed by a pretty young woman wearing a black pantsuit and a white silk blouse. She wore no overcoat, and the cold air had quickly reddened her cheeks. She had ash blonde hair and bright blue eyes which, I realized, were the same as Douglas's. She set a crammed leather briefcase on the chair as Aunt Betty introduced her to the members of our group, moving counterclockwise from Uncle Jim to me. "And finally, this is Alice. Alice Lynch, another grandchild."

Teresa Zorn held out her hand, and I shook it. She looked at me and smiled a dazzling white smile. "I'm Teresa Zorn, Alice." Then the smile disappeared. "And I was very sorry to hear about your mother."

This took me by surprise. I stammered, "Oh. Okay. Thank you."

Teresa sat on her chair, moved the briefcase into a space between her feet, and unsnapped its brass clasp. After a short pause, she began to speak in a clear, knowledgeable voice, "Let me start by sharing some information that I found in my research. Over two-point-three million marriages take place every year in the United States. Of those two-point-three million, between one quarter and one half end in divorce after seven years. You can imagine then how rare it is for a couple to make it to the fifty-year mark, the golden anniversary."

Teresa looked up at my grandparents, who didn't seem to be listening, so she switched to Aunt Betty and Uncle Jim. "There must be a very strong bond that holds people together for so long. A golden bond. And we at Memory Lane believe that is something worth celebrating. In fact, we'll be celebrating two golden anniversaries during your week alone."

Teresa then pulled out a brochure with a multi-column chart that showed the years 1955 to 1965. Each column was crammed with facts about one of those years such as its top TV shows, songs, and movies. Teresa looked at my grandparents and informed them, "Some of the earliest days of television are lost forever because no one thought to record the shows. It wasn't until the development of videotape in the early 1950s that most shows were recorded. This was the Golden Age of Television, and it's at this point that the Memory Lane experience begins.

"Television *is* daily life. If your TV is tuned to November, 1957, then so are you. The rest follows along—the cars, phones, radios, bikes, clothes, magazines, records. You'll be amazed! Most of the materials from that year are still available; what is not available can be reproduced exactly like the original. For all practical purposes, you *are* in 1957.

"Some of our most popular weeks at Memory Lane recreate summers when a father was twelve years old and his favorite team won the World Series. He can relive it all again, pitch by pitch. We are already booked solid for next October." She looked pointedly at Uncle Jim. "Especially October 11 to October 16, 1969?"

He answered quickly, "The 1969 Mets. Four games to one over Baltimore."

"Exactly right! Good job! Football, too. Mr. Blanchard knows a few things about that. He will be reliving three of the greatest days in Notre Dame football history at his house. We're looking forward to making that happen for him."

Teresa circulated the chart, beginning with me. She explained, "*Authentic* is what it's all about; every detail. We will draw you back into your time by total immersion. It really works!"

Teresa Zorn was positively beaming. She looked from my grandparents, to my aunt and uncle, to my cousins, to me. None of us said anything in reply. I passed the chart to TJ. Finally, Aunt Betty chirped, "That all sounds fascinating! Please tell my parents what you told me, about how you got started at Memory Lane. They'll like that."

I doubted they would, but Teresa Zorn was game to try. "Well, I went to college at Adelphi University, right here on Long Island. I majored in Education. I wanted to be a high school history teacher."

Aunt Betty interrupted her to say, "Like my sister Donna." (I should point out here that my mother never taught in a high school, and she never taught history.)

Teresa continued, "I went to a job fair and talked to some people from Global Entertainment about a new concept they were developing called Memory Lane. To make a long story short, they hired me, and I started working at the Memory Lane park in Effingham, Illinois. People out there relive growing up in the St. Louis and the Chicago areas. They have some great World Series memories!"

Uncle Jim added, "And some great Notre Dame memories."

"Yes, indeed. I spent five years as a cast member, acting as everything from a roller-skating waitress to a school teacher."

Aunt Betty laughed appreciatively.

"I was in the right place at the right time because Memory Lane soon became the most successful vacation destination in the Midwest. Back then, the Illinois franchise was the only one in existence. Now there is one opening here on Long Island, and there are plans to build Memory Lane parks in Hagerstown, Maryland, and in Bakersfield, California."

The chart had made its way quickly back to Teresa, so she stashed it in her case. She told us seriously, "In this post-nine-eleven world, people want to take their vacations close to home, in the United States. Our Memory Lane is set very close to here, on seventy acres near the MacArthur Airport."

Teresa then pulled out a vintage lunch box. It had a picture of a married couple with two young boys and the caption *The Adventures of Ozzie and Harriet*. She opened it and asked, "Would anyone care for a Tastykake, a Devil Dog, or a Ring Ding?" This got the boys' attention. Teresa opened the lunch box and passed out samples to them. Then she handed Aunt Betty a make-up bag packed with bottles and tubes. "Let's see how many of these 1957 products you can recognize."

Aunt Betty was delighted. "Well! A lot of them are still around, but they don't look like this anymore. Look, Jim." She held up samples of Pepsodent, Wisk, Ban Roll-on Deodorant, Listerine, Vitalis.

Uncle Jim reached in and pulled out a small bottle of Coke. "I'd like to buy the world a Coke."

Teresa smiled, puzzled. "What's that, Mr. Blanchard?"

"It's a Coke commercial. You know: *Have a Coke and a smile. It's the real thing.*" He picked up the toothpaste. "You'll wonder where the yellow went when you brush your teeth with Pepsodent."

Teresa beamed. "You see? You *do* remember. Well, little delights like those will come back to you—like what it was like to eat a TV dinner while you watched the goofy acts on the Ed Sullivan Show; how much fun it was to play Clue, or Monopoly, or Sorry."

My grandparents looked skeptical, like they had never enjoyed any of those things. But Aunt Betty was grinning happily, so Teresa continued. "Levittown is the perfect place to recruit guests for the first Memory Lane in the East. Levittown was the birthplace of suburban America, and therefore the birthplace of what we remember as the 1950s. The houses at our theme park are actually modeled on Levittown 'cape' houses. You will feel right at home!"

She laughed again, but no one joined her. We were clearly a tough crowd. "The park is having its soft opening next month. Do you know what that means?" She did not wait for an answer. "It's before the grand opening. During that time, we will introduce our park to a small, specially selected audience, and at a special price. Shortly after that, we'll roll into the big Thanksgiving and Christmas seasons.

"The guests on your street will be all local people. In addition, we have chosen a local hero's family to be the face of our marketing campaign—Captain Ed McCain, whose son died on September 11, 2001."

We all gasped at once. Patrick spit out part of his Ring Ding. Teresa looked puzzled, but she soldiered on. "There will be other families, too. They may be reliving the same year as you, or they may not. However, you will all be reliving the same ten-year span."

She explained, "Some park activities are for everybody, like the parades; the shops in the town square; the fireworks displays. But what is unique about Memory Lane is what happens *inside* your house. That is for you alone."

She turned to my grandparents. "You will relive *your* wedding week in 1957; nobody else's." She turned to Uncle Jim. "You will relive *your* football Saturday in 1966; nobody else's."

Teresa then got down to business. She reached into the briefcase and pulled out a map showing the street where we would stay. She pointed to the top two houses on the near side. "You will be here, in the first two houses." She moved her finger across the street. "Mrs. Nordstrom and her granddaughters will be over here. Mrs. Nordstrom is a very special lady. She competed on the United States Winter Olympics team in 1960. Believe it or not, she has never seen the CBS broadcast of those games."

Uncle Jim asked, "Where was it held in 1960?"

"Squaw Valley, California. It was the first Winter Olympics ever shown on TV. She has never seen herself march into the stadium, or perform in an event, or take part in any of the festivities that were captured by the TV crews. It's our honor to show her all of that, capsulized into five days of broadcasts." Teresa winked at the boys. "Mrs. Nordstrom has twin granddaughters, and they are fine figure skaters, too."

The boys didn't react any more than my grandparents. I decided to give Teresa Zorn a break. I pointed at the next house on the map. "So, who's here?"

Teresa's mouth twitched into a quick frown, then resumed smiling. "That would be Mr. Hoffman and his son, Ray." She exhaled, then added, "They will be reliving the assassination of President John F. Kennedy by Lee Harvey Oswald. Do you guys remember when that was?"

I doubted the guys did, so I answered for us, "November 22nd, 1963."

"Yes, correct. Gold star."

TJ muttered, "That sound like a fun week to relive."

Uncle Jim told him, "And I'll bet you a dollar they don't think Lee Harvey Oswald did it."

Teresa nodded. "You'd win that bet." She winked at TJ, "So save your money." Teresa pointed to the next house and announced, "The Hardys! Wonderful people. Mr. Hardy worked for the FBI for thirty years. He's retired now, but his wife and his daughter, Mrs. Whitman, are taking him back to re-live his first week on the job. They want to enjoy America as it was back then."

Her finger moved again. "Which is similar to what the Clarks are doing. Mr. and Mrs. Clark and their two children will be in this house. They have a teenage girl, too, and a cute little boy."

Uncle Jim asked, "What are they reliving?"

Teresa chose her words carefully. "Mr. Clark wants his family to relive a time when God was a more visible part of life in America. One thing he mentioned is that he wants his children to experience prayer in school."

Uncle Jim took a deep swig of beer. "I pray during football games: God. Country. Notre Dame. That's my religion."

Teresa laughed knowingly. "So I've heard!"

Uncle Jim then summed it up for us, "Well, it takes all kinds, I guess."

Teresa agreed. "It is a great mix of people, and of times. I hope you will get to know each other, and that you'll share what you learn."

Patrick was staring at the map intently. Then he spoke. "So where are the McCains?"

Teresa pointed at the last two houses on our side of the street. "The house next to you will be empty. The last house will be taken up by Captain McCain and his family. They are

40

having a fiftieth wedding anniversary mass the same day as you.”

Patrick burst out, red-faced, “No! That can’t be! There’s no way the McCains could afford this!”

Aunt Betty shushed him, “Patrick!”

“Well, it’s true, isn’t it?”

After an awkward pause, Teresa Zorn filled the gap. “As I said, they came to our attention as a local family who deserved a trip to Memory Lane.”

I asked, “How did they come to your attention?”

She shrugged, as if it hadn’t been her decision. “I’m not really sure. It was through our field marketing.”

My grandfather spoke up. “Through them bragging about themselves, I bet.”

Patrick demanded to know, “We don’t have to mix with them if we don’t want to, do we?”

Teresa smiled kindly. “No, of course not. You’re free to do or *not* do whatever you like.”

“And what about security? Like police?”

“Good question, Patrick. We have an excellent security staff. They are available twenty-four hours a day for police, fire, and ambulance services. You’ll see them cruising the streets in marked and unmarked cars. They’re never more than a minute away.”

We left it at that, for the moment, but Patrick and I had just gotten very wary about Memory Lane. And, despite Teresa

Zorn's polished and professional pitch, my grandmother remained totally unmoved. Teresa asked her directly, "So, Mrs. Abel, how is all this sounding?"

She muttered, as if it should be obvious to all, "I already lived through that week. I see no reason to do it again." She turned to my grandfather, "Do you?"

He didn't answer. However, to my surprise, he now seemed totally absorbed in the Memory Lane brochure. When he looked up, his eyes were alert. He turned the brochure outward and asked Teresa Zorn, "Would I get to work on one of these again?"

We all beheld a gorgeous green car, sleek and shining, with polished chrome bumpers, handles, and mirrors. Below it was a caption: *The 1957 Ford Fairlane*. Teresa Zorn seized the moment. "You would! You would have that exact car, parked in your own garage, with all the tools and supplies you would need to work on it to your heart's content."

My grandfather said, "That's great."

So everybody turned back to my grandmother. She was trapped. She shrugged and pointed at another item in the brochure—a *TV Guide* magazine. "I'll sit there and watch my soaps. If that's what you all want."

Aunt Betty added, "And you'll get married again! Renew your vows?"

My grandmother looked horrified. "No! I'll do no such nonsense. I'll go to mass on Sunday, as usual. It can be a wedding mass if you like. But it would be silly to have two old people climb up there and pretend they're teenagers getting married. We'll dress up nice and enjoy the mass, but that's all."

Aunt Betty conceded, "Well . . . Okay, if that's what you want."

"It is."

"And we'll have a nice little party after, just like you did the first time."

Teresa looked greatly relieved. She gushed, "Terrific!" She spread her hands outward and asked, "Now, you must all have questions, lots of questions. What can I tell you?"

No one spoke until I blurted out, like an idiot, "Will Douglas be working on our street?"

"Douglas?"

I already regretted it. I added stupidly, "Douglas Zorn."

She seemed puzzled. "Do you know Douglas?"

"Yes. From middle school."

"Oh, that's neat! Well, sure. He could be working on your street. Would you like him to?"

I backed off. "Only if he'd be there anyway. I was just wondering."

Teresa smiled knowingly, and let it drop. After a few seconds of silence, she said, "Let me tell you some of our frequently asked questions." She looked at me: "How are newspapers and magazines delivered?" She looked at the boys:

"How is the food delivered?" She looked at the three of us: "What about school? Do we get out of school?"

Patrick perked up at that one. "Okay. Do we get out of school?"

Teresa smiled. "You won't want to! You'll be going to a real school, with a real teacher." She paused to point at her own chest. "But it will be a school set in the past!" Teresa reached into her briefcase again. Was there no bottom to that thing? "While we're on the subject, I'll need to find out who will be volunteering to speak at the school." She explained, "We ask that one adult from each family visit the school to discuss the week they are reliving."

My grandmother asked abruptly, "What about the mass? Will it be a real Catholic mass?"

"Oh yes. And it will be said in Latin, as it was in 1957." Teresa Zorn and Aunt Betty exchanged a conspiratorial smile. "Since your brother, Father Dunne, officiated at your original wedding, we assumed he would officiate at this one. That's why I added him to your house."

Teresa laid down diagrams showing who would sleep where in each house. My grandmother stared at them. She muttered, "Father Dunne's been sick for a long time. He could be dying for all I know."

Teresa smiled. "I can tell you that he is doing well, despite some recent illness. I contacted him, and he agreed to participate. Agreed enthusiastically! He will hear confessions on Saturday and perform two wedding masses on Sunday."

My grandmother asked, "Two masses?"

"Yes. Yours, and the wedding mass for Captain and Mrs. McCain."

We all fell silent again, a reaction that was not lost on Teresa Zorn. She added, "But *their* 1957 wedding took place early in the morning. They will have the church from 10:00 to 11:00; *you* will have it from 11:00 to 12:00."

Teresa pulled out a fat, heavy book from that amazing briefcase. "I'll be leaving this with you. It's the 1957 *Sears Catalogue for Fall and Winter*." She plopped it down in front of TJ who flipped it open to a page of boys posing in underwear. Patrick snorted. "Inside, you will find some easy-to-use order forms. Each guest is to choose his or her outfits for your stay. Select anything and everything that you need—from underwear to outerwear and everything in between. Have fun with it!"

TJ asked, "So what kinds of things would we bring with us?"

Patrick muttered, "Your silk undies."

Teresa told TJ, "You don't need to bring anything! Select all the items you will need from the catalogue. Those items will be waiting for you on arrival."

"We can't even bring our own toothpaste, or deodorant?"

"No. Because they could be anomalies."

TJ smiled with delight. He clearly liked that word. "What are anomalies?"

"They're things that don't belong in a particular time. Like, imagine a painting of George Washington sitting on a motorcycle."

"Cool. So, what would be some anomalies for 1957?"

"Cell phones, iPods, laptops. None of those would be invented for another generation."

TJ repeated, "Anomalies."

After that, Teresa stood up. She smiled warmly and told my grandparents, "Thank you so much for your hospitality today." She told Aunt Betty and Uncle Jim, "I'll be in touch with you soon. And often."

Then I was surprised when she turned to me. "Alice, would you mind walking me out? I have a favor to ask of you."

I gulped and nodded yes. I had something to ask her, too. And as soon as we reached the curb, I did. "Is Douglas okay? Did he get injured?"

Teresa smiled quizzically. "Injured? No. Why would he?"

I didn't want to get into the whole story. He obviously had not been injured, or she would know about it. I asked instead, "Will you both be taking care of us at Memory Lane?"

Teresa deposited her leather case on the passenger seat. "I'll be the main facilitator for your stay. I'll be the teacher at the school; the sexton at the church; the operator on the other end of the telephone line. I'll take on whatever roles are necessary to recreate your special time down to the smallest detail. Douglas will help me do that. He will be the paperboy, the altar boy, and," she stopped to wink at me, "the cute boy in the neighborhood."

Then Teresa, very ceremoniously, handed me a journal-sized book. The book's cover showed a montage of scenes from Memory Lane and the words *Golden Moments* embossed in gold. "Here's why I asked you to come outside, Alice. I'd like you to be the chronicler of your family's time at Memory Lane. I'd like you to write in this book every night. Otherwise, you are sure to forget some of the things that happen."

I flipped open the book to a page of cheesy, paste-on stickers: a *sunrise, a dinner chef, a school bell,* et cetera. Teresa commented, "Aren't those neat?"

I nodded noncommittally.

She tapped the cover, smiled a hopeful smile, and said, "Don't think of this as a chore, Alice. Just write whatever you feel like, like in a diary. And sign your name, like in a diary. This will be *your* record of events. Just a few minutes each night should do it."

Teresa then handed me a DVD. "And get everybody to watch these TV shows. They're all from your week in 1957. They'll teach you a tremendous amount about that time."

"Okay. I will."

She slid into the driver's seat and called, "So! I'll see you back in 1957!"

"Yes."

I stayed outside for a moment. I watched her drive three houses down, get out, and enter the McCains' front yard. I just stood there muttering to myself, "My God. Why? Why the McCains?"

When I got back inside, the living room was empty. I could hear Aunt Betty in the kitchen, though, talking a mile a minute about Memory Lane. I headed up the stairs, turned left, and spotted Patrick and TJ. They had resumed their pre-lunch spots, but now Patrick was red-faced and fuming. He practically shouted at me, "This blows! This totally blows. We have to live on a street with the McCains? And is Matt McCain gonna be in that school? No way I'm going then! I'll be a 1957 drop out."

TJ added, "Beauty school dropout," for no apparent reason.

Patrick snorted. "And what's with this soft opening at the park crap? What's up with that? It's like they want people there to test the roller coasters? To see if they break?"

TJ pointed out, "It's not that kind of park."

I told Patrick, "It gets worse. You haven't even heard what the McCains did to Douglas."

"Who?"

"Teresa Zorn's brother, Douglas. You know him."

"I do?"

"He's at Division High."

"Does he play football?"

TJ needled him, "Why? Do you?"

Patrick ignored the remark and answered, "I think I know him. What? What did they do?"

"Douglas was riding through the neighborhood, giving out Memory Lane fliers like he was a paperboy. The McCains stopped his bike and started messing with him. They wouldn't let him go. It was looking really ugly, but I don't know how it wound up."

Patrick thought about that. "Maybe he wound up dead, you know? Like the paperboy on Jerusalem Avenue."

TJ added, "Like the kid who got run over, in the rain."

I wasn't surprised to hear this. That dead paperboy was a Levittown urban legend. I said, "Right. The dead paperboy. What else do you know about him, TJ?"

"I know that he was riding in the dark, in the rain, without a raincoat, not looking where he was going. He was going way too fast because he was late for work because he had stopped somewhere where he shouldn't have."

I answered, "Right."

Patrick added, "He was late because he stopped to buy some weed. And he smoked some, too."

TJ contradicted him. "No. I heard it was like a premarital sex thing. He was late because he was with a girl having premarital sex or something, so he was going real fast to get there."

I repeated, "Right. Right."

Patrick growled, "Is that all that you can say?" TJ just looked at me curiously.

I asked, "Would you be surprised to learn that most of what you've heard about that boy isn't true? It's a myth. An urban legend, spread by parents, based on their own agendas."

TJ was puzzled. "Their agendas? Like what?"

"Like to keep you away from drugs, or alcohol, or girls."

Patrick added, "Or boys."

"Those are the *myths* of the dead paperboy. I know the facts, if you want to hear them."

TJ nodded, but Patrick challenged me, "How do you know the facts?"

"Because my mom always encouraged me to find out the facts."

He held his hands out apologetically. "Okay. Okay."

TJ flopped back onto the bed; Patrick lowered himself down onto the floor. I stood before them and recited from memory: "Okay. The paperboy, of course, had a name— Timothy Strop. He was not only a paperboy; he was an altar boy and an Eagle Scout. He had arrived, alcohol-free, drug-free, premarital-sex-free at the drop-off spot for the *Newsday* truck. Back then that was the parking lot of the Hempstead municipal pool.

"He and a dozen other paperboys each collected a bundle of afternoon editions and set out on their routes. It was

Thursday, November 22, 1973. The headlines that day were: (1) President Nixon in trouble for the Watergate burglaries; (2) a boycott of Arab oil in the Middle East, and (3) ceremonies commemorating the tenth anniversary of the death of President John F. Kennedy.

"The people on Timothy Strop's route would never get to read those headlines. He was struck by a car and killed while trying to cross Jerusalem Avenue. Nobody saw it happen, except of course the killer.

"A Levittown policeman patrolling in the rain at five o'clock spotted a bicycle at the side of the road. He stopped to investigate. He saw a pack of newspapers, and then he saw Timothy Strop's body lying in the grass near the sidewalk, suggesting that the boy had the strength to crawl a few feet away. The police officer checked for vital signs and found that he was dead. A coroner later determined he died of massive head injuries, and that he had been dead for about thirty minutes, putting the time of the hit-and-run at about 4:30 pm.

"Two days later, the Levittown police arrested a man named Jack Gallahue for the crime. Mr. Gallahue pleaded no contest, and he served three years of a ten-year sentence in Sing Sing State Prison."

TJ nodded thoughtfully. "God, if I were those parents, I wouldn't know what to do."

"Well, that brings me to a bizarre footnote to the story: Timothy Strop's mother drove to the gates of the prison on the day that Jack Gallahue was released. She tried to run him over with her car! She was arrested for the attempt, but since Mr. Gallahue was not injured, and since she was understandably distraught, no charges were ever brought.

"As it turned out, she shouldn't have bothered. Jack Gallahue, drunk again, drove his pick up truck into a cement barrier on the New Jersey Turnpike, broke his head open on the front windshield, and died there in the fiery wreckage."

Patrick stirred himself enough to add, "Drunk drivers are such a-holes."

TJ hissed at him, causing Patrick to say, "What?"

"Duh? Her mother? Your Aunt Donna?"

Patrick then reddened and muttered, "Sorry, Alice."

I just said, "No problem. You're right. They are a-holes."

The Blanchards finally left at four o'clock. Aunt Betty and Uncle Jim seemed really pumped up about Memory Lane. Patrick and TJ seemed to have forgotten all about it.

I had a science paper to write on the human brain. I worked on it for about two hours and finished it, including the endnotes. Then I did a Google search of my own; a search for the McCains. I wanted to check Teresa Zorn's story about them being local heroes. I had some serious doubts, and those doubts turned out to be justified. Completely.

After that, I had some time to kill before bed. (There's a lot of time to kill at my grandparents' house.) Sometimes I call up

Paige to gossip about kids at school. This day, though, I turned my attention to My Little Pony. Yes, that's right. My Little Pony. The little plastic horse with the long flowing mane. It's true, and I'm not ashamed.

My mom and I had many things in common. One of them was this: We both acted like adults even when we were kids. Mom had a term for this: *prematurely mature*. Prematurely mature kids, and I speak here from experience, always have some really *immature* thing that they do as an outlet. Mom's outlet was playing with Barbies. Mine is playing with My Little Pony.

Mom would get a Barbie every Christmas, and she'd add accessories on her birthday. For example, she might get Busy Barbie for Christmas; then she would add the Barbie Beauty Center on her birthday. The next Christmas she might get Miss America Barbie, and so on. According to her, it was quite a collection, and she spent hundreds of hours secretly playing with it.

But I never got to see them. She threw them all out one day. For no apparent reason. For no reason that she would share with me, anyway. Perhaps I will do the same thing.

Anyway, I started my collection when I was four, so it's pretty big now. Kirsten and Rachel, who lived behind our house on Haven Lane, were heavily into it, too. Our birthday parties always featured My Little Pony stickers, games, and books. My favorite pony was (and is) Blue Belle. Kirsten's favorite was Blossom, and Rachel's was Snizzle. We'd get the three of them together sometimes, with all their accessories. But I preferred to play with Blue Belle by myself. I'd invent stories for Blue Belle to tell, and she'd tell them, either to an imaginary audience or to Mom. Mom always seemed really interested in the stories. She'd ask, "And then what happened?" whenever I came to a stopping point.

I was holding Blue Belle up and preparing to speak when my cell phone rang. I put her down, read the caller ID, and got mature again real fast. It was Douglas Zorn calling. I gulped and pressed the button. "Hello."

"Hi, Alice. It's Douglas Zorn! Teresa gave me your number. I hope you don't mind."

"Mind? No."

"I just wanted to tell you how great it was running into you the other day, and that I'm really looking forward to seeing you at Memory Lane. Really really looking forward to it. Okay?"

"Okay."

"Great. Bye-bye then."

"Bye." Douglas hung up, but I kept staring at the phone for a long time.

I finally put Blue Belle back in her drawer. I lay down on the bed and replayed the phone call over and over in my mind. Every word. What did all those words mean?

Anything?

Nothing?

I thought about the Elizabeth Kubler-Ross Scale. Here I am, one month after my mom's death. If I had to pick a stage, I'd say I had just arrived at *bargaining*. What am I trying to get out of this situation? What am I hoping will happen at Memory Lane?

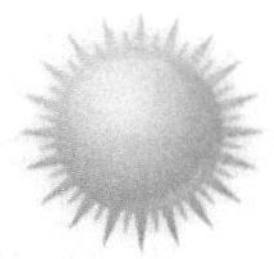

Chapter 2

Here we go.

I'll start my chronicling at sunrise today, with this cheesy sun sticker, because this is the day we all go to America's hottest new vacation destination, Memory Lane (The east coast version of it). Wisely, Aunt Betty told my grandparents that we *absolutely* had to be there at 8:30 for orientation. My grandparents were not ready on time, but the real orientation wasn't until 9:00, so it worked out perfectly. Uncle Jim didn't even pull up until 8:30, but my grandparents didn't catch on. They were too busy looking for lost stuff.

When we finally walked out into the cold morning air, I saw Patrick and TJ seated in the rear section of the SUV. Patrick was asleep, and TJ was just staring out of the window dreamily. That left the second bench seat empty for us. I thought about cramming in with the boys, but that seemed impolite. Instead I sat with my grandparents, in silence, like we were a row of crash-test dummies. Up in the front seat, Aunt Betty had her nose buried in a stack of Memory Lane documents, so the only sound in the car came from Uncle Jim singing TV commercials. Did he do that all the time?

We drove west on Highway 495 to Ronkonkoma; then we turned off and proceeded down a small road through a wooded area. We rounded a bend, and the road suddenly expanded into an impressive entranceway—a red brick wall that stretched one hundred yards across. In the exact center, the wall bowed up into a high arch. We drove under that arch, stopping inside at a security booth where Aunt Betty showed our documents. Beyond the booth, two very new asphalt roads diverged left and right. A computerized sign on each road indicated where it led, either to *1955—1965* or to *1966—1976*. Uncle Jim took the road to the left and followed it for about half a mile, passing several busy construction sites, until we saw our ultimate destination.

TJ whispered, "The Emerald City!"

We drove to a large building with *Town Hall* carved in granite across the top. More computerized signs were set up over a row of parking spaces. Uncle Jim steered toward the one that said *Blanchard* and pulled into it. The spaces on either side were already occupied—one with a Volvo station wagon and a sign that said *Nordstrom*; the other with a Prius and a sign that said *Hoffman*. As we disembarked, I scanned the other signs, and none of them said *McCain*. Was it possible that they weren't coming?

Aunt Betty took my grandmother by the elbow, and Uncle Jim did the same for my grandfather. They led the way into a cavernous space shaped like one half of a giant circle. The space had no windows. Light came from green-shaded bulbs hanging over a shiny, parquet floor. The inside wall, the diameter of the circle, had a long row of doors in it—there must have been forty of them—with a set of higher double doors in the center.

Small groups of people were already milling about. A woman, a girl our age, and a little boy were gathered around a kneeling man. The parents and the girl were wearing t-shirts that said, *R4R—Ready for Rapture*. The boy was wearing a gi—all white in front except for red lettering that said *Armageddon Karate*. They had their hands on the man's shoulders, praying. I whispered to TJ, "The Clarks."

He whispered back, "Duh. Do you think?" He pointed to the right. "Yikes! Swedish princess alert!" Two beautiful blonde girls, identical except for the colors of their tops, were chatting amiably with an old lady. She wasn't an old lady like my grandmother, though. She was spry and alert, and she had a big smile on her face.

Ten feet away from them stood a frail-looking man with two women. The man had a smile on his face, too, but it was the kind of smile my grandfather has on a bad day. He had to be Mr. Hardy; so the two women were Mrs. Hardy and Mrs. Whitman.

I checked out the rest of the space. There was still no sign of the McCains. Anywhere. Had Memory Lane come to its senses and kicked them out?

At exactly 9:00 am, a clock started to chime. After the ninth sounding, Teresa Zorn stepped out of a side door. She was followed by a tall, wiry man and a tall, wiry boy. They seemed to be upset about something, but Teresa was not letting that alter her happy face. She told them, "I'll take care of that immediately, Mr. Hoffman. You will have all three network feeds available to you. You won't miss one minute of the news." The father and son exchanged doubtful looks.

Teresa Zorn then started to greet people informally. She knew everybody there by name. As she moved from group to group, a photographer in a shiny brown, vintage suit followed her. His job, I soon realized, was to take photos of each family.

She greeted us with, "Mr. and Mrs. Blanchard! Mr. and Mrs. Abel! And Patrick, and TJ, and Alice!" (I had to give her high grades for names—straight *A*s.) "Welcome! Everything is ready for your trip back to November 20th to 25th, 1957, culminating in a golden anniversary wedding mass performed by Father Dunne." (Another *A* for our activities) "Let's get you set up for a photo, shall we? Barney?"

The photographer, Barney, approached us with a folded-out contraption called a Polaroid Land Camera. He lined us up and shot several pictures. Then he pointed at TJ. "You are quite photogenic, young man. Can I ask you to do something for me?"

TJ answered, "Sure."

"Come stand with these two girls." He directed TJ to a spot ten feet away where the blonde twins were already waiting. Barney then ran into one of the forty doors and returned with another camera. He told the girls, "This is my 1957 Hasselblad. It's Swedish, too. I've been waiting for a chance to use it."

Patrick muttered to me, "So is that why TJ's so weird? He's secretly Swedish?"

Barney lined up the beautiful blond girls on either side of TJ. I had to admit they made a very attractive trio. Barney placed a Memory Lane brochure in TJ's hands. Then he said, "Smile, kids!" and started taking flash photos. TJ looked a little uncomfortable, and he blinked at every flash, but the twins switched right into professional model mode—smiling, emoting, tossing their great hair around.

After about twenty flashes, the photographer called, "Okay, kids! Thanks!" He took the brochure back from TJ. The twins reverted to normal mode, nodding politely to TJ and returning to the old lady's side. TJ, still blinking, staggered back toward us, grinning as widely as I had ever seen. He leaned over to me and whispered, "Those girls *smell* fabulous, too. I hope their perfume's not an anomaly."

Right after that, Teresa Zorn positioned herself in the exact middle of the groups and spoke in a loud, perky voice. "The big day has finally arrived! We have been working for weeks behind the scenes preparing for your trips back in time." She suddenly smiled slyly and twisted her shoulders, like a naughty little girl. "But remember: This will be the *soft opening*, so please forgive us if we occasionally come up short. Also, it may seem a little strange at times to see more cast members around than guests, but we're all here to serve you."

She straightened up and pointed to the wall of doors. "Each door over there is a changing room. In that room is the first outfit that you ordered from the Sears clothing catalogue. You should leave all of your present-day possessions in that room, which will be securely locked. You can pick them up on the day you depart. The rest of your clothing choices have already been placed in the closets and dressers at your houses.

"Also remember, please, no anomalies. We have done everything we can to make your experience here truly authentic. Please do not undo that by slipping anything modern into your pocket. Believe me, you can live for five days without your cell phone!" (At this point, I felt a twinge of guilt, but not about my phone. More about that later.)

"Once you are dressed and ready, come back out and meet your personal guide. He or she will escort you to your house and help acclimate you to it." She stopped at that moment and winked at me. "Then while your parents and grandparents are rediscovering what home life was like on this day in history— the appliances, the foods, the magazines—you kids will be off to discover what school life was like."

Teresa pulled out a small plastic device about the size of a garage door opener, aimed it at the wall, and pressed a button. A name, spelled out in tiny blue bulbs, appeared above every door. The names ran alphabetically from the left to the right, beginning with the Abels and the Blanchards. I was happy to see that my own name had not been tacked onto theirs, like an orphan. The *Alice Lynch* door was positioned to the right of *Ray Hoffman* and the left of *Ann McCain*. I turned and looked at Patrick. He, too, had seen the McCains' names pop up on six successive doors, but the McCains themselves had still not shown.

I was getting excited, though, in spite of the McCains. I could barely remember what I had ordered from the 1957 Sears catalog, so I was eager to see what was waiting for me. I exchanged raised eyebrows with TJ, and we both took off toward our doors.

I turned the brass knob, pulled the heavy door toward me, and stepped into what looked like a large department store changing room. To the left was a tall, three-sided mirror. To the right was a closet divided into halves, marked *1957* and *2007*.

After a quick check to be sure that the door was locked, I undressed and stacked all my clothes on the 2007 side. I slid my cell phone into a jeans pocket. Then I slipped out my one anomaly (Let's keep it a secret for now.) and slid it into the pocket of my Sears Hideway-Hood coat. I set to work putting on all the 1957 garments, struggling just a bit with the hook on the Cordtex Teen Bra.

When I was finished, I turned and looked into the mirror. Except for my hair, which was long and tied back, I could have passed for a girl in the 1957 *Sears Catalogue for Fall and Winter*. (They were regular kids; not like the Swedish twins.) The dress was a green corduroy Empire Jumper, with a plain white blouse beneath it. It was smart and sensible, like me. I took my coat down from the hook, folded it over my arm, and turned the doorknob once again. As I stepped back into the cavernous room, I heard the door close and lock itself behind me.

The twins were already back, looking a little less glamorous but still very cute. They had chosen identical outfits—black-and-white checkered dresses with red bows tied at the top. The Hoffman boy was back out, too. He looked a lot more nerdy in dark brown pants, a button down white shirt, and a black, my-mother-made-me-wear-this, sweater vest.

He *was* tall, though.

Patrick and TJ stepped out at the same moment. Patrick had on black corduroy pants and a patterned shirt—some green and yellow thing with circles and lines. TJ, of course, looked fabulous. He had on gray pleated Gabardine slacks, blue suede shoes, and a light blue turtle neck sweater. I strolled over toward them, holding out the sides of my jumper with my fingertips. TJ was grinning delightedly, and he called, "Look at you!" Patrick was just staring at the floor, embarrassed.

The little karate boy threw open a door next to us and ran out. His sister, who must have been in there helping him, followed. The boy looked very cute in a green plaid shirt. The girl, who had been dressed very plainly before, looked about the same.

Teresa Zorn started circulating again, passing out compliments on people's clothing choices and, I suspect, looking for hidden anomalies like a nose ring, a modern wristwatch, or the telltale bulge of a cell phone in a pocket. I avoided her gaze.

Everybody took a few minutes to gawk. The adults, I was surprised to see, hadn't changed much. Aunt Betty's skirt was a little longer, and a little wider, but she and Uncle Jim and my grandparents looked basically the same.

Teresa Zorn got our attention again. "You all look terrific! Truly authentic! If you will follow me now, we will take a short, magical journey. We will pass together from the present time into the past."

Teresa pulled out that clicker device again and pressed it. The double doors in the center opened, like the mouth of a cave. The other side was filled with dazzling light. We all entered it slowly, slightly awestruck, pointing and blinking like mole people.

This side of the circle had continuous glass windows looking out on a perfectly restored 1950s town. I knew from my Memory Lane map that I was looking at the 1955—1965 Town Square. I could pick out the school, the church, some shops, and the movie theater. Behind the Town Square, barely visible from where we stood, were the pointed roofs of our houses.

Everyone in our group was chattering and smiling as we exited the Town Hall into the park, even my grandparents. Our vintage car, the 1957 Ford Fairlane, sat waiting for us at the curb. Teresa materialized with a set of car keys. She offered them ceremoniously to my grandfather, but he just stared at them, bewildered, and looked at my grandmother.

Uncle Jim tapped him on the arm and said, "I'll take those for now, Pop." Uncle Jim opened the car's huge front door and climbed in. He turned the key, and the engine roared to life. Then he reached over and turned on the radio by pressing a fat, white button. It blared out, "And here's the news for Wednesday, November 20, 1957!" He pressed another button and a pop song came on. We listened to it while our grandparents made their way over. The song was about two teenagers who went on a date and fell asleep, so everyone assumed they had sex, but they didn't.

Aunt Betty opened the passenger side door. She identified the song for us: "That's 'Wake Up, Little Susie' by the Everly Brothers!"

TJ answered, "I figured that, Mamà, right after they sang 'Wake up little Susie' for the one hundred and forty-seventh time."

A second car pulled up next to ours. This one was a red 1959 Chevrolet Impala, and it was even longer and sleeker than the Ford. There at the wheel, wearing a blue windbreaker with *Memory Lane, Douglas* on the pocket, was Douglas Zorn. He rolled down the passenger window by hand and called to me, "Hey Alice. Good to see you again!"

I smiled. "Good to see you, too." And it really was. He was better looking than ever.

"I think you might get a little cramped in the Fairlane. Do you want to ride over with me?"

TJ whispered, "Go for it, honey."

I smiled again. "Sure."

TJ added, "Just don't wake up like little Suzie."

Douglas addressed the others. "Mr. Blanchard, will you be driving the Fairlane?"

Uncle Jim answered, "Yeah. I guess so."

"It's got a three-speed manual transmission. Is that okay?"

"Sure, no problem."

"Okay then. You can follow me." He leaned over and opened the passenger door from the inside. "Your chariot awaits." I thought that was a lame thing to say, but he was so handsome, and the car was so beautiful, that I didn't care. Douglas explained, "I am your family's personal guide. I'll be with you every day, as much or as little as you like."

I slid into the seat beside him. "You will? What about Division High?"

Douglas flipped his hands out. "Work study. I have to do a project for this semester, and what could be better than this?"

He looked over at me, his blue eyes flashing diamond bright. "I am so psyched to see you here, Alice!"

"You are?"

He pounded the steering wheel. "Yeah!"

Stupidly, I asked, "Can you say *psyched*? Did they say that in 1957?"

He laughed. "I don't know. They might have said *keen* or *neat*." As he put the big car into gear and pulled out, he added, "You look really great, Alice."

"I do?"

"Yeah."

"Let me show you some stuff: This is the Town Square. It's where everything happens. You come down here at night to watch fireworks, see 1950s characters, meet other guests, and have fun." He pointed through the front window. "Here's the church. Here's the school. Here's the Bijou Movie Theater."

Suddenly, for some strange, self-destructive reason, I felt the urge to make a complete fool of myself. I clasped my hands together, interlocked my fingers, and chanted, "Here's the church. Here's the steeple. Open the doors, and see all the people."

Douglas didn't laugh. He just looked at my wriggling fingers and smiled nervously. He had no idea what I was doing. I wanted to die.

We soon reached a tidy, gray-shingled cape house (See cheesy sticker.) and parked out front. Uncle Jim pulled around us and drove the green Ford Fairlane into the garage. He and his passengers entered the house through the side kitchen door. Douglas and I, with me keeping my mouth shut tight and my fingers at my side, entered through the front living room door.

Just inside was a wooden sign on an upright stand. It said: "Welcome to Wednesday, November 20, 1957. Dwight D. Eisenhower is the President of the United States. There are 48 stars on the flag. The number one pop song is "Jailhouse Rock" by Elvis Presley. The Best Picture of the Year Oscar went to *The Bridge on the River Kwai*. The TV Emmy for Best Actor went to Robert Young for *Father Knows Best*. The Soviet Union has just launched Sputnik, the first man-made satellite, causing Americans to fear that the Soviets may next launch a nuclear attack."

Douglas gathered everyone into the living room and read the sign aloud. Then he said, "This house is a classic Levittown cape, short for Cape Cod. It is outfitted for this week in November, 1957, with magazines and books and newspapers. The TV and the radio are programmed to play back the authentic transmissions of that day. Totally authentic. The newspaper is an exact replica of that day's *Newsday*, your paper of choice. All of your appliances, clothes, and foods are authentic, or at least authentically packaged. We're not going to serve you fifty-year-old corn flakes, but we will serve you fresh corn flakes in a replica of the 1957 box!"

Douglas pointed to a strange pile of metal next to the couch. "These are your aluminum tray tables. You can set them up to eat Swanson TV Dinners. I recommend the fried chicken." He pointed at our Admiral TV. "The contraption on top of the TV is called a rabbit-ear antenna. Over there is your home entertainment console—a radio and a record player combined. Notice that this cape has a built-in bookcase under the stairs with bestsellers from 1957." He slid a fat novel part way out. "I'd avoid *Atlas Shrugged*, though, unless you're staying with us for a month. It's, like, a thousand pages long."

He pointed at the front door. "The milkman will deliver glass bottles of whole milk into the insulated box outside. The mailman will deliver mail through the slot in the door—maybe a long overdue letter." He winked at me. "Maybe it didn't have a three-cent stamp on it."

Douglas started for the kitchen, and we followed. He pointed out various contraptions. "This is your Bendix clothes washer, and this is your GE fridge. Over here is your rotary dial telephone. It's a party line, which means you are not the only ones who use it. In your case, it's connected to the Blanchards' house. All you have to do to talk to each other is pick it up. All you have to do to talk to a Memory Lane operator is dial *O*."

Douglas then led us on a quick, informative march through the rest of the house. At one point, we all crowded into my upstairs bedroom—a cape bedroom with ceilings that sloped down on the sides. The room had a wooden homework desk, a four-drawer dresser, and a bed with a pink coverlet. There was a green Hula Hoop leaning against one wall. There was a red *Silly Putty* egg on the dresser, sitting on top of a note that read: "You can find more wonderful toys and games at the F. W. Woolworth 5 & 10 cent store in the Town Square."

Now, I mentioned earlier that I had smuggled one anomaly in with me. It was Blue Belle. I had kept my hand over her inside in my coat pocket to keep her from being discovered. And confiscated. I waited, stealthily, as Douglas led the crowd out of my room and down the hall. Then I opened the top drawer of the dresser. Inside were seven pairs of underpants, each stitched with the name of a day of the week. I quickly stashed Blue Belle under them and hurried to catch up to the others.

Douglas had led the group out the front door and was now standing on the lawn. He was still talking away, but he stopped at a weird sight. A vintage fire engine turned onto the street and drove right past us.

And the McCains were on it.

The older McCains were seated in the cab. Dennis's weasely father was standing in a space just behind the cab, along with several other people. Dennis and Matt were hanging on at the back.

We watched the McCains disembark at their Memory Lane house, just two doors down from the Blanchards. Uncle Jim approached Douglas. "Wait a minute. How many people are they trying to fit into that house? Teresa told me there was a six-person limit."

Douglas answered. "Yes, sir. There is. Only six of them are staying. They have special permission for others to come to the Golden Anniversary mass on Sunday."

"Sunday? Well, this is Wednesday."

"Yes, sir. It must have something to do with a photo shoot." He explained, "The McCain family will be doing photo shoots for marketing purposes. That's something I helped to arrange."

I saw that Barney the photographer was one of the people standing behind the engine cab. He hopped down and started to arrange the McCains around the fire truck. He tried to, anyway. Even from where we stood, it was obvious that Captain McCain was giving him a hard time.

After that, we walked down to the Blanchards' house and completed a shorter tour. They had basically the same stuff, except it was slightly more modern. And the boys had received different toys and games. TJ picked up a Slinky as soon as we walked in. He climbed half way up the staircase and let it flop its way back down. It was pretty cool. Patrick struggled doing tricks with a Duncan yo-yo as Uncle Jim commented, "If it isn't a Duncan, it isn't a yo-yo."

Uncle Jim even received a toy of his own—an official NCAA football. He tried to talk Patrick and TJ into throwing it around on the lawn, but they refused to go outside because of the McCains.

At 10:00 am, it was time for Patrick, TJ, and me to go to school. I was actually excited about that; the boys were not. They wanted to stay and play with their stuff, but Aunt Betty shooed them out. Douglas walked us across the roadway, past the neighbors' houses, and back to the Town Square. We stopped outside a two-story building that had *School* carved over its granite entranceway. Behold the sticker:

Douglas turned and pointed behind us. "The kids on your street are the only students for now, but soon all those other houses will be occupied. And then all the houses in the sections beyond it." He turned back. "We'll need to use seven or eight classrooms per week." He gestured to our right. "The playground will be totally packed at recess."

The playground was an area of black asphalt with a few hopscotch squares drawn in white chalk. It was surrounded by a green cyclone fence. I lowered my voice and asked Douglas, "Who will you be then? The playground monitor?"

He laughed. "Maybe. I'll be whatever I need to be."

"Oh? Will you be walking kids to school?"

He looked right into my eyes. "That all depends on the kids. I'll sure be walking you." We held that pose for a moment. Then he raised his hand and pointed. "Turn left when you go inside. That's your classroom." He winked at me and added, "I think you'll like your teacher."

I watched him walk away. I was smiling, giddily. But I was also thinking to myself, *Come on. What teenager winks?*

I pulled open the right side of the double doors and led Patrick and TJ inside. We found ourselves in a tall entranceway with glass trophy cases full of what-had-to-be-bogus trophies. We turned to the left and entered a high-ceiling classroom. To my surprise, several students were already in their seats.

I took a moment to look around. The floor was a checkerboard of large green and white squares. Long slate blackboards ran the length of the front and the right walls. The blackboards had aluminum trays along their bottoms holding white sticks of chalk and gray erasers. The left wall had four windows, without screens, that looked out onto the road. The back wall served as a coat closet. It had gray, accordion-like doors that folded into each other when you pulled them open. The boys followed me back there, and we hung up our coats.

There were sixteen desks in the classroom, arranged in four rows of four. Each desk was made of metal and wood, and you had to slide in from the left side to sit. A teacher's desk faced us at the front of the room. It was made of a darker wood. It had a pencil holder and a large ink blotter on top. An American flag with 48 stars stood to the left; a green metal trashcan sat to the right.

Teresa Zorn entered the room quietly and winked at me. What was it with these Zorns and their winking? She was wearing a long blue skirt with a very plain white blouse, secured at the throat by an opal broach.

TJ whispered to me, "That outfit screams *schoolmarm*."

As Teresa fidgeted with some papers, I led the boys to our seats. I chose a window desk for myself, the third one in the window row. TJ sat next to me, and Patrick squeezed into the desk behind me. Then we looked around.

The Swedish girls were seated in the first two desks in the left rows. I had expected to hate them on general principle, for being blonde and perfect, but they turned and said hi to us so sincerely that I forgave them right away. I waved and said hi. So did TJ, but Patrick just sat there.

That tall boy from the Town Hall was seated right in front of me. He was staring out the window, apparently bored, but his posture was so ramrod straight that I knew he was aware of us.

The two kids from the prayer circle sat in the first two desks in the right rows. The girl was pleasant-enough looking. But she had a very short haircut, and no make-up, and not a hint of jewelry. I thought, *schoolmarm two*, and I was about to whisper that to TJ when she turned and waved politely. So I felt instantly bad again, waved back, and kept my mouth shut. The little boy next to her was very much at ease; simply delighted to be there. He was looking around and smiling, taking it all in.

Teresa seemed to be killing time, and we soon found out why. The McCain boys burst in, loudly, like that was amusing somehow; like anyone cared that they were there. Matt flopped into the last seat near the wall; Dennis took the seat next to him. They had a fun-sucking effect on the room; only the little boy continued to smile.

Teresa finally spoke. "Now that we're all here, let me tell you how delighted I am to be your teacher for the next three days. If you do not remember me, my name is Teresa Zorn. 'Miss Zorn' would be appropriate for our time period, as I am not married. I am a certified teacher in New York State. We will be learning about life in our state and in our nation." Miss Zorn projected a giant wink to the whole class. "There will, however, be no homework!"

The McCains hooted and slapped five. Miss Zorn smiled at them nervously. "I'd like to begin by asking you all to introduce yourselves to your classmates." She pointed at the blonde girl by the window. "Let's start with the first seat and move across."

The first girl said, "I'm Pia Nordstrom, and I am the twin sister of Petra."

She stopped, so the next girl said, "I'm Petra, and I'm no relation to her."

Everyone laughed nervously. Teresa asked, "You two have cool names. What do they mean?"

Pia answered, "One means *pious*, and one means *stone*." She turned slightly to include the class. "Let's see if anyone can guess."

The boy in front of me answered immediately, "Petra means stone, because petrified means turned to stone."

Pia favored him with a smile. A really straight, really white smile.

Then Teresa looked at the little boy and asked with a giant grin, "What's your name, sweetie?"

"I'm Robby Clark."

"What can you tell us about yourself, Robby?"

"That Jesus Christ is my savior."

"Okay. What else?"

"There's nothing else."

"Okay." Teresa, still grinning, turned stiffly to the girl next to him.

She answered without prompting. "I'm Rosemary Clark. I'm a born-again Christian, too, like my brother. My brother might have added, though, that he is an accomplished karate kid, with all kinds of belts and awards."

Teresa nodded gratefully. "Thanks. And can you tell us something about yourself?"

"Well, I am further along in my walk with the Lord, of course, being older. And I took karate, too."

"Okay. Okay, thanks."

Teresa started to turn away, but the little boy called out to her, "Aren't we supposed to start school with a prayer? That's what our dad said."

Teresa seemed momentarily flustered. Then she answered, "Yes, of course. You're right. We are. Let us all bow our heads and start this school day with a prayer."

To my surprise, the McCain boys led the way with that. The only one who did not bow his head was that boy in front of me. After about ten seconds, Miss Zorn pointed at that boy and asked, "Okay. What is your name, please?"

He answered defensively, "Me? I'm Ray Hoffman."

"Tell us a little bit about yourself, Ray."

"I'm a CT." He explained right away, "A CT is a Conspiracy Theorist, a researcher into the death of President John F. Kennedy and its cover-up by the U. S. government. I am not a Conspiracy 'Buff.' I don't even know what that term means. I am of course not an LN, or Lone-Nutter, which describes someone who believes that President Kennedy was killed by a lone nut named Lee Harvey Oswald. That never happened."

I had the feeling that he might like to continue, but Teresa said, "Thank you, Ray. That's very interesting."

She then pointed at me. I said something dumb. "I'm Alice Lynch. I go to school in Levittown. I want to be a teacher."

Teresa smiled. "Neat. Just like me." She pointed at TJ. "How about you?"

"I'm TJ. I like to draw. I was home schooled for the last three years because I had exercise-induced asthma. I don't have it anymore, so I won't be home schooled anymore."

Teresa nodded. "Thanks." She nodded at Patrick. "And you?"

Patrick pointed at me, "I'm her cousin." And at TJ, "And his brother."

"Okay. What's your name?"

"Oh, sorry. It's Patrick."

"Thanks, Patrick."

She moved to her left and smiled at the McCains. Before she could speak, Matt interrupted. "I'm Matt and that's Dennis." He looked around defiantly. "You don't want to know about us."

Teresa, still smiling, concluded, "Okay then. That's that, and thank you all. In case you were wondering, you *will* get credit for attending my class. I have already contacted your schools and arranged for it." Teresa gestured broadly. "In this classroom, we will have some readings, some film strips, some slides. But a very important part of your education here will come from our guest speakers. Each of you has at least one fascinating family member who has agreed to speak to us."

Dennis McCain asked, "About what?"

At this point, my mom would have told him to raise his hand before he spoke. Miss Zorn ignored the behavior. "We will ask each guest speaker the same two questions: 'What days are you here to relive? And why?'"

Matt said, "I know the *why* part. Because it's all free!" He exchanged another high five with Dennis.

Dennis spoke out again, "So this is supposed to be . . . what? A school in a time warp?"

Miss Zorn answered politely, "This is a public school in the late 1950s."

"Is that why there's no blacks? No Hispanics?"

Matt added, "No Ricans?"

"That's a good question." Dennis and Matt high-fived again. I was already tired of that. Teresa continued. "Here in 1957, Hispanics make up only about five percent of the U. S, population. And blacks, although the Supreme Court ruled school segregation to be illegal in 1954—" Teresa suddenly broke off to ask the group, "Can anybody tell me the name of that Supreme Court ruling?"

I knew the answer, but I wanted to see who else did. Ray, without raising his hand, muttered, "Brown versus the Board of Education of Topeka, Kansas."

Teresa shot a dazzling smile his way. "Excellent, Ray!" She turned back to Dennis. "But blacks would not truly be integrated into the public schools until the 1960s."

Matt asked, "So, do you have any blacks here at all?"

"What do you mean? Where?"

"Here. In this Memory Lane place."

"In the whole park? Oh yes. We have African American guests."

"How come I haven't seen any?"

"That's a good question, too." Another high five. How pathetic. "It may be that African American guests avoid our 1950s decade because of the issues we just discussed. They might not want to relive that particular time."

"Yeah. Right. Like who wants to walk around all day gettin' called a nigger?"

Teresa's face tightened, but she stayed in schoolmarm character. "I believe the term today, in 1957, is *colored*."

"My boys on the baseball team don't call each other colored. That'd be an insult. They call each other *niggah*. And it's cool. They just don't want me calling them that."

Teresa turned away from them. "That sounds like good advice." The classroom door opened a crack. Douglas stuck his head in and gave Teresa a thumbs-up sign. Teresa said, "Okay.

Excellent. We're ready for our first guest speaker. Let me introduce her to you now."

Douglas opened the door wide and stepped back to let the guest enter. She was the lady we had seen in the Town Hall, Pia and Petra's grandmother. She was dressed in dark blue sweatpants and sweatshirt. The shirt had *USA* emblazoned in white with red piping across the front. She stopped in front of the twins' desks, and they giggled together like three teenagers.

Teresa Zorn announced, "It's my pleasure to introduce Mrs. Ingrid Nordstrom who, as Miss Ingrid Swenson, was a member of the United States Olympics Team." All of us clapped spontaneously, even the McCains. Teresa continued, "Mrs. Nordstrom, can you tell us what days you are here to relive, and why?"

Mrs. Swenson smiled sweetly. "I am here to watch my very young self march into the Olympic stadium in Squaw Valley, California. That happened on Thursday, February 18, 1960, at the opening ceremonies of the Eighth Olympic Winter Games." We clapped again. "I am also going to watch myself compete in the Ladies 3,000 Meter Speed Skating." She smiled sheepishly. "I finished in fourteenth place, by the way. But still, it was all very thrilling, and all very memorable."

She stopped there and looked at Teresa, so Teresa turned to us. "Excellent. Thank you, Mrs. Nordstrom. Now, who has a question about the 1960 Winter Olympics?"

Ray's hand went up casually. He asked, "Did President Kennedy come to the games?"

Mrs. Nordstrom pointed out, "I believe Dwight Eisenhower was the President then."

Ray seemed stunned. Then he slapped his own forehead, really hard. "You're right! JFK wasn't sworn in until 1961. January 23, 1961. Sorry."

Teresa surveyed the class. "Excellent. Anyone else?"

Matt McCain pointed at Mrs. Nordstrom and blurted out, "Let's see your medals!"

Petra turned and corrected him, "Let's see your manners."

Matt started to reply, "Let's see your—" and stopped, causing a burst of smarmy laughter from Dennis.

It looked like the twins both wanted to go off on the McCains, but Mrs. Nordstrom steadied each of them with a look. Then she answered graciously, "As I believe I implied, I did not win an Olympic medal. I have lots of other medals and trophies, but I have not brought any of them with me. Perhaps some other time."

Teresa stepped toward her and said, "Thank you, Mrs. Nordstrom," and we applauded again. The old lady grinned at the twins and started out, pausing just a moment to tousle Robby Clark's hair. That boy was irresistible.

Teresa stared at the classroom clock. Then she asked Dennis McCain, "Do you know where your father and grandfather are? They're also scheduled to speak this morning."

Dennis shrugged. "No."

"Do you know if they are coming?"

Matt spoke up. "They're coming! Don't worry about it. If they said they were coming, they're coming."

Dennis added, "My father always has to be on call."

I thought, *Why? In case someone needs a lying little weasel?* But I didn't say it. When it became apparent that there was no second speaker, Miss Zorn began a school-type lesson. She pulled out an old textbook titled *Our Nation's Story*. She used a projector to show slides about the USA and the USSR being locked in a struggle to the death.

It was all pretty scary, but Teresa Zorn described it with the same smooth delivery as her sales pitch. "Here in 1957, both we and the Soviets understand that a nuclear war means mutually assured destruction. Whoever starts a war can be certain that the other side will retaliate, and all life on earth will end. We Americans must live with the possibility of an atomic missile attack every day and every night."

The lesson continued like that until just before noon when Douglas opened the door again. Teresa suddenly left nuclear destruction behind and called out, "Great! Lunch is here!"

Douglas had wheeled up a black cart. On top of the cart was an assortment of metal lunchboxes based on 1950s TV shows. Teresa explained, "The outsides of the lunchboxes are different, but the insides are all the same. Today we are featuring Oscar Mayer Sandwich Spread on white Wonder Bread, whole milk with Bosco chocolate syrup, and Ring Dings. Everyone pick up a lunchbox and take it out to the entranceway. You can eat there, relax, and get to know each other."

Robbie got up first. He seemed delighted to get a *Lassie* lunchbox. When my turn came, I grabbed an *Adventures of Ozzie and Harriet* box because, I must admit, Ricky Nelson looked cute. TJ took the same one. Patrick grabbed himself a *Davy Crockett* box. Since there was no *John F. Kennedy Assassination* lunchbox, Ray Hoffman settled for *Superman.*

We all filed out and ate in the entranceway, by the trophy case. No one really relaxed, possibly because there were no seats. I guess the idea was for us to mingle, but we all sat on the floor within our own groups. Some kids were definitely stealing glances, though. Ray Hoffman couldn't keep his eyes off Pia and Petra. Neither, for that matter, could Matt McCain. The twins, however, seemed to have eyes only for TJ.

The uncomfortable, unhealthy lunch finally ended when Miss Zorn opened the door and asked, "Isn't that sandwich spread great? And who can beat chocolate milk and Ring Dings?"

Only Robby Clark felt compelled to shout, "Yeah!"

Teresa told us, "You can leave your trash right where it is and come back in."

A minute later, we were all back in our seats staring at a rickety white movie screen while Teresa fiddled with a sixteen-millimeter projector. When she got it working, she turned off the lights. This caused Matt to whisper to one of the twins, to either one I guess, "Come sit on my lap for the movie."

They both ignored him completely, as if he had never been born. Nicely done. But both McCains continued to talk throughout the film. What a pair of jerks. Miss Zorn, despite being a certified teacher in New York State, let it all go.

The first film was titled *Duck and Cover*. It was really a cartoon, but it was deadly serious. The main character, Burt the Turtle, was walking along when a monkey with a stick of dynamite dropped from a tree branch. The monkey, I guess, was the Soviet Union, and the dynamite was an atomic missile. Burt pulled his head into his shell to be safe. The rest of us, however, couldn't do that. We had to learn to duck and cover.

Okay.

The next film was titled *All About Fallout*. It showed what to do in the days and weeks following an atomic attack. Deadly radiated particles will fall to the ground when an atomic bomb goes off. But if you duck and cover, and then hurry to a fallout shelter, those particles will soon start to lose their deadliness. By the next day, they will only be one one-hundredth of their original strength.

Great. No problem.

At the end of that film, Ray Hoffman turned around and looked me with an expression of complete incredulity. He whispered, "Do you believe a word of this crap?" I raised my shoulders up and down noncommittally. He added, "It's just government propaganda."

Miss Zorn queued up a third film titled *A Day Called X,* about a nuclear attack on Portland, Oregon. Shortly after it started, though, the classroom door opened and Douglas led two men inside.

My blood boiled on seeing them again. They were Dennis McCain's father and grandfather, our missing speakers. The father, the shorter of the two by a full head, reached over and turned on the light switch, causing the film to basically disappear on the screen. He spotted Teresa at the projector and announced, "We're supposed to be speaking here, right?"

"Yes! You're Captain McCain and Lieutenant McCain."

"Yeah. That's us."

"We'll be right with you."

Teresa started to shut down the projector, but he responded rudely, "You'll be with us now if you want to do this. We could get called away at any minute."

I believe my mom would have told them to get lost at that point, but Teresa dutifully stepped away from the projector and joined them at the front of the class. Captain McCain spoke up in a loud, old man voice that I remembered from the first time I heard him. "What did you want us to talk about? Fire fighting?"

Teresa smiled. "First, we want to ask the questions we ask all guests: What days are you here to relive? And why?"

The old man announced, "It's my wedding anniversary."

"Oh? A special anniversary?"

"The fiftieth." He looked out at us as if he was expecting applause for that, but he didn't get any.

There followed a long, awkward pause. Teresa finally prodded them, "Would you like to tell us a little bit about yourselves?"

The short guy spoke up. "My father here is a retired captain on the FDNY, the Fire Department of New York. Me and my brother are firefighters, too. Or, in my brother's case, he *was* a firefighter. He died a hero on nine-eleven." He pointed at Dennis and Matt. "Maybe some day these young men will join the department, too." The McCain boys hooted and clapped.

Teresa Zorn looked at us. "Excellent. Are there any questions from the class?"

The next pause was even longer, to the point where it got embarrassing. I found myself drifting back in my mind to the office at Jonas Salk Middle School. I remembered the scene in great detail. I heard these two screaming at everyone in there. I saw my mom come in and have to take their abuse. I watched the principal do nothing to help her. Suddenly, I realized that I did have a question, based on my Google research. And I raised my hand.

The short guy looked at me, but he didn't speak. Finally Teresa did. "Go ahead, Alice. Ask your question."

I stood up and locked eyes with the short guy. "What was your brother's name?"

"Captain William McCain." He pointed at Matt and Dennis. "Their uncle, and an American hero."

I asked, "Was he born on Long Island, in 1958?"

His little weasel head stretched upward, surprised. He answered, "Yeah."

The grandfather felt compelled to repeat, "And he died on September eleventh."

I turned toward him. "Really? Are you sure about that?"

The Captain just blinked at me for several seconds in astonishment, so I turned back to the father. "And are you sure that he held the rank of captain?" He, too, became speechless. "Because I recently did a search online. I found an obituary in *Newsday* for a firefighter named William McCain. He was born in Levittown in 1958. But he wasn't a captain, or even a lieutenant; he was still at the rank of firefighter." The short guy squirmed as I went on. "He died at Hempstead Hospital, of heart failure, on August 27, 2001. Is that the same guy? It must be the same guy, right?"

The two of them exchanged a furious look, but they didn't

reply. They couldn't, because I had them dead to rights. "Because that would be—what—fifteen days before September eleventh, wouldn't it?"

The short guy snapped at Teresa, "That's enough of this! This is disrespect."

The old guy was staring at me with a look of pure hatred. I stared right back. He finally found his voice, his old-guy-scary voice. "Who the hell do you think you are, talking about my son like that?"

I faced him down. I answered as calmly as I could. "Who am I? I am Alice Lynch. My mother was Mrs. Donna Lynch from Jonas Salk Middle School. Do you remember her? She died on September twenty-fourth, and that's true. She was an American hero, and that's true, too. *I'm* not lying about it."

Captain McCain stared at me a few seconds longer; then he broke away, unable to meet my gaze. He lumbered toward the door and exited quickly, followed by his weasely son.

Matt McCain rose half way out of his seat, his fist clenched, like he was going to come after me, but Dennis grabbed his elbow and held him still. I heard Dennis whisper, "Later." He looked at me with the cold calculation of a snake.

Teresa just stood there, totally clueless. Finally, she tried to direct our attention back to her lesson. "So, what have we learned? Captain McCain is here to celebrate his golden wedding anniversary. He and his wife married in 1957, one of the years we are studying today. Let's get back to our film."

The lights dimmed again, and the old projector whirred, but I don't think anyone was paying attention to the nuclear attack on Portland, Oregon. TJ poked me and whispered, "You go, girl!"

I turned to him and nodded. Then I noticed Patrick. He had his head down. He appeared to be hyperventilating. I leaned over, "Patrick, are you okay?"

"No. I am not okay. Are you crazy?"

"What?"

"The McCains! Do you think they're going to come after you?"

"I don't really care."

"That's because they're not! They're not, because you're a girl. They're going to come after me."

TJ whispered, "Don't be silly."

I tried to defend myself by saying, "All I did was tell the truth about those creeps. What's wrong with that?"

Patrick didn't answer. As I sat back and thought about it, though, I knew he was right. He could be facing big trouble now with the McCains. We all could.

When the school bell rang at three, we got a lucky break. Teresa announced, "I need Dennis and Matt to stay behind for a photo shoot. The rest of you can go. See you tomorrow!" She winked at me. I really wish she would stop doing that. She added, "Unless there's a Soviet attack." She pointed to Robby. "And if you see a flash in the sky, what should you do?"

Robby Clark shouted, "Duck and cover!" and Teresa laughed. The rest of us detoured wide around the McCains, grabbed our coats, and exited. We ran through the schoolyard and down the street like we thought atomic bombs could fall at any moment.

The boys hurried past my cape house and disappeared into their own. I didn't, though. I slowed down and turned into our driveway, hoping to check out the garage. (I was the only one who hadn't seen it.) It looked like a small version of the house—the same slate gray color with white shingles. The big door was pulled down so I peered through the side window. My grandfather was on his knees polishing the front bumper of the '57 Fairlane; polishing it with extraordinary care.

I decided to let him be, and I walked back to the kitchen door. From the stoop I could hear the TV set blaring. When I entered the living room, my grandmother looked up at me and spoke, very loudly, over the sound of a soap opera, "That Douglas boy was here all morning. He got your grandfather started working on that old Ford. He got me started watching my old stories." Her voice took on a tone of wonder. "I remember them all, Alice! I remember everyone in them; everything about them."

"Cool. And how's it going at Aunt Betty's house?"

"She said Jim just wants to watch football for three days, and drink beer. So Betty spent most of the day over here. She likes the soaps, too, and the magazines, and the catalogues." This was more enthusiasm than I had ever heard from my grandmother. Ever. About anything. Memory Lane was already a big success.

I sat on the couch next to her and watched the TV screen. A middle-aged woman was looking into a mirror like she was about to cry, while violin music played in the background. I waited for a commercial to come on. Then I said, "I've been meaning to thank you, Grandmom, for your gift."

She looked at me, surprised. "What do you mean?"

"The house! Half of your house."

"Oh. That was always the plan, from the time Betty and Donna were little. They were always going to get the house."

"Still, it's very generous of you."

She waved my words away. "It wasn't *my* money. It was what your grandfather made at his garage."

"But you managed that money well, I'm sure."

She conceded, "I did what I could."

The commercial ended, and the show came back on, but I persisted with my questions. "So, what's this show called?"

"*The Secret Storm.*"

"Uh huh. What's it about?"

She seemed a little distracted, but she did answer. "It's the same as all the others—*The Guiding Light, Love of Life, As the*

World Turns. They're all about women trying to hold their families together."

"Uh huh. So, what kind of stuff happens to the women?"

"Stuff? Well, problems. Family problems. Nobody else in the families can solve them, so the women have to."

"What do they do?"

She was getting impatient. "They do what they have to do! They face the problems, they make the decisions, they hold their families together."

I said, "Okay, I see. Thanks." And I stopped talking.

The show ended a few minutes later with a great swell of violins. My grandmother got up and announced, "I'm going to rinse out the glasses and cups. You should always do that." I was tempted to say, 'We can call Douglas to do it,' but it sounded like she really wanted to clean something.

I switched the TV over to another channel. (It only had three.) This one was playing *The Mickey Mouse Club*. I watched for a while; I learned that Wednesday is "Anything-Can-Happen Day."

Then I switched it off and stood at our bay window for a few minutes, observing the street. A *Charles Chips* truck rolled by from the right. It was delivering potato chips, I guess. Then a police cruiser with a little red light on top came from the left. I leaned forward slightly and pressed my face against the glass, looking left. I had expected Patrick and TJ to stop by, but there was no sign of them. Eventually, I turned the TV back on and found myself watching *Queen for a Day.*

Queen for a Day turned out to be a truly evil show. Three women were forced to beg a studio audience for help to survive personal tragedies in their lives—a child with cancer, a husband who needed an iron lung, and so on. Two of the women would lose and get absolutely nothing. Or maybe a case of baked beans or something. But the third would get an ermine robe, a gold crown, the iron lung, and an endless list of 1950s products. I watched the show unfold like a fatal car wreck.

Just before six, I heard a rap at the kitchen door. My grandmother opened it, and I heard Douglas's friendly voice. "Hello, Mrs. Abel! Your dinner has arrived."

I switched off the TV and hurried in there. Douglas and another guy were standing outside holding up aluminum trays of food. The other guy had short, curly hair and the blackest five-o'clock shadow I had ever seen. His blue windbreaker said *Memory Lane, Francis.*

My grandmother took a step back and told them, "You can put it over there. I'll get some plates and glasses."

Douglas explained to her, "No, Mrs. Abel. Your work ended when you filled out the dinner menu last month. All you're supposed to do now is sit and enjoy yourself." He held out a copy of *Newsday.* "Here, you can read today's paper."

My grandmother looked at him like he was talking nonsense, but she did take the copy of *Newsday,* and she did back out of the way. Douglas and Francis set to work immediately. And silently. Douglas didn't say anything else until he was ready to leave, and then it was just, "Enjoy your dinner, folks. Pick up the phone and dial *O* when you're finished, and either Francis or me will pick it up."

I smiled and replied, "Okay," but I couldn't help but think, '*Francis or I; not Francis or me. You wouldn't say, Me will pick that up*, would you, Douglas?'

I turned back and saw that my grandmother, for lack of any chores to do, had already taken her seat at the white Formica table. She sounded a little annoyed when she asked me, "Aren't we supposed to eat at six o'clock? All of us? Where are the others?"

The phone rang. I picked it up to hear, "Hi! This is Teresa Zorn. Is this Alice?"

"Yes."

"Okay, Alice, this is very important: Be sure to remind everyone to share family stories at dinner tonight. That's how you start your trip down Memory Lane."

"Okay."

"Everybody should take a turn. You kids should start with your earliest memories. That will help your grandparents remember when you were young, and when your parents were young, and so on, back to 1957."

"Okay."

"Do you promise to remind them?"

"Yes."

"Great! Have fun with that!"

Aunt Betty, Uncle Jim, and the boys arrived five minutes later and took their seats around the table. The main course laid out before us consisted of pot roast, baked potatoes, green bean casserole, and apple fritters. Drinks were bottles of Coca Cola and, for the two men, bottles of Budweiser.

We sat and waited for my grandfather for a minute; then Uncle Jim went out back to get him. When they returned, my grandfather stopped at the sink to wash his black hands. Uncle Jim told us, "Man, Grandpop really loves that car! I practically had to drag him away from it."

Aunt Betty looked over at the sink. "That's nice, Pop." My grandfather didn't reply. Uncle Jim asked, "So what exactly are you doing to that car, Pop? Changing the spark plugs?"

My grandfather took his seat and explained, "It's all cleaned up. No dents at all."

"That's good. A '57 Fairlane, in mint condition? Do you know what that's worth?" My grandfather took a swig of beer, so Uncle Jim answered his own question. "About fifty grand." He smiled at me. *Have you driven a Ford lately?* Right?"

We bowed our heads, and my grandmother led us in a quick prayer. Then I did my duty, passing on Teresa Zorn's phone message. "Teresa called and said we're supposed to share family stories about the past. That's how we begin our trip down Memory Lane. Everybody has to tell his or her earliest memory."

Aunt Betty beamed. "I love that idea! Who wants to start? Patrick?"

Patrick shoved a forkful of pot roast into his mouth and forced out, "No."

"Okay. TJ?"

"I'd rather not, Mamà."

Everyone concentrated on the food—passing things, filling their plates, but not speaking. Uncle Jim finally rescued the moment by saying, "I remember something. I remember that Patrick had a very hard head as a child. Hard as a cannon ball. He would use it as a battering ram in peewee football." Uncle Jim and Aunt Betty laughed. "Remember? He was the star of his team because of that hard head."

Then Aunt Betty said, "I remember TJ in sports, too! In karate class. He would always break those boards. Lots and lots of boards."

TJ held up his hand and turned it, showing off its edge. "If not for me, those boards would be alive today. They would be planks now."

Aunt Betty continued, "And I remember both boys in Cub Scouts, with their little blue uniforms." She turned to me. "And Alice! I remember when Alice was in preschool—she couldn't have been more than fifteen months old. She was already talking, and in full sentences."

Aunt Betty held her gaze on me, so I figured it was my turn. I contributed this: "I have an earliest memory. It's on my third birthday. I remember my dad standing in our kitchen with his hand on the light switch." I paused to think about that moment: I was thinking about my *real* family—Mom, Dad, and baby me—not these strange people around this strange table. That thought made me feel so empty, but I finished up, "Then Mom entered with a chocolate cake. With yellow candles. They both sang *Happy Birthday to You.*"

Aunt Betty said, "Nice;" then asked, "Okay, what is your earliest memory, Jim?"

Uncle Jim thought for a moment. "It has to be sitting in front of the tube watching football with my dad and my brothers. That was a real event back then. There was no DVR, no TiVO; no tapes even. No way to record a game. You were either there in front of the TV or you were not."

Aunt Betty's eyes suddenly teared up. "I'd like to share a memory about my sister Donna. I remember us playing school in the backyard. I was eight and she was five, but she was the teacher and I was the student." Aunt Betty turned to my grandmother, "What do you remember about her, Mom?"

My grandmother looked surprised to be included, and not at all happy. "What do I remember about Donna? Donna always wanted to be a mommy. That's what I remember. She was always playing with dolls."

That didn't sound right to me. Aunt Betty then asked, "And what's your own earliest memory, Mom?"

My grandmother exhaled, clearly tired of this activity. She finally answered, "I remember a family vacation. My family went to Luray Caverns in Virginia."

Aunt Betty asked, "Is that when you got claustrophobic down in the caves, and you panicked, and you had to be taken out by a park ranger?"

My grandmother looked appalled. "Nonsense!"

"But that's what you told us."

"I never said any such thing because it's not true. We had a lovely time."

Aunt Betty countered, "That's what you told me when I wanted to go on a class trip to Crystal Cave, Pennsylvania. And you wouldn't let me go. I remember that."

My grandmother waved her hand emphatically. "Bah! You remember it wrong. You were too little." She turned away from Aunt Betty with finality, as if to say, *That's my story, and I'm sticking with it.*

So the family sharing ground to a halt right there. After everyone had finished dessert, an apple pie with raisins, Aunt Betty picked up the black phone and dialed *O*.

Five minutes later, Douglas and that I-need-a-shave guy arrived to clean up. This time, though, they were accompanied by Teresa Zorn. She entered through the front door and staked out a spot at the far end of the kitchen.

She raised one hand to keep us all in there. "Mr. and Mrs. Abel, I have something for you." She held up a DVD inside a white, paper sleeve. "This is the first of three DVDs we have produced *just* for you." She attempted to hand the sleeve to my grandmother, but my grandmother looked away. Teresa then pressed it into my grandfather's hand. He just stared down at it, letting it flop loosely in his grasp like a white rag.

Teresa continued, "Fifty years ago tonight, you two were planning your honeymoon to a special destination, a place you loved to go to when you were dating—Atlantic City, New Jersey. Well, tonight's DVD is all about that city. I hope you enjoy it!"

TJ asked her, "How are we supposed to play a DVD? They haven't been invented yet."

Teresa flashed him a brief wink. "It is an anomaly, TJ, but for a very good cause." She turned back to my grandparents. "Your Admiral TV has been outfitted with a DVD slot in the back. You never even noticed it, did you? You may only use it to view these specially produced, personalized DVDs."

Teresa pointed to the living room. "Now go in there, all of you, and take your seats. The crew here will save any leftovers in Tupperware containers for a midnight snack." She assured TJ, "Tupperware was invented in 1946," to which he replied, "Thank goodness."

She then handed Patrick a thin box full of wrapped, multicolored candies. "And here's the perfect snack for tonight's viewing—a box of genuine Atlantic City salt water taffy."

Teresa took my grandfather's arm and started him toward the living room. "There's not a thing for you to do, Mr. Abel, except come in here, sit down, and enjoy this trip down your personal memory lane."

We all dutifully followed them in. Patrick, TJ, and I sat on the floor and opened up the salt-water taffy. The adults found seats on the couch and chairs. Teresa took the DVD from my grandfather's grasp. She walked to the back of the Admiral, slid the disc into a slot, and pulled the on/off knob. It took a few seconds for the set to warm up; then the screen displayed a *Memory Lane Productions* logo and this message: *A film produced especially for John and Margaret Abel.* That screen faded, to be replaced by the image of a long wooden boardwalk and the words *Atlantic City, New Jersey.*

Teresa slipped quietly into the kitchen as an announcer's voice began, "John and Margaret Abel, welcome to Atlantic City, New Jersey, the site of your honeymoon on November 24th, 1957!"

My grandmother commented, to no one in particular, "We spent one night there. It was freezing. Then we came back." She looked at my grandfather, "It was November. I never knew why you took me there in November."

My grandfather's tone sounded like he was agreeing with her, but his words said something else entirely. "Yeah. It was a great place."

I held up the box of salt-water taffy for the adults to take some. Aunt Betty and Uncle Jim did, but the old people shook their heads no. The announcer described all the great entertainers who appeared in Atlantic City, including Ricky Nelson, "who sang before over forty thousand fans." A song called "On the Boardwalk in Atlantic City" came on. It played over a montage of 1950s celebrities visiting the place.

My grandfather really came to life when the screen showed an old hotel, and the voice announced, "This is where you stayed, John and Margaret! The Skyscraper of the Sea, the twenty-four story Claridge Hotel."

My grandfather pointed at the TV and confirmed, "That's where we stayed!" Then he reminded my grandmother, "We used to drive down there a lot, over the summer. We'd stop in and have a drink at the Claridge. So we said, 'Let's come back here for our honeymoon.'"

My grandmother seemed frozen solid, so Aunt Betty replied, "That's nice, Pop."

Then the screen showed a bizarre sight—a frightened horse being forced to dive into a small swimming pool forty feet below. My grandfather called out, "The diving horse!"

The announcer confirmed that and explained the phenomenon of "the world famous diving horse."

TJ muttered to me, "Shouldn't we call it the 'world-famous, pushed-off-a-platform-and-trying-not-to-drown horse?'"

I muttered, "Yes. That'd be more like it."

The DVD rolled on with a segment on the Miss America Pageant—a montage of women in bathing suits with frozen smiles and lacquered hair—walking up and down to the tune of "There She Is, Miss America." The segment ended comically with a photo of my young grandmother in a bathing suit on the beach. It was supposed to be funny, but none of us dared to laugh, or even to look at her.

After that, the song, the segment, and the DVD came to an end, and the *Memory Lane Productions* logo reappeared. We all kept staring at that logo, unsure what to do, until Teresa Zorn popped her head in from the kitchen. She demanded to know, "So? What did you think of that?"

Aunt Betty answered right away. "It was very special. Very memorable."

Teresa Zorn's eyes scanned the room, looking at each of us. She decided to let it go at one answer. As Patrick, TJ, and I got to our feet, Teresa added, "Don't forget to go to the Town Square tonight! Have a soda at the Soda Shop; buy a new game at Woolworth's." She looked right at me. "Meet some boys." She turned to include everyone else. "And see some outstanding fireworks."

Since it was still early, Patrick, TJ, and I decided to go to their place to play some board games. We pulled on our Sears Catalogue coats—my Hideaway Hood, TJ's Sheepskin-lined

Mackinaw, and Patrick's Reversible Three-Season. We exited by the front door and walked down the long cement pathway to the street. Several cool, long cars were cruising by with Memory Lane cast members at the wheel. Patrick didn't seem to notice them. (Was he really that dense?) TJ did and commented, "What's with the fins on the cars? Did they help with gas mileage or something?"

I told him, "I don't think so. I don't think they cared about gas mileage."

"So . . . They were just fins for fins' sake?"

"Yeah. I guess you could say that."

"Cool."

Because Uncle Jim was spending part of his time in the 1960s, the Blanchards' house had some different touches inside. Instead of the built-in bookcase under the stairs, they had a built-in TV set. Their couches, lamps, and carpeting were all more modern. Their radio console, a Philco Phonarama, was really big—with storage space in its bottom for a dozen board games including Clue, Battleship, and Sorry. After a quick vote, which I lost, we started to play Battleship.

We had just finished setting up on the floor when the front door opened and Aunt Betty and Uncle Jim entered. As she unbuttoned her coat (a blue Splash Tweed), Aunt Betty warned us, "There's just one rule, kids. After each game, you have to pick up the pieces."

I answered, "Okay" for all of us.

They went into the kitchen. Uncle Jim came back holding a can of Rheingold beer in one hand and a can of Schaefer beer in the other. He announced, "Time for a taste test. He watched us play for a few minutes, alternating chugs from his cans. Eventually, he said, "So? When you're done here, are you going to go mingle with the other kids?"

Patrick's arm shot up and pointed to the west. "I'm not mingling with the McCains."

Uncle Jim assured him, "No. Maybe not the McCains. But you should meet some of the others. They all looked pretty nice."

Aunt Betty called in, "Those blonde twins are gorgeous!"

TJ nodded. Then, to everyone's surprise, Patrick said, "That other girl was nice, too."

TJ's jaw dropped. "Who? The bible girl?"

Patrick looked at him. "Yeah."

"Like, Miss Parting of the Red Sea, 1957?"

"Shut up!"

I said, "I thought she was really nice, too, Patrick. And her brother's a little doll. Let's go to their house first."

We finished the game, picked up the pieces, and put it away. We walked out into the cold night air and crossed the street to the Clarks, dodging two more super-long, super-shiny cars.

I led the boys up to the Clarks' front door and knocked. A tall lady with brown, wavy hair opened the door and smiled. She was wearing a dress and an apron, like a classic-TV sitcom mom. I said, "Hello, Mrs. Clark. I'm Alice Lynch. These are my cousins, Patrick and TJ Blanchard."

Mrs. Clark looked delighted. She took a step back to let us in. "Teresa Zorn called and said some of the neighborhood kids might be out mingling. I didn't know if anyone would come here." She pointed to the living room. "Wait in there a moment, and I'll get the children."

Patrick, TJ, and I shuffled into the living room. It was like ours except for one thing—there was no TV set, blaring or otherwise. There just wasn't one at all.

Rosemary Clark descended the stairs followed by Robby. Was she ever without him? I had to admit she looked nice, in an I-don't-wear-makeup kind of way. She was about my height, too, which I liked. She seemed genuinely surprised to see us. Surprised and happy. "Hi, you guys! Thanks for coming."

Neither of my cousins replied, so I said, "Sure. We thought we'd stop by and mingle, like Miss Zorn said."

Robby asked me, "What's mingle?"

I replied, "It's when you talk to a bunch of new people, and you get to know them."

He giggled. "Mingle."

Rosemary took our coats and hung them up in the kitchen.

When she returned, Patrick said something, but it wasn't good. "Don't you have a TV?"

Rosemary shook her head. "No."

"Not at all. Not upstairs?"

"No. Not anywhere. For that matter, we don't have one at our real house, either."

Patrick's mouth fell open. "How can you not have a TV? What about a computer? Do you have a computer?"

"No."

"No Internet?"

Robby shouted, "It's the devil's tool!"

That killed the conversation for a few seconds, but Patrick persisted, "What do you do for news? Like, current events?"

"We read the newspaper," Rosemary told him. "*Newsday*, just like you. And magazines."

"Christian magazines?"

"Some. We read *Christianity Today*. But we read *Time* and *Newsweek*, too. We have several issues in the magazine rack over there, all from 1962."

Mrs. Clark glided in from the kitchen with a plate of chocolate chip cookies, and Patrick's face lit up. We ate the cookies and mingled with the Clarks for another fifteen minutes. Then Rosemary looked at the clock and said, "Come on, Robby. We promised Dad we would be back for prayer circle." She looked right at Patrick. "Anyone is welcome to join us, but we'll certainly understand if you'd rather not."

Patrick seemed to be considering it, but he finally replied, "Maybe some other time. We gotta get going now."

Rosemary hurried into the kitchen to get our coats. As she handed Patrick his, she suggested, "Maybe we'll see you at the Town Square."

He asked dumbly, "The Town Square?"

"The place with the shops and stuff. We're going up there later."

"Great!" he answered. "We'll see you there." He even turned to her brother. "See you, Robby!"

Robby yelled, "Bye! Thanks for coming to mingle!"

I led the boys out of the house and to the left, to our next stop—the Hoffmans. The situation there was very different. Ray Hoffman opened the door, but he did not seem very happy to see us. He finally managed to mumble, "Hi. Come on in," as he backed up.

The Hoffmans' house had a modern, 1960s look, with low furniture and wall-to-wall carpeting. *Three* console TVs were set up the living room. Each was tuned to a different network. Ray's father sat at a point equidistant between them, frowning. He seemed totally focused, but he did say, "Hi, kids. Welcome to 1963 and all that. Take off your coats. Ray, get them some sodas." Then he slipped back into total immersion.

Ray indicated that we should follow him into the kitchen. He pulled open the refrigerator door and pointed out a wide variety of soda bottles: Coca Cola, Pepsi Cola, Lemon Squirt,

Seven Up, Hires Root Beer. We all made our selections and took seats around the table.

I said, "Is it just you and your dad here?"

"Yeah."

"Is that your family?"

"What?"

"Is it just you and your dad? Are you, like, a semi-orphan?"

Ray seemed offended. "No. I'm not a semi-orphan. I have a mother and a sister. They did not make the trip. They backed out at the last minute."

Mr. Hoffman called in from the living room. "They backed out! We never made any pretense about what this trip was about, did we? November 22, 1963? Does anyone *not* know what happened that day?"

Ray countered with, "Does anyone *know* what happened that day?"

Mr. Hoffman answered, "No! No one really knows." His voice turned angry. "By the way, these are not the authentic network feeds; nowhere near. They've messed around with this lineup, I know they have. I am increasingly unhappy with this place, Ray. Or decreasingly happy with this place, if you prefer."

Ray confided to us, "They'd better watch out. The Memory Lane people want my dad to write good things about them on his blog. He gets hundreds of hits. They want him to tell other CTs to come here and relive other events."

The left side of TJ's mouth curved up almost to his ear. "Other events? Like what?"

Ray looked toward the living room. "I don't know. Whatever they're into. It could be the assassination of Bobby Kennedy or of Martin Luther King; the Watergate hearings; the impeachment of Richard Nixon. Any event that went on for a few days and got extended play on television."

TJ interjected, "Those all sound like fun."

Ray continued, "Or nine-eleven, maybe. Nine-eleven and its immediate aftermath. All those white-dust zombie people wandering around Manhattan."

"Funner still."

Mr. Hoffman appeared in the doorway, still frowning. "Well, at least they got my bike right."

Patrick assumed, "A motorcycle?"

"No. No. My bicycle, from back when I was your age. I had a Western Flyer that I absolutely loved. I rode it until I got my first car." He pointed toward the garage. "I'm going to go adjust the seat and handlebars now. Ray, you can watch something else on TV."

"Really?"

"Yeah. There was still network programming on November 21, 1963. The programs only got preempted for major news—the assassination itself, Oswald's murder, JFK's funeral. Otherwise, the boob tube marched on."

Patrick asked, "So if today's only November 21st, what do you watch? The President hasn't been shot yet, right?"

Mr. Hoffman reached into a cabinet and pulled out a short stack of discs. "Right. We have some classic DVDs to warm up with: *On Trial: Lee Harvey Oswald.* That's a good one. *Four Days in November, The Day the Nation Died, The Dallas Tapes.* All strong." His frown deepened. "Look at this, Ray. They stuck Oliver Stone's *JFK* in here. He shook his head rapidly. "Trashy, stupid nonsense. Damaging to the cause. Very damaging." Mr. Hoffman stashed the DVDs back in the cabinet and exited through the kitchen door, still muttering.

We all took our sodas into the living room. Ray slid a DVD of his own into a slot behind the center TV, an RCA Victor Lowboy. Then he pulled the knob and we waited for the screen to reveal *The Amazing Adventures of Superman.* He confided to me, "I love this show. 'A never-ending battle for truth, justice, and the American way.' That's what it's all about."

"Are we going to watch it now?"

"Nah. I've seen them all dozens of times. Let's watch something new." He fast-forwarded to *The Adventures of Ozzie and Harriet* and asked, "Do you know this show?"

I said, "I saw it on Teresa Zorn's DVD."

"Is it any good?"

"Well, the title is based on a very broad definition of 'adventures.' They never actually do anything."

Suddenly, Mr. Hoffman burst back in. He practically yelled at the TV. "Wait! Wait! I know this theme song! I know this show! *Ozzie and Harriet*. Right?"

Ray answered, "Right."

"It's about the Nelsons, this supposedly all-American family. They're a real family, but they have this show where they play TV versions of themselves. It's bizarre. It's like they're the Bizarro-Nelsons."

TJ said, "So it's real, like a documentary?"

"No. It's the opposite, because nothing that you see is real. They're pretending to be this perfect, role-model family for America. But, in their real lives, Ricky Nelson was dating a seventeen-year-old girl, and he got her pregnant. Technically, that's statutory rape. They had a shotgun wedding, and the girl disappeared for seven months; then she reappeared with a baby. So do you know what Ozzie did?"

I asked, "What?"

"He actually altered the baby's weight on the birth certificate and announced that it had been born prematurely. At seven months. The result was a baby acceptable to the American public."

I didn't know what to say, so I just smiled politely. But I was thinking, *I didn't need to know all that.*

Ray leaned his long frame forward and turned off the TV, muttering, "Maybe this isn't the best show to watch right now."

Mr. Hoffman disappeared into the kitchen, but he returned right away with a Coke. He asked us as a group, "So, do any of you have questions about what Ray and I are doing?"

I sure didn't, but I was surprised to see that TJ did. "Are you two, like, trying to catch the real Kennedy assassins?"

Mr. Hoffman stared at TJ with piercing dark eyes. "Exactly, young man! That's exactly what we're trying to do. Because—" and here he looked at Patrick and me, "the real assassins are still alive!"

Patrick stirred himself and spoke. "Really? I thought Lee Harvey Oswald did it."

Mr. Hoffman pulled his head back. He sneered, "Then you must believe in the Magic Bullet Theory."

"Huh?"

"That one bullet could pass through President Kennedy's head, turn left and pass through Governor Connelly's wrist, then disappear for awhile and then magically reappear on the President's stretcher at Parkland Hospital."

Patrick looked away. Offended, I think.

I asked, "Mr. Hoffman, wouldn't the real killers be in their seventies or eighties now?"

"They would."

"So isn't it too late? Those would be some very old guys."

"No. It's not too late!" Mr. Hoffman's eyes flashed. "There has always been a great hope, a hope in something called *the deathbed confession*. There are people alive today who know what happened. They are very old; they are at the end of life, but that may be the very reason why they want to set things straight. To tell the truth at last."

The rotary phone rang in the kitchen, so Ray went in to answer it. He returned in ten seconds and told us, "That was Teresa Zorn reminding us to go to the Town Square."

His father asked, "What for?"

Ray answered, "You're gonna love this. She said the Nelson family is visiting the Soda Shop."

"You're kidding!"

"Nope. Ozzie and Harriet and David and Ricky."

"And they're doing what exactly?"

"I don't know. Nothing, I guess. Just sitting in the Soda Shop."

Mr. Hoffman shook his head bitterly. "The Nelson family. Phony role models for a phony age." He looked up at us. "But go! Go! It's all part of your authentic theme park experience."

Ray said, "Yeah. Well, maybe I will go. Just for a bit."

Five minutes later, we were all strolling through the beautiful, retro Town Square. We passed the Bijou Theater, which had a poster outside for *The Bridge on the River Kwai*. Then we passed the F. W. Woolworth store, which had *5c and 10c* painted on the window. We stopped in front of the Soda

Shop, which had *Come in for a Lime Rickey!* painted on its window. A teenage boy with a paper hat was working inside.

Patrick pointed. "Hey, I know that kid. He played football last year."

I peered through the painted letters and focused on the boy. He had on a white apron and a badge that said *Soda Jerk— Randy*. He was polishing the top of a lunch counter that had six stools.

I looked to the left. As advertised, a table near the door was occupied by the Nelsons—Ozzie, Harriet, David, and Ricky. Four actors pretending to be them, anyway. They were all eating hot fudge sundaes. (It suddenly struck me, as they spooned ice cream into their smiling mouths, how much they were like the Blanchards—Jim, Betty, Patrick, and TJ.)

I asked Patrick, "Do you guys want to go inside?"

He looked nervous. He shook his head. "Nah. Not really."

TJ said, "I do! I want to have a Lime Rickey."

I knew that if I asked Ray, he would shrug. But I wanted to be polite, so I did ask him, and he did shrug. I pushed the Soda Shop door open and started in, so they followed.

Randy the soda jerk snapped to attention. If he recognized Patrick, he did not show it. He called out, as if from some goofy, soda jerk script, "Hey gang! How about a Lime Rickey?"

No one else answered, so I told him, "Sure. Make it four." We all climbed up onto the counter stools. I unbuttoned my coat and let it slide onto the back of the stool; so did TJ, but Ray and Patrick kept theirs on. A Lime Rickey, as it turns out, is a green drink that's served in a frosted, tubular glass. It is made of crushed ice, lime syrup, and soda water. Ray took one sip and pronounced it, "Disgusting."

I hung in there a little longer, not getting disgusted until the third sip, at which point I whispered, "Whoah. Massive sugar overload."

Ray smiled at me. (Was that the first time?) He pointed out, "Your tongue is green." I checked it in the mirror behind the counter. It was true. Ray's reflection stuck his tongue out. "I'll bet mine is, too. Yeah."

Then the guy playing Ozzie Nelson called over to us, "Are you kids enjoying your stay here at Memory Lane?"

I smiled. "Yes. Very much. Thanks." Ozzie, Harriet, David, and Ricky all smiled back at me with gleaming teeth.

Ray muttered, "So that's the ideal American family? They all look like they're on Prozac."

I agreed. "They do look kind of extra-special happy." I ventured one more sip then pushed the frosted glass away, shaking all over in disgust. I stuck my tongue way out to get some air on it. Then I continued, "My family doesn't fit into that mom-dad-sister-brother mold. It never did. It was mom-dad-me; then it was just mom-me; now it's just me." I added ruefully, "Little Orphan Alice."

He stared at me intensely. "Yeah? Really? That's true?"

"Yes."

"You really are an orphan? Or a semi-orphan?"

"I really am an orphan. A full orphan. Why?"

"You used that term before, semi-orphan. I thought you were mocking me."

"No. Not at all."

We sat there for another minute. Ray kept looking back at his house nervously. Was he really afraid of missing something? Something that happened in 1963? Or was he just afraid of his dad? He finally announced, "Well, I'd better get back."

I answered indifferently, "Okay. Goodbye."

He muttered, "Bye" and hurried off. Really hurried.

The Clarks came in soon after and walked up to the counter. They got the same scripted greeting from the soda jerk, and then from Ozzie Nelson. I watched Rosemary Clark very carefully. I intuited, as only girls can, that she was striking a pose for Patrick.

But Patrick didn't notice. He had his head down. I was about to tell him to look at her when he muttered to me, "This place really blows. Really bad. I'm going back, too."

"Back where?"

"I dunno. Home? I'll watch football with Dad, I guess."

"Okay. If that's what you want to do."

"Yeah." Patrick slid off the stool. "That's what I want to do." He shuffled out with his head still down. He didn't even look at the Clarks.

That left two empty stools between TJ and me, but they didn't stay empty for long.

The three Nordstroms entered, looking very happy once again. The girls approached the counter, striking Randy the soda jerk dumb with their blonde beauty. He just stood there with his mouth hanging open, but the girls only had eyes for TJ.

Pia or Petra, I'm not sure which, gave me a quick smile and a, "Hi, Alice" as they climbed up onto the stools. They both turned to TJ and started to chat.

Mrs. Nordstrom sat down a table near the wall. I watched her pull out a *Golden Memories* book, just like mine. Was she their family's chronicler? Obviously. She made notes for about one minute and then put it away. (I wondered if she used the cheesy stickers.)

I sat and stared at my tongue in the mirror for a while. When I tired of that, I pulled my jacket back on and slid down from the stool, not saying a word to anyone (not that anyone had noticed).

I exited quickly through the Soda Shop door, turned right, and set off toward home. But I did not get far. As I passed F. W. Woolworth's, I spotted Patrick's large frame inside. He was just standing there, looking lost. I entered the store and called over to him, "So? No football with Dad?"

He explained, "Not yet. I saw some games through the

window. I got a note in my bedroom about buying games and stuff in here."

"Yeah. I got that, too."

Patrick pointed to a game called Pick Up Sticks. "I might get that."

"Yeah," I told him. "You should."

"I don't have any money, though. So I don't think I can."

I assured him, "You can. There's a way to buy stuff here, or they wouldn't be advertising it in our bedrooms." I turned to a smiling saleswoman. "Excuse me. Can he buy one of these games?"

The woman's smile widened. "Of course."

"How does he pay?"

"You just tell me your name, and we add it to your account."

"Okay. Thank you." I poked Patrick in the side. "You see? It's that easy."

Patrick still looked stressed, so I spoke directly to the saleswoman. "His name is Patrick Blanchard." Then I looked back at Patrick and pointed at the box. He reached out, picked it up, and carried it over to the counter.

The woman took care of the rest, punching up the sale on an old cash register and sliding the Pick Up Sticks into an F. W. Woolworth paper bag. Patrick took the bag, muttering, "Thank you." He started toward the door, turned, and told me, "Maybe I'll see you later."

"Okay. I'll be home in a bit. Stop by."

"Yeah."

I strolled around the store scanning the shelves of toys, looking for one particular item, but I did not see it. I asked that helpful woman again, "Do you have any Barbies?"

She pointed behind me. "Look around the corner, with the 1960s toys."

I did, and I saw a whole display—Barbies, Skippers, Kens, Christies. I wondered if my mom had owned any of those, and had suddenly ditched any of those, for no apparent reason. I studied them for a while, intrigued, but then I left the store without purchasing anything.

Right before I reached our street, I saw a flash of blinding light; then I heard an explosion. (I thought, *Duck and cover!* but only for a second.) I looked up and saw that the fireworks had begun. I could hear people—TJ, the Nordstroms, the Clarks—cheering the first blast.

The fireworks display started out slowly, but it built to an impressive finale. I stood and watched it by myself. As the last sparks fell, I noticed that the Hardy family had strolled outside to watch. So had the McCains, from the far end of the street (and there were definitely more than six of them). The adults in my family, though, did not show their faces.

Twenty minutes later, TJ, Patrick, and I had congregated back in my room. TJ was totally giddy; Patrick was totally depressed. Was there any middle ground with these guys? TJ offered to do another braid for me. I hesitated for a moment, thinking about Mom, but then I said okay. I sat on the floor, and TJ kneeled behind me. Patrick flopped down by the door.

After a moment, I asked them both, "So, end of day one. How's everybody liking Memory Lane?"

"I liked the Town Square," TJ said. "But I did not like school. Bor-ing."

Patrick agreed, "The school blows. The dinner was decent."

I gave my opinion. "But that dinner-time, memory-sharing thing was so bogus!"

TJ asked, "Why?"

"Why? Didn't you hear Grandmom? 'Donna always wanted to be a mommy.' No she didn't! My mom always wanted to be a teacher."

Patrick said, "Yeah. The thing about me and football was bogus, too. I was no star. I was one of the worst players on the team." He dropped his voice. "I was the kid they didn't put in when the game got close."

TJ and I looked at him with pity. TJ said, "I guess I don't have to confess that I was a pretty crappy karate kid."

Patrick curled up his lip in that I'm-about-to-insult-TJ way. "Why were you in karate anyway? Was ballet class full?"

TJ ignored him. He told me, "I was only in karate for

about thirty days. And Cub Scouts? I was in that even less. All I remember is that I hated it." He looked at Patrick. "You hated it, too."

Patrick sneered again. "Yeah. We both dropped out. But TJ's sorry he missed Webelos." He then added, in case I didn't get it, "We blows."

TJ worked on my hair in silence; then he asked, "So why would Mamà claim I was good at karate if I wasn't?"

I suggested, "She might really remember it that way."

TJ thought for a moment. "What? People can remember things that aren't true?"

"Sure they can. And they do."

TJ finished the braid very quickly, and very ably. The conversation soon switched to our new living arrangements back in the real world—in Grandmom and Grandpop's house. TJ said, "I suppose Patrick and I will be in the small bedrooms, because Miss Alice will need the large boudoir for her many lovers."

I sputtered a laugh. "Oh, right."

"They will be waiting in line."

"Right. Please take a number for better service."

"I'm serious, Miss Alice. You are getting so very attractive."

"You are getting so nearsighted."

"Come on! Tell the truth. The boys are after you. What about that Douglas boy?"

"Douglas is just doing his job."

"No way. He treats you very special."

"He does?"

"Oh yeah." TJ playfully reached over and covered Patrick's ears. "You know what he wants, honey. And you know you want to give it to him."

Patrick swatted his hands away as I sputtered again. "Forget that. Not me. I'm a sexually inactive teen."

"Get out! I don't believe it."

"Believe it."

"No, I don't. I won't. We shall have to investigate. We shall have to play *Truth or Dare*. Okay, Patrick?"

"No! That game is stupid."

TJ turned to me. "Okay. That just leaves us. And play we will! Ask me a question, beginning with the words *truth or dare*."

I said, "Okay. Truth or dare: Do you really want to be at Memory Lane?"

He rolled his eyes in a sweeping arc. "That is the most boring question ever asked in the history of this game! Who cares? Ask me a question about sex! This game is all about sex."

I had a sudden thought. "No! No! Wait a minute. We can't play *Truth or Dare*."

He rolled his eyes back the other way. "Don't be such a priss."

"No, we can't play because it's an anomaly."

"It is?"

"Yeah. That game is like a nineties thing. And we, of course, are in the fifties."

"Well, they must have had something like it!"

I shook my head. "No. I don't think they talked about sex."

TJ pondered that. "Okay. How about doing sex? Did they do it?"

"I don't know. I guess Ricky Nelson did it. At least once."

TJ decided, "We can call it something else then. Truth or . . . Or what?"

"Duck and cover?" I suggested.

"Yes! Or just duck! *Truth or Duck*! That's it. Either you tell the truth, or you have to duck under your desk, like in duck and cover. And you have to assume the I-have-my-hands-over-my-head-so-I-can't-get-killed-by-an-atomic-bomb position. Okay?"

"Okay."

"So ask me."

"Okay, TJ. Have you—"

"You have to start with *truth or duck*!"

"Okay. Truth or duck: Have you ever had sex?"

"No. I have never had sex—with a girl, or with a boy, or with a duck, for that matter. Now it's my turn. Truth or duck: Have you, Miss Alice, had sex?"

"Yes. Yes, I have. I made out with Richard Hess on a school trip."

"Really? How far did you go?"

"For a long time, like ten miles."

TJ tugged on my braid. "How far did you go anatomically? Baseball . . . base-wise? First base, second base?"

"Oh I don't know. I never understood that base stuff. It was heavy kissing, like I said."

"And you call that sex?"

"It was very sexy kissing. Tongues were involved."

"No. That doesn't count. Next!" He turned to Patrick, who growled, "Leave me out of this!"

TJ, of course, did not. "Truth or duck, Patrick: Would you like to make out with Miss Rosemary Clark, in the Alice Lynch, on-the-school-bus, sense of the word?"

"That's none of your business."

"Have you ever made out with anyone, either in the Alice Lynch or any other sense of the word?"

"Shut up!"

Suddenly, we all looked up to see Aunt Betty and Uncle Jim standing in the doorway. I froze, with my mouth open. This was worse than making a total dork of myself with Douglas. How long had they been standing there? Did they now think I was going to be having sex in their house? In our house? Sneaking boys upstairs to my boudoir?

Fortunately, no. They didn't. They didn't seem to be tuned

in to our conversation at all. Aunt Betty clapped her hands, like a kindergarten teacher, "Okay, Patrick. Okay, TJ. It's time to go!" She bent and kissed me on the cheek, "Good night, Alice." Uncle Jim gave me a small wave. Then they filed down the stairs and exited quickly through the front door.

I walked over to the window and peered out, waiting patiently for them to come into view. When they did, I thought: *There they are! My new sitcom family—Jim, Betty, Patrick, and TJ Blanchard. My own personal Nelsons.* I tried to imagine myself walking along the street with them, but I could not. They were still too weird. They were still too unknown to me. I had a mother and father—a real mother and father. Their names were Donna and Alex Lynch. But they were gone now.

I had a sudden urge to write or draw something that showed my real family; that got it down on paper. I hurried over to my 1957 desk. I opened the top drawer and pulled out a sheet of *Memory Lane* stationery and a Dixon Ticonderoga pencil. I started to draw a family tree, but I soon stopped. It was too depressing. I was the only living Lynch, out on a branch, off to the side like some lonesome monkey.

I turned the paper over. This time, I started drawing circles, and those worked better. I drew three, one inside the other. Here is what each one means: The first circle is for immediate family. The first circle is inhabited by you, your parents, and your siblings. That's it. No exceptions. Even if your grandmother comes to live at your house on the day that you are born and spends eighteen years babysitting you and making you healthful snacks to eat after school, she is still not in that first circle. She is in the second.

The second circle contains your blood family. It is inhabited by grandparents, aunts, uncles, and cousins. That's it. There are no exceptions here, either. Even if your aunt had two children with a bad man who died, and then remarried a very nice man and had two more children with him, only the aunt, the dead husband, and the first two children are in the second circle. The others are in the third circle, which is your part-blood family. The circles can then radiate outward into people who are like family, close friends of the family, good neighbors, and so on. You can add as many circles as you like.

I am now alone in my first circle, peering out at the world like that lonesome monkey, or like that poor little goat in *Jurassic Park*, the one who got tied up and had to wait for a T-Rex to come and eat it. I hated that scene. It reminded me of when Mom and I went into a pet store in the Walt Whitman Mall and I saw a little mouse sitting in a glassed-in box. I asked my mother what the little mouse was doing in there, but she didn't answer. Then a bigmouth boy nearby blurted out, "He's snake food. He's waiting for the snake to come eat him."

I got so upset that I started to scream and cry. Full toddler meltdown. We had to leave the mall, and I couldn't eat dinner that night. I still get upset when I think about it. I would like to think that the mouse somehow survived.

I would like to think that my mom somehow survived, too. I guess that means I have moved up the Elizabeth Kubler-Ross scale to *denial.*

—Alice

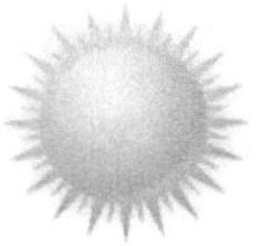

Chapter 3

This morning, Douglas and Francis delivered a high-carb, high-calorie breakfast featuring fried eggs and some mystery meat called scrapple. They also stocked a shelf in the kitchen cabinet with some truly deadly cereal choices, including Sugar Frosted Flakes, Sugar Smacks, and Sugar Pops. I chose Nabisco Shredded Wheat. I ate a handful of it dry, with a glass of Tang, which I consumed alone, like that monkey.

Then I pulled on my coat and exited through the kitchen door. I could hear the sound of a radio playing in the garage, so I turned left and headed back there.

I entered through the side door and spotted my grandfather. He was on his knees in front of the Ford Fairlane. Elvis Presley's "Jailhouse Rock" was playing on a small plastic radio, which was perched on a shelf along with several car-care products. My grandfather saw me and struggled to his feet. He looked very agitated. He pointed at the radio. "That damn kid turned that thing on, and then he left! I don't know how to turn it off."

"What, the radio? I can turn that off for you, Grandpop." I squeezed behind him and approached the shelf. "You probably just have to press a button."

"No! No!" he snapped at me. "You don't have to turn it off!"

I stopped beside him. "Okay."

"Leave it on. I don't care. But I'm not the one who turned it on. It wasn't me. It was that kid."

"Douglas?"

"I don't know his name." My grandfather had a soft cloth in his left hand which he was gripping tightly. His right hand was holding a bottle that said *Turtle Wax with Brillium*. He waved the cloth forward in the direction of the car. "So? How does it look?"

"Great. It's just beautiful."

"No, the bumper! How does the bumper look?"

"Oh. Great, too." He stared down at it. I asked, "Are you waxing the whole car?"

"Yeah. Give it a uniform look. Make it look the same all over. So you're saying the bumper looks perfect?"

"Yeah. Absolutely. The whole car looks perfect."

He nodded thoughtfully. "Okay then."

I asked him, "So what are you going to do next?"

"What do you mean?"

"I mean, are you going to work on stuff under the hood? Like when you had your garage? Are you and Grandmom going to take it out for a spin?"

He looked alarmed. "No!"

Unfortunately, that was about it for me and car talk. I couldn't think of anything else to say, so I listened to that Elvis Presley song. It was about a hot, all-male dance party inside a prison. Rock on, 1957. Then I remembered a line that Douglas had used, so I used it, too. "The car has a three-speed manual transmission. Right?"

My grandfather nodded rapidly. "Yeah. Yeah, it does."

"Well, maybe you could work on that?"

"Yeah."

I hung around for a few more minutes. Ricky Nelson's "I'm Walkin'" came on the radio. That one was about love, I think. When it was over, I announced, "Okay, Grandpop, I'm going to go to school now. Enjoy your day working on the car."

"Yeah."

I squeezed past him again. I noticed, as I did, that he was unscrewing the top of the Turtle Wax bottle. By the time I had exited, turned left, and was passing the window, he was back on his knees polishing the front bumper. It was not going to be one of his good days.

Douglas was already waiting at the kitchen stoop. He shouted out, "Hey, Alice! You did your hair different!"

I thought, *Differently*, but I answered cheerily, "Yes! It's a French braid. TJ did it for me."

"Really? It looks great."

"Thank you."

He asked, "Do you want to wait for TJ and Patrick?"

"No. They can find the schoolhouse. It's pretty large."

Douglas laughed. Had he actually understood one of my jokes? He replied, "Okay. Good. It'll just be you and me then."

I must admit I was flattered by that. I was flattered enough, and confident enough, to ask him, "Hey, can we hang out later? Maybe after school?"

The muscles in Douglas's face tightened into a frown. "Uh, well, I'm afraid I have to go to the other section of the park later. There's always something else for us to do. We don't have any down time at all."

I was instantly embarrassed. Closer to mortified. I muttered, "No. Sure. I understand."

"The other section is filling up fast. People love that time period—*1966 to 1976*. You know? The Beatles, the hippies, the astronauts landing on the moon; all that." I didn't say anything else, so he went on. "You should see the kids over there. They're wearing mega bell bottoms and stuff."

We walked in silence for a long, excruciating minute until we entered the schoolyard. I told him, "Thanks. I'll be okay from here."

"Cool. See you later."

I wandered over toward the wall, hoping to hide, feeling like a total idiot. The door flew open and Matt McCain stepped out. He actually nodded at me, said, "How's it going?" and continued on around the corner. I don't remember if I answered him or not. Probably not. I was too upset.

Patrick and TJ arrived a minute later. Patrick demanded to know, "Why didn't you wait for us?"

TJ answered before I could. "Because she walked here with her boyfriend—Ricky Nelson or Wally Cleaver or Bud Anderson—I couldn't tell. I was too far away."

The best I could do for a reply was to snarl, "It was Douglas. And he's not my boyfriend."

"What? Did you break up? Do tell."

"I don't want to talk about it." The boys let the matter drop and leaned against the wall behind me. Ray Hoffman joined us next, looking about as unhappy as I felt. Was he ever happy?

Matt McCain suddenly reappeared from around the corner. He walked past us as if we were not there. He stopped at the gate and stared at the rising sun; stared like he had never seen it before.

Ray pointed to him subtly and whispered to Patrick, "Do you know that dude?" Patrick shrugged. Ray continued, "He was in my baseball league. He's scary and violent and needs to take massive medications, but I don't think he does."

Patrick shuddered. "I'm just staying out of his way."

Ray then revealed a very interesting piece of information: "My mom's a school counselor. She knew him at Gateway."

I was so surprised that I asked him to repeat it. "Your mom's a what?"

"A school counselor."

"Really?"

"Yeah."

"And she told you confidential stuff about him?"

"No, not exactly. But you overhear stuff, you know?"

"Yes. I know how that goes."

"He got kicked out of Gateway for sexual assault."

"That's why he got kicked out of Gardiners Avenue, too. Did he grab another girl?"

Ray shook his head slowly. Reluctantly. He muttered, "No. Actually, I heard it was a boy."

"No!"

"That's what I heard."

"God. This gets weirder and weirder."

The iron school bell high on the wall started to clang. Ray pulled the door open and we all filed into the classroom. Miss Zorn was already in place at her desk, smiling. Everybody settled in quickly except the McCains, who ran in theatrically and dove into their seats. My mom would have nailed them right then and there. Miss Zorn just continued smiling; then she rose to speak. "Good morning, class. I'd like to start today the same as yesterday, with silent prayer, and then some class sharing."

Miss Zorn shut her eyes and held very still, like she was

sitting before a birthday cake and thinking up a wish. I didn't see anyone else do that; we all just stared at her. Her eyes popped open a few seconds later, and she smiled. "Okay. Now let's share!"

TJ whispered to me, "Anomaly. They didn't *share* in 1957. Nobody shared until Oprah."

Miss Zorn explained, "This time, I want to know how you prepared yourselves for your visit to Memory Lane."

She pointed at Ray. "Ray, you and your father are reliving a week in November of 1963, correct?"

"Correct." He claimed, "I didn't do anything extra. I've been preparing to relive this week for five years, ever since I became a CT."

"I'm sorry. What does that mean again?"

"A Conspiracy Theorist."

Dennis McCain muttered some crude remark that I couldn't quite hear, but it made Matt laugh convulsively. Teresa looked back there. "Okay, Matt, your turn. You and your family are reliving 1957, correct?"

"I don't know. If you say so."

"How did you prepare?"

"How did we prepare?" He turned to Dennis. "Did we prepare?"

Dennis nodded emphatically. "We prepared."

Matt looked back at Teresa. "Like he said, we prepared."

Dennis added, "We prepared by . . . preparing."

Teresa smiled faintly. What was she thinking? She gave up on them and asked, "Okay. Pia? Petra?"

Pia answered, "We learned to figure skate, with our grandmother."

Teresa commented, "I bet that was fun."

Her sister replied, "It's harder than it looks. You have to be very precise. You have to keep your skate blades exactly on the lines of the figures. Like skating in two circles to form a number eight. That's why they call it figure skating."

Matt blurted out, "Not because you girls have hot figures?"

Dennis added. "No, man. Those two aren't hot. They're cold. Definitely cold."

My mom would never have let remarks like that go unchallenged. Those McCain boys would have been removed from her class. But Miss Zorn elected, once again, to ignore them. I could tell by the reddening of the girls' ears in front of me, Rosemary included, that they were getting upset. But Miss Zorn just kept going. "Okay. Rosemary?"

Rosemary answered, "We read some Bible stories. And we went to another theme park to learn about Bible culture."

"Oh? Where?"

"Holy Land. In Orlando."

The McCains sputtered. Even Miss Zorn sounded doubtful. "Really? There is such a place?"

"Oh yes. It's a theme park, like this. It's an authentic reproduction of the world where Jesus walked two thousand years ago."

Matt stage-whispered, "He shoulda rode a mule."

Dennis answered, "He shoulda rode Rosemary."

Robby Clark spun around in his seat and glared at them. He started to get up, but Rosemary casually put a hand on his shoulder. She whispered, "Think, Robby. What would Jesus do?"

It was my turn next. Teresa pointed at me. "How did you prepare, Alice?"

"I did research about memory."

"Excellent. What did you learn?"

"I learned that memory comes from an area of the brain called the hippocampus."

Dennis McCain turned to me. "Hippo campus? Is that, like, where fat chicks go to college?"

I ignored him as thoroughly as the twins had. "The hippocampus records life memories. It has a little bump on the back of it, called the amygdala. The amygdala records highly emotional memories. Too much stress can overwhelm both the hippocampus and the amygdala, and you can't remember anything at all."

"That's excellent. Excellent information. Now how about your cousins."

She smiled at Patrick until he muttered, "We, uh, watched Notre Dame football movies. Like *Rudy* and *Knute Rockne: All American.*"

TJ contributed, "I watched *Davy Crockett*. And *Queen for a Day*."

Dennis whispered loudly, "I'll bet he did. I'll bet he is a queen for a day."

Teresa Zorn took another stab at classroom management. "Is something wrong back there?" When the McCains didn't answer, she persisted. "Dennis, did you want to share something with the class?"

Dennis stared at her coldly. He pointed to Matt. "Yeah. In fact, I do. We do. Our uncle was a firefighter and a hero. Somebody disrespected him yesterday. Somebody owes us an apology."

I spoke up right away. "Respect? You creeps don't deserve respect."

"What you said is a lie! Our Uncle Bill died on September 11th, 2001. You got your dates mixed up."

TJ dared make a remark. "You should let that drop. It's an anomaly. You're talking about something that happened in 2001, and this is supposed to be 1957."

Matt barked at him, "Shut up, queen for a day!"

Teresa held up her right hand like a traffic cop. But rather than confront the problem, she changed the subject. "We will start this morning with a film on the Red Menace, the efforts of communists to destroy the United States from within." She turned a switch on the sixteen-millimeter projector, and it started to whir around noisily. "If I can get this projector to cooperate, we'll watch two fine films about this topic. Then later we will have our guest speakers."

The first film was about the FBI's battle against communism in America. As it turned out, so was the second film. Nobody paid much attention to them, not even the Clarks. Patrick fell asleep. TJ make pencil sketches of the twins, of the backs of their heads anyway. I just sat there. It was a total waste of time.

Fortunately, lunch came early. Douglas wheeled the cart full of lunchboxes into the classroom and we all lined up, selecting the TV show of our choice. I grabbed one at random that turned out to be *Leave It to Beaver*.

Lunch today consisted of Oscar Mayer wieners and Jell-O, which we all ate standing up in the entranceway. The food prompted some crude remarks from Matt McCain about mustard on his Oscar Mayer wiener. Dennis snorted his approval of each pathetic witticism.

I was willing to ignore all of it but, to my surprise, Rosemary Clark was not. After one such remark, she rounded on the McCains with almost biblical fury. "You have no right to talk in front of girls like that!" Patrick, who had been hovering near her, suddenly drifted away, leaving Rosemary in a face-off with Dennis McCain.

Dennis snarled, "What did you say, bible girl?"

Rosemary stood her ground. She said, right to his face. "You heard me, nine-eleven boy."

Dennis sputtered. He also took a step backward. Then he just muttered lamely, "Why don't you go home and read your bible?"

Rosemary leaned forward, totally not intimidated. "Never mind what I do. Watch what you do. You have been warned."

Robby took up a karate stance just to the side of Dennis. The Clarks now had him surrounded. Dennis's ferrety eyes darted around looking for Matt, but he was busy shoving another hot dog into his mouth.

Luckily for Dennis, Teresa appeared holding a Memory Lane application form. She motioned for both of the McCains to join her by the double doors. When they did, Teresa pointed to the application and said, "You have written here that you are brothers. But you're not really brothers, are you?"

Dennis replied simply, "No. And we didn't write that."

Teresa looked at him and then back at the form. "Well, someone wrote it because that's what it says here on your form, signed by your father."

"That someone would have been Douglas."

"What?"

"He's *your* brother, right?"

"Yes."

"Well, I told Douglas that Matt and me were cousins, but we were like brothers. He must have misunderstood that when he wrote it down."

"Douglas wrote this?"

"Yeah. He filled the whole form out for us. Kind of as a favor. Gosh, I hope he didn't make any other mistakes."

Teresa nodded tightly. Then she backed away, still looking hard at the form. She kept backing up all the way into the classroom. The rest of us followed, leaving our trash behind.

Right after we were seated, Douglas appeared again. As he had done the previous day, he announced cheerfully, "Miss Zorn, your guest speakers are here."

Douglas then stepped back to allow a little old man to enter. He was clutching a small stack of white index cards. His wife and daughter entered right behind him. Teresa said, "Welcome, Mr. Hardy, Mrs. Hardy, and Mrs. Whitman." She indicated that the two women should sit behind Rosemary and Robby.

Just a few seconds later, Mr. Hoffman hurried in carrying a white book. Miss Zorn acknowledged him, "Ah! Mr. Hoffman!" and pointed him to the seat next to Ray. Then Teresa turned back to the old man. "Mr. Hardy? I'll ask you the two questions we ask all of our guest speakers: What days are you here to relive? And why?"

Mr. Hardy just smiled at her. Mrs. Whitman raised her hand and spoke up. "My father is here reliving the week he became an FBI agent." She added, as an explanation, "That's the Federal Bureau of Investigation. We're reliving the week of November 19th to 23rd, 1962. My mother and I thought it would be good for him to immerse himself in that time again. He seems to remember it very clearly." She lowered her voice. "Actually, he remembers it more clearly than he remembers the present time."

Teresa nodded sympathetically. "Yes, indeed. I understand. That is another wonderful aspect of Memory Lane. People can go back to a time long ago that is, remarkably enough, still very fresh in their minds. They find great comfort being surrounded by things that they remember."

Mrs. Whitman nodded appreciatively. "My father has prepared some remarks about his early days in the Bureau. He and my mother worked on them together. He's eager to share his memories."

"Excellent. And we're eager to hear them. Go ahead, Mr. Hardy."

Mr. Hardy looked at his wife, who pointed at him to start. He read slowly and quietly from the note cards. No one could hear him very well. He talked about "Director Hoover" and about "un-American activities" and about "rooting out communists," just like on the filmstrips.

The McCains started making noises, like barnyard animals. What total morons. At one point, Mr. Hardy's wife and daughter both turned and *shushed* them, and Matt muttered, "Sorry."

Miss Zorn never said anything. She just waited for Mr. Hardy to turn over his last note card and look up. Then she concluded, "Thank you for that very interesting talk, Mr. Hardy." She turned to us. "Are there any questions from the audience?" No one had any questions, so Teresa thanked Mr. Hardy a final time "for describing what life was like inside that great American institution, the FBI."

Mrs. Whitman got up and guided her father back to the empty seat behind his wife. Teresa then turned to Ray's father. "Mr. Hoffman," she began, "would you tell us what days you are here to relive? And why?"

Ray's father, holding the white book in his left hand, walked to the front and faced us. With his right hand, he pressed down on his eyes, like he was struggling with a massive migraine. With his eyes still closed, he told us, "Before I answer those questions, and before I get to my planned remarks, I feel compelled to tell you the truth about the FBI." He opened his eyes and continued. "The FBI, under its founder J. Edgar Hoover, waged a relentless battle against anyone who disagreed with anything the U. S. government said or did.

"J. Edgar Hoover was a phony man who attempted to create a phony nation. A homosexual who persecuted other homosexuals. A secretive, bitter loner who championed happy, loving family life. A compulsive liar, evidence tamperer, and violator of our Constitution who pretended to stand for truth, justice, and the American way."

Ray raised up a finger and got his father's attention. This prompted him to add, "Oh yes. He may even have approved a plan to assassinate President John F. Kennedy. As a result, the United States has been living a lie since 1963. And we can't move forward until we admit that."

I don't think Mr. Hardy understood a word of it, but his wife and daughter did. They looked daggers at Mr. Hoffman, but he didn't seem to notice. He switched gears smoothly to his real topic.

"Anyway, my son and I are here to relive the week of November 20th to 25th, 1963, the week of the assassination of President John F. Kennedy.

"In a nutshell: Incompetent police work, both at the FBI level and the local level, allowed the real killers of President John F. Kennedy to go free. The Dallas police let an armed mafia hit-man enter their station house on the morning of November 24th and murder the only suspect in the case, the lone nut named Lee Harvey Oswald.

"This incompetent police work was then followed by an incompetent congressional investigation known as The Warren Report." Here he held up the white book. It was thin and floppy, like a mini phonebook. "A congressional commission, headed by Chief Justice Earl Warren, was supposed to tell the

American people what really happened.

"Well, it didn't.

"The Warren Commission interviewed all the eyewitnesses. They *all* indicated that the shots came from the front side of the motorcade and were fired by several gunmen. The commission then concluded, somehow, that the shots came from the *back* of the motorcade and were fired by *one* gunman."

As Mr. Hoffman took a breath, Robby, with genuine enthusiasm, shouted out, "A lone nut!"

Mr. Hoffman smiled. "Yes, young man. You are correct."

"Lee Harvey Oswald!"

"That's the name. And the beauty of the Lone Nut Theory, of course, was that the nut was already dead. They did not need to have a trial in which Lee Harvey Oswald would continue to say what he had said from the very beginning: That he did not do it."

Mr. Hoffman held up the white mini phonebook again. "What we have here is an acceptable version of events, a made-up account of what happened. It is acceptable to the Dallas Police and the FBI and the U. S. Government. It is not concerned with the truth of what happened to the President of the United States on that fateful day."

He stopped here to point at Ray. "But *we* are concerned. Many of us are. We believe there is such a thing as the truth, and it is comprised of evidence and eyewitnesses and facts." He tossed the Warren Report dramatically, angrily, contemptuously, into the green trash basket. "And we will not accept anything less than that truth."

Everyone except the Hardys broke into applause. Mr. Hoffman nodded to Teresa to indicate that he was finished. She said, "More excellent information." She again asked us, "Are there any questions from the audience?"

Dennis McCain's hand shot up. "Kennedy. Wasn't he Irish?"

"He was."

The McCains exchanged high fives. "Didn't he, like, bang a lot of chicks?" He looked at Pia and Petra, but they were not looking back. "Didn't he, like, do a different babe every night?"

Mr. Hoffman answered him seriously, like he wasn't a total moron. "He did, as you imply, have involvements with *many* women. And at least one of them may have been involved in his death—Judith Campbell, the girlfriend of mafia boss Sam Giancana." He asked the class in general, "How might that information connect to other information you have heard today?"

Robby's hand shot up. "The mafia hit-man!"

"Good. Good."

"The one who snuck into the police station."

"Yes. You're on your way to becoming a CT."

To my right, I noticed that Mr. Hardy's wife and daughter were exchanging whispered messages. Then they rose up together from their desks. They tapped Mr. Hardy on the back, so he rose, too. Teresa stopped the proceedings and said, "Just a moment, everybody. Let's have a final thank you for Mr. Hardy for speaking to us today."

We all muttered, "Thank you" as the three of them walked out quickly. And angrily. They did not even look in the direction of Mr. Hoffman or, for that matter, Miss Zorn.

The Q and A went on for fifteen minutes after that, with just about everybody asking a question or making a comment. When Ray's father exited, he heard a much more enthusiastic chorus of *thank yous*.

After the three o'clock bell, as the class was filing out, Teresa Zorn pulled me aside. "So, Alice," she asked, "how are you liking school in the 1950s?"

"I'm liking parts of it." Patrick and TJ stopped and stood by the door. I waited for the McCains to leave before I told her, "I'm sure not liking the McCains."

Teresa nodded sympathetically. Then she explained, or tried to, "Dennis and Matt just like to say gross guy stuff. But that's what high school guys do. They try to out-gross each other. I'm sure you've heard that kind of talk in school."

I told her the truth. "No. Not at my school; not in my classes; not from the guys I know. The twins don't seem like they've heard that kind of talk before. And there's no way Rosemary has. You need to stop their behavior. It's out of hand. You need to raise the bar in here."

Teresa Zorn nodded seriously. Then she tried to tell me, "This is something I have done many times, Alice. I can promise you, it's going to get better."

But I wasn't buying it. "No. It's not going to get better. It's going to get worse. Much worse."

She had nothing to say to that.

Patrick, TJ, and I walked briskly back toward our houses. The McCains were nowhere in sight. TJ followed me up the walkway, but Patrick kept on going, with his head down, into his own house.

My grandmother glanced up briefly as we came in. She was totally immersed in a blaring soap opera. *The Secret Storm?* TJ and I sat on the floor behind her and browsed through some old magazines. I opened *Crime Detective* from November 1957 and whispered to TJ, "Listen to these titles: *Passion Killing of the Blonde Model, Young Nurse in the Desert Grave, Scarf Slaying of the Burlesque Dancer.*"

"Sounds like you're doing some serious research there, Miss Alice."

"A lot of young women were getting killed in 1957."

"Well, come on!" TJ raised his eyebrows. "A model, a nurse, a burlesque dancer? They were all asking for it."

"And they were all blonde and young."

"Like the Nordstrom twins."

"Yes."

"Maybe someone will try to kill the twins while we're here. Maybe the McCains."

"And you'll rescue them?"

"I'd give my life for them." I read for a while, but TJ quickly tired of the magazines. He crawled past me to the entertainment console and rooted through my stack of games: Go to the Head of the Class, The Game of the States, Cootie. (That one had something to do with building a large black bug. No thanks) He said, "Oh! You have Dominoes! I wish we did."

"You could buy it at Woolworth's."

"Really? We can do that?"

"Yes, oh helpless one."

He opened the box and let all the dominoes cascade out onto the carpet. Then he set them up in a curving line, every single one of them, running from the couch to the kitchen entranceway. After about ten minutes, he whispered to me, "Watch this." He touched one domino at the end; it hit the next one, which hit the next one, and so on, so that the dominoes all toppled, one after the other. He laughed in delight.

My grandmother got up after *The Secret Storm* and left, but the TV blared on with commercials for Mr. Clean, Wisk, and Ivory Soap. Then, without warning, the TV emitted a high-pitched whine that made TJ and me stop and stare at it. The whine lasted for about twenty seconds as the screen showed a test pattern and the word CONELRAD. When the noise stopped, a deep, authoritative voice announced, "This has been a test. This has been only a test. Had this been an actual emergency, you would have been given instructions to report to the nearest fallout shelter."

I got creeped out by the announcement; TJ just got annoyed. He stood up and smacked the on/off knob with the side of his foot, like a karate kid. "Enough with the Red Menace already. Hey, where's that disgustingly horrible magazine?"

"What?"

"The one with the blonde girls."

"Oh, *Crime Detective*? It's in the magazine rack." TJ dug it out and immersed himself in one of the lurid tales. I got up, pointed to his line of dominoes, and reminded him, "Just don't forget to pick up the pieces."

TJ waved me away, and I headed into the kitchen. Suddenly, I heard the muffled sound of voices. Angry voices. I realized they were just outside the door, so I crept over to listen. One voice belonged to Francis, and he was complaining bitterly. "I have served the last five meals to them. When is it going to be your turn?"

Douglas's voice answered, "I've served just as many meals as you. And cleaned up just as many."

"But not to them! You haven't served *one* to them, or cleaned one up."

"I'm a personal guide, Francis. I've got other things to do."

"Yeah, well, the McCains' house is not a one-person job. Help me, or get someone else to help me."

"All right, I will. Keep your voice down."

Douglas rapped on the glass, causing me to shrink back. I took a deep breath. Then I smoothed the front of my jumper, reached out, and opened the door. Douglas and Francis were now hoisting up two large trays. And they were all smiles. Francis said, "It's 5:50 pm, Miss. Do you know what that means?"

I once again failed, utterly, to control my own mouth. I retorted, "It means that your five o'clock shadow is fifty minutes late?" They exchanged a worried look. I was mortified. "I'm just kidding!" Their look changed to puzzlement. I had done it again. I babbled, "You're not late! Not at all. You're right on time."

Douglas piped up, "Great! We hope you're hungry, Alice!"

I stepped back, wishing I could keep stepping back all the way to my room. Douglas handed me the afternoon newspaper with a small, comical bow. Then he and Francis threw themselves into their task, laying out a dinner with trimmings. Once the last napkin was in place, Douglas smiled, said, "See you later, Alice," and led the way out the door. I snuck over and leaned my ear against the glass in case they started squabbling again, but I couldn't hear anything.

My grandmother arrived right after that. She surveyed the set table, frowned slightly, and took her seat. TJ and I sat with her, trying not to giggle, as she fumed silently over another late start. I guess this is the dinner sticker:

The rest of the Blanchards walked through the kitchen door at 6:05. Uncle Jim was starting to look a little worse for wear, making me wonder: How much football was he watching? How much beer was he drinking? He was followed by Patrick, who smacked his lips appreciatively at the assortment of foods on the table.

After him came Aunt Betty accompanied by a ghostly old man. The man had on a large overcoat that was unbuttoned, revealing a black suit and a white Roman collar. It took me a few awkward seconds to realize who it was. Aunt Betty finally said, "Come on, Alice! Boys! You remember Father Dunne." I did, but I could hardly recognize him. We all got up and made a show of hugging him and saying hi. He managed a smile and a soft hello in return. He seemed really frail; really tired.

By 6:10, we had settled into our places around the table. We bowed our heads and, out of habit, looked at my grandmother. After a pause, she raised her eyes and said, "I'll be inviting Father Dunne to say grace tonight, he being the priest."

Father Dunne dutifully led us through a quick recitation of "Bless us O Lord and these Thy gifts." He then managed a smile. He held out his hands, like Jesus in the Last Supper, and added, "And *pax vobiscum*. Peace be with you."

We all replied, "Amen."

My grandmother started to ladle out wedges of chicken potpie. As she did, she asked, "So Father, where have you been keeping yourself?"

Father Dunne accepted the first plateful. Then he replied cryptically, "I've been wandering in the desert, Margaret, for forty days and forty nights, like Jesus did."

None of us knew how to respond to that. Aunt Betty decided to change the subject. She told him, "Memory Lane has a wonderful tradition, Father. We share true stories of the past while we eat dinner. We did it last night, and it went very well."

He sounded doubtful. "It did?"

"Oh yes. We shared nice memories about all the children, and some about the grown-ups, too."

"But which was it, Betty? Were you sharing true stories or nice memories?"

Aunt Betty looked confused. "Well, they were the same thing."

Uncle Jim drained the contents of a bottle of Schaefer beer. He set it down hard and pushed back from the table, commenting, "It's the one beer to have when you're having more than one." He then belched loudly, causing Patrick to laugh. But Uncle Jim covered his mouth, thoroughly ashamed. "Pardon me, Father. Pardon me, everybody. I didn't mean to do that."

He stood up. "I'd better go do my job. It looks like Pop's working late again." Uncle Jim made his way unsteadily to the door and exited. The rest of us ate in silence for a minute, gulping down chicken potpie, creamed onions, and corn fritters from several large bowls.

A minute later, Uncle Jim led my grandfather in through the kitchen. Father Dunne greeted him cordially, "How are you holding up, John?"

My grandfather growled, "The paperboy never came today! Jim's paying good money to stay here, and they say they have real newspapers, but ours never arrived!"

"Oh? Sorry to hear that."

Aunt Betty suggested, "We can call Teresa. Which paper did you want, Pop? *Newsday*?"

"Yeah. What else?"

I informed them, "*Newsday* is here. Douglas delivered it with dinner."

But my grandfather was not appeased. "That boy never gets the paper here on time. Why should we have to wait until dinner?"

Uncle Jim laughed. "He has a point, you know. The truth is: That paper was really delivered fifty ago. We should be able to look at it whenever we want." My grandfather pointed at him in agreement.

"Okay," said Aunt Betty. "I'll speak to Teresa about getting it delivered earlier."

I interrupted, "But *Newsday* is an afternoon paper. Or it was in 1957."

TJ muttered, "Anomaly" under his breath.

Aunt Betty winked at me as if to say, *Let's pretend we're doing something about this, but we're not*, so I let it go. The rest of the dinner passed without incident, but without any sharing of nice memories, either. Aunt Betty and Father Dunne discussed his schedule of masses and confessions in the coming days. Once we had consumed a lemon meringue pie for dessert, people started to get up.

Curiously, the cleanup crew, Douglas and Francis, arrived on their own, like they had been hovering outside. This time, Douglas himself delivered the specially produced DVD. He handed it to Aunt Betty; then turned to include my grandparents as he recited, as if from a script, "A love that lasts fifty years is something to celebrate. This DVD celebrates your love when it was young. It's called *Love Songs of 1957*. We hope you enjoy it."

Instead of the box of salt-water taffy (which was very good, by the way), he handed me a bag of those little Valentines Day hearts with words and sayings on them. I guess you could buy those back in 1957, too. They tasted gross back then, too.

Douglas and Francis set about their cleaning task, figuring that we would all go into the living room and watch the DVD, but that didn't happen. My grandparents kept right on walking through the living room and down the hallway. My grandmother called over her shoulder, "We don't need to sit through another one of those things. You kids go ahead."

I thought Uncle Jim might be offended, since he was paying for 'those things,' but he totally agreed. "Yeah, we're gonna pass tonight, too."

I looked at Aunt Betty in surprise. "What? You don't want to learn about the love songs of 1957?"

She cocked her head toward the kitchen. "I promised Father Dunne we'd check out his wooden confessional at the church. The DVD is ours to keep. Right?"

I assured her, "Right."

"So I'll be able to watch it whenever I want."

Just like that, Uncle Jim, Aunt Betty, and Father Dunne were gone through the side door. I figured, then, that my cousins would watch with me, but TJ emerged from the kitchen wearing his coat and fluffing out a wool hat. I asked him, "What? You're leaving, too?"

"Oh yes. I promised the twins I'd stop by after dinner. They've been telling me about some 1950s party games." He leaned toward me and whispered naughtily, "Kissing games, if you must know. They have a list of them, and we're going to try them all tonight."

"Kissing games? Like what?"

He recited the names, as if each one were a forbidden delight, "Spin the Bottle. Post Office. Seven Minutes in Heaven."

"I've never heard of that last one. Where's heaven supposed to be?"

"It's in a closet."

Patrick snorted, "You'll be right at home in there, T-Gay."

I cast a weary glance over at Patrick. He was sliding the DVD into the back of the Admiral. Apparently, just he and I were going to watch it. I opened the front door for TJ and said, "Okay. Have some naughty 1950s fun."

He whispered throatily, "Oh, I will. I will," and headed out.

Patrick sat back heavily on the couch. He looked at me and shook his head. "Amazing. What on earth do two hot, blonde chicks see in him?"

I don't think he was expecting an answer, but I gave him one. "Well, let's see: He pays attention to them. He likes things that they like. He's fun to be with. And he's drop-dead gorgeous."

"He's drop-dead gay!"

"Apparently, they haven't noticed that. Or if they have, it is not an issue."

Patrick snorted. "I'll bet they were home-schooled, too. You can always tell. They're all home-schooled geeks."

I had heard enough. "You know, never mind about them. Let's talk about you for a minute."

"Let's not and say we did."

"No. We're going to do this. We're going to talk about you. Let's start by making a list of your best qualities, Patrick. Okay? What are they?"

His big hands turned palms up. "My best qualities?"

"Yes."

Patrick sounded annoyed. "Uh, let's see: That I'm not gay?"

"That's it?"

"That I'm not a home-schooled geek?"

"Okay. Anything else?"

Patrick looked at me accusingly. "What? What is this?"

"Okay. So this is the list of your best qualities: I'm not gay. I'm not home-schooled. And that's it? Two things that you are *not*. But you had no control over those things, did you? So you get no credit for them."

Patrick's face turned red, but he answered coldly. "Yeah. Whatever. Are we gonna watch this thing or not?"

I eyeballed him for a moment longer; then I reached down and turned on the TV. I took a seat at the far end of the couch and waited as the *Memory Lane Productions* logo came into view. It was followed by some fifties-type music and the message: *A film produced especially for John and Margaret Abel—Love Songs of 1957.*

We watched the opening segment in silence as a group of black guys dressed in suits sang a song for a group of white teenagers. The next two segments were like that, too, but with different black guys. The songs had titles like "To the Aisle," "The Book of Love," and "It's All in the Game."

I watched and listened with great interest. Each song laid out the rules very simply: Two people meet; they fall in love; they get married; boom-boom-boom. That's what my grandparents did; that's what my parents did. It's the same for every generation. I thought: *The story doesn't change; only the characters.*

After the third song was over, I glanced at Patrick. He didn't look angry anymore, or defensive. He looked miserable, and hopeless. I said, "So? What do you think?"

"Of what?"

"The DVD."

"It sucks."

"Yeah? Why?"

"Because life sucks."

"Really?"

Patrick looked away from the TV, but he pointed to it. "Those love songs aren't for guys like me. They're for other guys, I guess."

"They could be for you."

"Oh really? But you just told me I'm a complete loser."

"No, I didn't."

"You just said I don't have one positive thing about me on my list."

"On that particular list. That *you* made. About yourself. But you can make another one."

He shook his head. "Forget it. You don't understand what I'm talking about."

I actually sputtered. "Wait a minute. I *do* understand. I understand completely. I don't think any guy is ever going to love me that way. Not like in those songs."

He looked surprised. "You don't?"

"No!"

"Why not?"

I held up my fingers and checked off my reasons: "I am too tall. I act too old for my age. I'm too uncool." Patrick just stared at me. I reached over with my foot and poked him in the side. Hard. "Hey! You'd better start contradicting me!"

He winced at the pain in his side, but then he laughed. I demanded he tell me, "Those are my reasons. What are yours?"

"I don't know."

"You do. Give me the list."

"Another list?"

"Yeah."

"Okay." He held up his stubby fingers like I had done. "I'm too fat, ugly, sweaty. I'm also uncool." He paused; then added, "Oh yeah, and I'm tongue-tied. But only in front of girls."

I nodded—sympathetically, I hope. I pointed to the TV and asked, "So what did we learn?"

"From the DVD?"

"From talking to each other about the DVD."

"Uh, that we both have low self-esteem?"

I threatened another kick in his side, causing him to cover up. "No. Everybody has low self-esteem. Everybody. That's a fact. But everybody goes out there anyway, and tries, and meets someone, and falls in love anyway. It's just how things work, whether we are good at it or not. We still have to try."

Patrick didn't reply.

I got up to turn off the TV, but the phone rang so I detoured into the kitchen. Ray Hoffman was on the other end. He didn't even say hello. He just asked, "Do you guys want to come over and play Clue?"

I turned my head from the receiver. "Hey, Patrick! Do you want to go to Ray's and play Clue?"

He muttered, "Whatever," so I replied, "Okay. Patrick and I will stop over."

A minute later—after waiting for two huge, wood-paneled station wagons to pass by—we crossed the street to the

Hoffmans. Ray's father was standing outside. He was hunched over, with his face turned away, like some kind of conspirator. When he saw me, he muttered a final word into a cell phone, snapped it closed, and stashed it in his pocket. He pointed at the front door. "Go ahead. Just walk in."

I opened the door slowly and found myself looking right at Ray. He was on a chair in front of their middle TV, an RCA Victor, watching a commercial for Lucky Strike cigarettes. He pointed to the TV and then to a glossy magazine in a rack. "Lucky Strikes on the tube, and Seagram's Seven whiskey in the magazines. My lungs and my liver don't stand a chance in 1957."

I asked, "Can they really advertise those things on TV?"

He gestured toward the set, as if to say, *See for yourself,* but he answered comically, "Yep. They have yet to discover that cigarettes and whiskey are bad for you."

I pointed to a familiar-looking book in the magazine rack. "Is that your *Golden Memories* journal?"

He snorted a laugh. "Yeah. It is. It remains unopened. No golden memories yet."

"No? Who's the chronicler for your family?"

"My dad, I guess. It sure isn't me." He leaned forward and turned off the TV. "You guys ready to play? I have it set up in the kitchen."

The three of us gathered around the kitchen table where a Clue board and cards had been spread out. We drank sodas and played the game for about fifteen minutes without any problems. But then Patrick, out of pure habit I suppose, started to make disparaging remarks about TJ. He pointed at the three facedown cards and pretended to solve the mystery, "T-Gay, in the library, with *The Big Book of Fairies*."

Ray laughed, loudly. So, a minute later, Patrick tried another one. "T-Gay, in the kitchen, with the quiche." This really cracked Ray up. It was nice to see him laugh, but it bothered me that it was at TJ's expense. Patrick bragged, "I could go on all night."

I told him, "Please don't."

But Patrick had one more: "T-Gay, in the bedroom, with the Vaseline jar."

Ray started laughing uncontrollably at that one. I had heard enough. I told Patrick, as calmly as I could, "You shouldn't be making fun of your brother like that. Especially when he's not here."

Patrick just shrugged. Ray looked suddenly guilty, but he couldn't stop laughing completely for several more seconds.

"I mean it. Especially in front of Ray."

Patrick frowned. "Relax. I'm just having some fun."

"Fun? Fun for whom?" He didn't answer, which made me madder. I decided to tell him the truth. "Do you want to know what's really going on here?"

"No. Not really."

I told him anyway. "You want kids to laugh at TJ. Otherwise, they'd be laughing at you."

He looked surprised. "For what?"

"You tell me."

Patrick frowned deeply. "Oh, I see. Okay. Are we back to my list?"

I didn't say anything else. I didn't have to. We completed the game with no further T-Gay jokes.

After we picked up the pieces, I asked Ray, "Do you want to come with us to the Clarks?" He seemed to hesitate, so I added, "Remember how much Robby liked your dad's speech? I think he's a future CT."

Ray admitted, "Yeah. Okay. They won't make us pray, will they?"

"They might ask us, but they won't make us."

"Okay. Why not?" He looked at Patrick. "And you're hot for Rosemary Clark. Right, big guy?"

Patrick reddened. "No."

I decided to forgive and forget. I said, "Come on, Patrick. It's okay. She likes you, too. I can tell." Patrick's eyes scanned mine, looking for a hint of mockery, but I was serious. I told him, "She's been checking you out; admiring your powerful build."

Patrick sputtered, "Cut it out!"

"It's true."

Patrick pushed away from the table. "Don't talk about her like that."

As it turned out, the Clarks were already praying when we got to their door. We could hear them from outside. We were about to leave when the voices stopped abruptly, so I went ahead and knocked. Mrs. Clark opened the door wearing a perfect *I Love Lucy* housedress. She smiled kindly and let us all in.

Like the previous time, it was a little awkward at first. Ray talked to Robby a little about Umbrella Man and Babushka Girl who, I gathered, were eyewitnesses to the JFK assassination. Robby giggled about their names.

Patrick was a bit tongue-tied but, after several minutes, he managed to ask Rosemary, "Do you have plans for after high school? For college?"

Rosemary told him, "Yes. I may be able to attend college. Maybe IBC."

Patrick asked, with interest, "What's that?"

"The International Bible College, in Stoney Brook."

"Stoney Brook, Long Island?"

"Yes."

"That's not far!"

"No."

I thought they were making a connection, like in "The Book of Love." I guess Mrs. Clark thought so, too. As she set down a tray of white cups, she commented, "You may be able to do that, Rosemary, but you can't count on it."

Rosemary agreed right away, "No. I can't."

"The signs are coming too fast."

Ray joined the conversation. "The signs? What signs are those?"

Mrs. Clark explained, "The signs of the end times."

Ray replied, a little too quickly, "And those are?"

Mrs. Clark handed a cup of hot chocolate to Ray. "Those are many."

"Okay. Can I hear some?"

Mrs. Clark passed cups to the rest of us. Then she answered, "All right. Here are a few of the signs: the reunification of Israel, the rise of one global economy, the increase in natural disasters, the war in the Middle East."

I wanted to signal Ray that it was time to stop asking questions, but he was too fast for me. He asked, "And how does this affect Rosemary going to college?"

Mrs. Clark remained polite, but her friendly smile had turned into a wary one. She asked him, "I'm sorry, young man. What is your name again?"

"My name is Ray. Ray Hoffman."

"Well, Ray, it affects everything our family does now, and will do in the future. There is not much sense in planning for a distant future when there will not be one. Not for the faithful."

Ray opened his mouth to ask something else, but I let him know, "That's enough, Ray!"

He looked at me with wounded innocence. "What?"

"You're asking too many questions."

He looked back at Mrs. Clark and conceded, "Sorry. I was interested."

After an awkward pause, Robby pointed to the clock. He announced, "Break time is over!"

Mrs. Clark told us, "We have to excuse ourselves now for prayer circle. The children will come down to the Town Square after we've finished." She looked at Patrick. "Unless you want to join the group. You are welcome."

Patrick didn't say anything. I waited as long as I could before answering for our group, "Not this time, I guess. Thanks."

We set down our cups, bundled up, and left quickly. As soon as we reached the end of the walkway, Patrick rounded on Ray. "What the hell do you know, Hoffman? Except all your conspiracy crap, that nobody gives a damn about anyway?"

Ray seemed shocked at this outburst. "What? What are you talking about?"

"Why were you so rude to Mrs. Clark?"

"I wasn't rude. I was just asking her questions." He looked from Patrick to me. "You have to admit, that's all pretty bizarre."

Patrick was near his boiling point. "You're bizarre! You're an idiot!"

Ray shook his head. "What is this? You're on *their* side?"

"I'm sure as hell not on yours!"

"Fine. Then you're even dumber than you look."

Patrick grabbed for his coat lapels, but Ray jumped back. I yelled, "Hey! Boys, boys!"

Patrick shouted, "I'd rather listen to Mrs. Clark any day than to you and your crazy father."

"Crazy?"

"He sits in the middle of three TV sets? Talking to himself about conspiracies? He's nuts!"

"*He's* nuts? No, no. Your girlfriend's family is nuts."

I had to step in and shove the boys apart, but they continued to snarl at each other all the way up the street. As we neared the Town Square, I spotted TJ up ahead. He was watching the Nordstrom girls roller-skating in perfect circles in front of the Soda Shop.

Patrick kept walking until he was standing next to him, but I stayed back with Ray. I asked, "Is your little spat over now?"

"My spat? Your cousin is now a born-again Christian? Since when? Since the Clue game?"

"I don't know. You hit a nerve, I think. Let's just forget it." I changed the subject. "Do you know what's happening here tonight?"

"Here? In the authentically bogus Town Square?"

"Yes."

"Something about cars. Muscle cars." We both reacted to a loud, rapping noise to our left. Mr. Hoffman was standing in the window of F. W. Woolworth, looking very agitated. He rapped again and waved at Ray. Ray let out a sigh. "I'd better go see what he wants." He walked into Woolworth's, so I followed.

Mr. Hoffman held up a plaid work shirt and started to harangue the woman behind the counter. "How is this an authentic 1950s work shirt? Can you tell me that? It's not 100% cotton; it's a blend. They didn't have synthetics, like rayon and nylon, in the 1950s."

The saleswoman replied cheerfully, but firmly, "Oh yes we do. Synthetics became very popular during World War Two, and they continue to be popular here in the fifties."

Mr. Hoffman looked stunned; like no one had ever told him he was wrong before. He ignored the woman and told us, "And the label doesn't tell you that this was made in China, but it surely was." He shot a challenging glance at the woman, who just smiled back. "The Chinese weren't producing anything in the 1950s. Except maybe more Chinese."

With that, Mr. Hoffman put down the shirt and stomped out of the store. Ray and I followed, but first I gave that saleswoman an apologetic smile, and a subtle thumbs up.

The Hardy family had now taken up a position across the street. Mr. Hardy was smiling, but the women were not. They were watching Mr. Hoffman on his angry trek home. The women whispered together as they had in class. Then the daughter broke away and crossed the street toward us. She started in on Ray, through clenched teeth, "Does *your* father realize that *my* father spent thirty years of his life protecting him?"

Ray stole a quick glance at me. "Uh, I don't know."

"I doubt that he does, or he would never say such false and malicious things!"

"Okay."

"What does your father do, anyway?"

Ray mumbled, "He's a teacher."

She looked Ray up and down. "A communist teacher, I'll bet." She whirled around and marched away.

Ray watched her go. He didn't seem too upset. Or too surprised. I thought, *Does this happen a lot?* I asked him, "Your father's a teacher? Where?"

"At Hofstra."

I bugged my eyes toward Mrs. Whitman. "She was really mad."

Ray shrugged. "Yeah, well. My dad can have that effect on people."

"I'll bet." I chose my next words carefully. "Do you realize that people think you and your dad are . . . ."

"What?"

"A little weird, to say the least. To be spending your time at a theme park watching a murder on TV."

"An assassination. The greatest crime in American history. A still-unsolved crime."

"A lot of people think it *was* solved. Case closed."

"A lot of people think smoking Lucky Strikes and drinking Seagram's Seven is harmless."

"Good point."

"People believe what they want to believe."

We left it at that. Soon, the four members of the Clark family strolled into the Town Square. So did Mrs. Nordstrom. Only the Abels, the Blanchards, and the McCains remained shut up in their houses.

The evening's entertainment began when the door of the Soda Shop opened and two actors stepped out. One was done up as Marilyn Monroe and the other as Elvis. The Marilyn Monroe girl giggled coquettishly. The Elvis guy looked around and curled his lip.

A few seconds later, a Memory Lane employee pulled up to the curb in a beautiful blue Thunderbird. The driver got out and held the door for Marilyn Monroe to walk around and climb into the driver's seat. Right after that, another employee pulled up in a humungous, pink Cadillac. He performed the same ritual for Elvis. Then they both drove off in a slow loop around the Town Square.

I asked Ray, "Didn't Marilyn Monroe and Elvis both die of drug overdoses?"

He shook his head knowingly. "Elvis did, but the FBI killed Marilyn Monroe and made it look like a drug overdose. That's because she was having an affair with JFK."

"Get out!"

"It's true. J. Edgar Hoover wanted to blackmail Kennedy about it, but Marilyn wouldn't cooperate, so he got rid of her."

"No way!"

"Hey, don't believe me. Believe that it was just an accident. People die in accidents all the time—" He suddenly stopped talking.

And I knew why: My mother. I assured him, "You don't have to stop talking about death around me. I can handle it."

"Okay. Sorry."

An awkward silence followed. Then Douglas Zorn appeared. Apparently, he had a role to play in the parade. He started to speak loudly, for everyone to hear: "From the golden age of Detroit, these are the models that made America the automobile capital of the world—the 1958 Cadillac El Dorado, the 1959 Chevy Bel Air, the 1960 Ford Thunderbird." As he named each car, it appeared from behind the Town Hall and rolled past us.

With every car that drove by—and there must have been two dozen of them—Ray got more and more agitated. He suddenly stepped away from me and interrupted Douglas, speaking in the same way, drawing the listeners' ears toward himself instead. "A golden age for Detroit indeed, because they had a stranglehold on the American auto market. You had no choice but to buy from Detroit, and they stuck it to you every chance they could."

Ray paused, so Douglas resumed, as if the interruption had not happened. "The styles of these cars have never been duplicated. They remain works of art—"

"No seatbelts!" Ray shouted. "Speedometers that reached over one hundred miles per hour, and they weren't kidding. Cars that were guaranteed to break down right after the warranty expired as part of a system called Planned Obsolescence. Leaking oil, spewing black smoke, unsafe at any speed!"

Ray turned toward Douglas again, as if to say, *Your turn.* But Douglas had had enough. He just stood there, his blue eyes blinking.

Ray walked back over and muttered to me, "Okay. I'm not sure why I did that, but . . . okay." He glanced nervously toward the cape houses. "I gotta get back to my dad. Tomorrow's the big day."

"The assassination?" I asked.

"Yeah. That's what we've been waiting for."

I replied with some sarcasm of my own, "Really?" But he didn't seem to notice.

"Yeah. See you." Everybody was glaring at Ray as he departed. He didn't seem to notice that, either.

Douglas and I were left standing together in silence. I was actually feeling a little sorry for him because of Ray's heckling. After a long pause, I asked, "How are things going in the *1966 to 1976* section?"

He looked relieved to have a new topic. He answered like his old self. "Pretty good. It depends on which part you're living in, you know? The beginning or the end. Either you're living all hippie natural, or all polyester disco." Then he added, "I've got three families I recruited over there. Just like here."

For some reason, I didn't like the sound of that. I asked him, "What do you mean?"

"I recruited three of the families there."

"What do you mean, 'Just like here?'"

He smiled a bright, confused smile. "What?"

"Who are the three families you recruited here?"

"Well, yours of course. The Abels and the Blanchards. That was huge."

"Why?"

"Because you're occupying two houses."

"So that's twice as much money."

"Yeah, I guess."

"And do you get a percentage of that?"

Douglas started to squirm. "I'm sorry. They don't allow us to talk about park policies."

"Just yes or no."

"Well, yes. Whenever you're the one who brings in a family, you get a bonus."

"I see. So you got a bonus for bringing us in."

Douglas exhaled loudly. "This is why we're not supposed to talk about park policies."

"Right. Got it. So who was your other family?"

"The McCains."

"I thought they were staying here for free."

"They are. But they're working for it. The McCains are this season's marketing tools."

I assured him, "Yeah. They're tools all right." I thought: *How could I have been such an idiot? This was all about money. Nothing else.* I added, tightly, "By the way, you don't have to walk me to school tomorrow. I've got the route all figured out."

"Oh. Okay."

The cars and celebrities continued to orbit around us, but I had seen enough. I turned and started to walk home, quickly, hoping to get to up my room unnoticed; hoping to pull out Blue Belle and have some private time with her. But I had no sooner left the Commons than I heard footsteps behind me. Before I could reach the door of the house, Patrick and TJ had caught up.

TJ said, "What's the rush? Is something good on TV?"

What a ridiculous question. I snapped at him, "No! Nothing good is on TV!"

It didn't matter. He went right on in TJ-mode. "Listen: I found out about the perfume! The twins normally wear Coco Mademoiselle, but that's an anomaly here, so they've switched to Chanel Number Five." He finally looked into my teary eyes. He stopped babbling to ask, "Hey, what's wrong?"

"Nothing's wrong. I wanted to go home. That's all."

Patrick muttered, "We wanted to hang out."

"With me?"

"Yeah."

"Patrick, why don't you hang out with Rosemary? TJ, why don't you hang out with the twins?"

TJ raised up his shoulders? "I have been. Don't you want to hear about the kissing games? My Seven Minutes in Heaven?"

Patrick grumbled, "Forget it. We should go home."

I felt instantly guilty. "No. No. We're here now. Let's all go inside."

By the time we reached the top landing, I had managed to push Douglas Zorn out of my mind, at least temporarily. As we walked into my room, the flash of the evening fireworks lit up the walls. I stood at the foot of the bed, struck a full crucifixion pose, and fell backward onto the mattress.

After staring through the window for a while, TJ sauntered over toward me. "So. Let's talk about sex. I have more input now."

Patrick remained by the window. "Let's not and say we did."

"Since my cousin Alice has revealed herself to be a school-bus make-out queen, I think she should begin."

I told him, "You should take a deep breath, TJ."

Patrick added, "Yeah. And hold it until you're dead."

TJ persisted. "Come on! You now have two love interests in play, Miss Alice."

"I do not."

"Please! So coy; so innocent! Douglas continues to court you as the boy next door, while Ray longs for you from afar."

"Forget that. Douglas *courts me* to make money. No other reason. And Ray longs for the Nordstrom twins, like every other guy."

TJ twirled an imaginary moustache. "Aha! But they are mine. The spinning bottle has pointed to me."

Patrick grunted. "God, what a waste."

TJ turned on him. "And you, oh unrequited one. Have you even admitted to yourself that you love the sweetheart of the Old Testament, Miss Rosemary Clark?"

Patrick answered truthfully, "Yes. I have."

"Aha!"

I suggested, "You should invite her over, Patrick. Maybe for the wedding party."

He shrugged. "Maybe I will."

The fireworks show flashed away for a few more minutes. Patrick and I remained adamant, refusing to talk about either sex or love with TJ. After the finale, we all went downstairs to play a board game—my choice this time—Go to the Head of the Class.

Near the bottom of the stairs, though, I spotted Father Dunne, sitting in the living room with his coat on. He wasn't reading, or watching TV, or talking to anybody. I asked, "Is everything okay, Father?"

He turned to me with a faraway look. But then he focused and smiled. "Yes, everything's going fine. What are you three up to tonight?"

TJ answered, "Not much. Alice wants to play teacher."

"Ah. Just like her mother."

"Yeah," I admitted. "Like my mother."

Father Dunne stood up. "That's nice to hear. I'll get out of your way then."

I asked him, "Have you been outside?"

Father Dunne looked at his sleeves, surprised to see he was still wearing a coat. "Oh! Yes. I heard a noise outside, so I went to take a look. The McCains are on their lawn. Doing whatever it is that they do." He suddenly looked right at me. "Would you like to see?"

"Me? Uh, I don't know."

Patrick blurted out, "I would not!"

"We wouldn't have to get close."

TJ said, "Yeah. Come on! Anything's better than that teacher game."

Father Dunne again addressed me. "I've been trying to talk to your grandparents about the McCains, but they're not interested." He looked at Patrick and TJ. "Neither are your parents. So I'll have to talk to you children." He pointed at TJ and me. "You two, anyway. We'll drop Patrick off at his house, if that's all right."

Patrick assured him, "That's all right!"

Patrick, TJ, and I got our coats. Then I had an idea, so I ran upstairs and grabbed a piece of stationery and a pencil. As we exited the front door, I told Father Dunne, "I do want to learn about the McCains. You know, they got a free trip here in exchange for being in a marketing campaign. It's because they're firefighters and heroes—nine-eleven and all."

He stroked his chin. "Well, they are firefighters. I guess that part is true. But the McCains aren't exactly New York's finest."

I played dumb. "No? Why?"

"Well, Captain Ed should have retired as a Deputy Chief or at least an Assistant, but he didn't. And his son William did even worse. William barely made lieutenant after twenty years in the department. And even that didn't last. He got busted back to firefighter before he died."

I added, "Of a heart attack. On August 27, 2001. It wasn't on nine-eleven as they claim."

Father Dunne's eyes widened. "You don't say!"

"I do. I researched it."

We had now pulled even with the Blanchards' house. Patrick broke from our group, hurried up the path, and disappeared inside. TJ and I kept walking west, though, under the benign protection of Father Dunne. We passed the empty cape house and came to a halt just at the edge of the McCains' property. One of those big shiny cars was parked at the curb. Francis was hoisting a large garbage bag into its trunk. The bag clinked like it was full of glass bottles. Francis smiled at us nervously, but he didn't say anything.

Father Dunne commented, "That's a lot of beer bottles."

TJ deadpanned, "Our dad is doing his best to keep up with them, but alas, he's only one man."

Father Dunne frowned. We all looked diagonally across the lawn. Six McCain men were crowded around the doorway. There were also three women in identical black raincoats. One of the women turned and spotted Father Dunne. I thought she might yell something, or make an obscene gesture at him, but I was completely wrong. She raised up her right hand and moved it crossways in a slow wave. Father Dunne saw it and waved back to her the same way.

I asked, "Who is that, Father?"

"That's Ellen McCain. Captain Ed's sister."

"Her name's McCain? So she never got married?"

"Oh, she got married. She married Jack Gallahue."

I snapped to attention. I asked, "Who?"

"Jack Gallahue. Jack died a long time ago, of course."

"Uh . . . Did they have children?"

"Yes. Two. Including Jack Junior. He's Matthew's father."

I stared at the men on the lawn. "Matthew's father! Which one is Jack Junior? Where is he?"

Father Dunne shook his head. "No one knows. He took off right after Matthew was born. It's very sad. Ellen has had much sorrow over the years." He concluded softly, "It's all very sad." Father Dunne then started to point to the other McCains and to explain who they were and how they were related.

I handed the stationery to TJ, and begged him, "Please, TJ! Sketch this out or I will never remember it."

"Sketch what out?"

"The McCain family tree. Draw a tree and fill in all the names that Father Dunne tells you. Make sure you put them on the right branches."

TJ took the paper and smoothed it out across my back. As Father Dunne recapped his descriptions, I could feel him sketching and labeling away. When he finished, TJ folded the paper once and slid it into my side pocket, announcing, "There you go."

I whispered, "Thank you."

Eventually, the McCain men pushed through the doorway and staggered into the living room, making growling sounds. The women followed with no further waving.

We took that as our cue to go home. Father Dunne and I delivered TJ at his door and then continued on together. After a short pause, he told me, "Alice, I was sorry I could not say mass at your mother's funeral. I certainly wanted to. They had me in chemotherapy and radiation. I was in no condition to travel."

"Of course, Father. I understand."

"Donna was a very special person. I knew her since she was a baby. I baptized her; I gave her first communion; I said the funeral mass for her husband—your father." He repeated, "Your father;" then he shook his head back and forth several times. "Al's death was shocking enough. I couldn't believe it when I heard that Donna had died, too." We turned up the walkway to our house. "It really makes me wonder."

"Wonder what?"

"Wonder . . . about fate, and the turn of the wheel, and who gets the good luck and who gets the bad. And if you get all bad luck when you're young, do you get all good luck when you're old? It seems to me that it all has to balance out at the end." He opened the door for me.

"Well then," I observed, "it sounds like I'm going to be one lucky old lady."

He laughed delightedly. "Yes! You should start playing the lottery."

"I will. Good night, Father."

"Good night." Father Dunne walked down the hall and into his room, still wearing that big coat. I turned right into the kitchen. I selected a short, green bottle of Seven Up from the refrigerator and popped the top with a steel opener.

That's when I heard the sound—weird, singsong voices outside the kitchen window. I opened the door wide enough to listen. I recognized the two voices right away: Matt and Dennis McCain. I stepped out onto the stoop and leaned right to see better.

Matt and Dennis were outside now, on the sidewalk in front of the Blanchards' house. They were yelling a series of stupid things like, "Come out and play, boys! Come out and mingle! Miss Zorn said to mingle! Come on out!" Over and over. Like the morons they were.

They stopped the noise when the Blanchards' front door opened. I watched Uncle Jim walk out dressed in a plaid bathrobe and bedroom slippers. The McCain boys froze in place. Uncle Jim spoke to them quietly, but firmly. I couldn't quite hear him, but he was obviously telling them to leave. He kept walking forward, so the McCains started walking backward. Obviously, backpedalling was too complicated a skill for them. Dennis tripped over Matt's foot and fell. He started yelling at Uncle Jim, "My leg! You hurt my leg!"

Uncle Jim stopped at the top of the sidewalk. Both McCains started heaping verbal abuse on him for "hurting Dennis."

This went on unabated, with the McCains yelling and Uncle Jim quietly standing there, for a long time. Then another figure entered the scene from the McCains' yard. It was an old lady in a black raincoat. Ellen McCain? She snapped, "Get inside, both of you! That's enough of this foolishness." The boys did what she said right away, shutting their stupid mouths and skulking back into the house. The woman turned and followed them without so much as a glance back.

Uncle Jim waited until they were all out of sight; then he turned and trudged inside. I considered calling out, "Good for you, Uncle Jim!" but I didn't. I didn't know if he would appreciate that or not. I didn't know if he would stop and talk to me or not. I didn't know much about him at all.

I closed the kitchen door, locked it, and headed upstairs. Once settled in my room, I sat down, pulled out the folded piece of stationery, and studied the sketch TJ had made.

Looking over the McCain family tree made me sad—sad for the Jack Gallahue side, anyway. Jack Gallahue died at the same age as my mom, but my mom died as a respected teacher, as a pillar of the community. Jack Gallahue died in disgrace.

And in flames. And I don't think anyone, anywhere cared.

His wife changed back to her maiden name, and she had her kids' names changed, too. She disowned him completely, all to avoid being associated with that most heinous of criminals, that urban legend, the hit-and-run killer of the dead paperboy.

It's all so sad. I must now be at the stage of *depression.*

—Alice

Chapter 4

Friday, November 22, 1957

I waited for Douglas and his breakfast crew to clear out before I went downstairs. I cut open a small box of Sugar Pops along the dotted lines, folded back the waxed paper, and poured milk into the carton as if it were a bowl. When I finished eating, I dumped my box in the trash, pulled on my coat, and stood outside waiting for the boys. It was very very cold, and the sky was threatening to snow. A milkman in an open truck drove by. He had to be freezing. So, I imagine, did his milk.

Patrick, TJ, and I walked to the school in silence. As we got closer to the playground, I could see Ray talking animatedly to the Nordstrom twins. They didn't seem to be listening, though. Dennis McCain, weasely as ever, was standing a few feet away from them, and the Clarks were a few feet behind him.

I led our group through the gate and up to the double doors. I tried the right one and found it to be locked. Then suddenly, as he had the day before, Matt McCain appeared from around the corner. He stood next to me for a long, uncomfortable moment. Then he looked straight at me and remarked, "That Kennedy guy was good, huh?"

I pondered whether he meant Mr. Hoffman or the actual President Kennedy. I figured it didn't matter, and I answered, "Yeah."

He spoke again. "I wonder who it'll be today."

Just then, I heard the sound of a metal lock clicking. The right door swung open, and Miss Zorn appeared just long enough to call out, "School's open, everybody!" before she hurried off.

Dennis McCain ran from behind and pushed past me. What a rude jerk. Matt followed him. Then the rest of us took turns walking through the door like civilized people.

Miss Zorn began the day's activities with another quick, silent prayer. She seemed to be the only one praying. After about five seconds, she opened her eyes and told us, "We will hear two speakers this morning. But first, since this is our third and final day in school, I was hoping we could go around the room one more time and discuss what you have learned about our time period. You can talk about things you have learned here, or at home, or somewhere in between."

Matt McCain's hand shot up. Teresa gamely pointed at him, commenting, "Okay. Let's start in the back of the room today."

"The beer cans don't have pop tops! What's up with that?"

Teresa held up one finger, stepped to her desk, and pulled out a small piece of metal. "You are correct, Matt. To open any kind of can, you need one of these, a can opener." She held it up like some ancient artifact. She asked Matt, "And do you now what its slang name is among beer drinkers?"

"What?"

"A church key." Both McCains let out loud, braying laughs. "All right, Dennis. How about you? What have you learned?"

"Uh, that the girls back then were ugly. Or frigid. Or both."

Apparently Miss Zorn had finally heard enough, after three days, to reprimand him. "That is not an appropriate remark, Dennis."

He replied unctuously, "Well, of course, I'm not talking about anybody in here."

She turned away from him, to me, with a plea in her voice. "What about you, Alice?"

But I was having none of it, and I told her so. "Speaking for my cousins and me, we are not going to say anything else in front of these two losers. And we don't want to hear anything else from them, either."

Rosemary turned toward me and called out, "Amen to that!"

Dennis replied, "You know, I was lying when I said there weren't any ugly girls in here."

The twins turned around. Petra spoke for them. "You *are* losers. And creeps. Keep your stupid mouths shut."

"I was lying about the frigid girls, too."

Suddenly, Robby Clark jumped out of his seat and stalked

back to Dennis McCain's desk. He looked him right in the eye. "You'd better stop talking bad about the girls in here."

Dennis looked over at Matt and replied, "Go away, Beaver Cleaver." Robby shifted his weight and snapped into a karate stance. "What're you gonna do? Karate kid me?"

Rosemary hurried to the back and placed a hand on Robby's shoulder. "That won't be necessary, Robby. Go back to your seat." After a final, steely glance (which, if I were Dennis McCain, I would have taken very seriously), Robby did as he was told.

Then TJ suddenly raised his hand. He didn't wait to be called on to say, "Here's what I've learned, Miss Zorn. I've learned that you get what you pay for. My family paid a lot of money for this trip, so we're getting a lot out of it. But these two," he stopped to indicate the McCains, "paid nothing to be here, so they are getting nothing out of it."

Dennis whispered to Matt. "Check it out. It's T-Gay."

Matt answered, "Yeah," ominously.

My blood turned cold. *T-Gay?* Why would they call him that? Where did they hear that name?

Teresa nodded nervously. "Thank you."

Just then, Douglas opened the door and smiled his phony smile. He informed his sister, "Miss Zorn, today's classroom guests have arrived."

Douglas stepped aside to let two men walk in. Mr. Clark appeared first, looking strong and confident. Father Dunne followed, looking like he was on death's door.

Teresa indicated that they should both stand up front. She said, "As always, we'll begin by asking the questions: Mr. Clark, Father Dunne—What days are you here to relive? And why?"

Mr. Clark and Father Dunne exchanged a glance that confirmed that Mr. Clark would go first. He said, "I will answer that question, Miss Zorn, but if I may, let me begin by asking you one: Have you prayed in here today?"

Teresa smiled. "Yes, sir."

"Ah, good. What was the prayer?"

"It was a silent prayer."

Mr. Clark did not look pleased. He told Miss Zorn, "So I have heard. That will not do. That is not what you promised." He turned to all of us and intoned, "All right. Please bow your heads and pray with me."

We all bowed our heads this time, even Ray, as Mr. Clark prayed: "Almighty God, we acknowledge our dependence upon Thee, and we beg Thy blessings upon us, our parents, our teachers and our country."

The Clark kids answered, "Amen," so the rest of us followed.

Mr. Clark then explained, "What we just did will be illegal some day. Yet here, in the 1950s, that prayer is said every day in *all* public schools in New York State."

Father Dunne walked back and eased himself into the seat

next to me. Mr. Clark addressed him. "Except for in Catholic or Christian schools. Right, Father?"

Father Dunne replied, "Or in Jewish schools. Or in schools sponsored by any other religions. Whoever pays the bills gets to decide which God you pray to."

"Yes. Well, in the 1950s, Americans were praying to God the Father and to His son, Jesus Christ. It seemed to be working, too, as America literally ruled the world. But then, ten parents sued the New York Board of Education in a case called *Engel versus Vitale*. The case worked its way up to the United States Supreme Court on April 3rd, 1962. The Court, under Chief Justice Earl Warren—"

Robby shouted out, "We just learned about him. He believes in the Lone Nut Theory!" Mr. Clark just stared at his son, puzzled, so Robby elaborated. "The theory that a lone nut shot President John F. Kennedy."

Mr. Clark nodded and muttered. "I see. Okay, Robby. But let Daddy finish here." He regained his rhythm. "So to answer your question, Miss Zorn, I have brought my family here to relive the last time they could pray legally in an American public school. The Supreme Court will soon rule that organized prayer in public schools violates the United States Constitution. And that 1962 decision remains the law of the land. In our present time, your teacher may legally pass out condoms to you—"

The McCains hooted, "Yes!"

"And she may pass out brochures telling you where to get the cheapest abortion in town, but she cannot lead you in a prayer, like I just did. And I submit to you, ladies and gentlemen, that that is why the United States no longer rules the world. We have lost our moral compass; we have lost our connection to God."

He then walked over and sat in the desk behind Rosemary, actually getting a "Yeah!" and a thumbs-up from the McCains.

Teresa smiled tightly and said, "Okay. Father Dunne?"

Father Dunne slipped out of his desk carefully and made his way to the front. He took a moment to compose himself. Then he told Miss Zorn, "As you know, I am here to perform one wedding ceremony and to help celebrate another one."

Teresa smiled.

"But what's really on my mind is . . . the desert." Father Dunne stared at the floor for several long seconds. I was starting to worry about him, but then he finally began. "Yes, the desert." He looked back up. "You see, the three largest religions in our country today—Judaism, Christianity, and Islam—are all desert religions. So let us ask ourselves as we sit in the lush, green forestland of North America, with our abundance of rivers and lakes, *why* do we emulate them?"

He pointed at Ray. "You! Does your family sell camels?"

Ray answered seriously, "No."

He pointed at Robby. "Do you draw your drinking water from a desert oasis?"

Robby shouted, "No!"

He looked at the Nordstroms. "Are either of you nomads?"

The twins shook their blonde heads in tandem.

"So why do we follow the religion of those who were? Of those who did such things, and who lived such lifestyles, thousands of years ago? Why do we follow the religion of those who only knew a harsh, brutal, narrow world? Can any of you tell me that? Aren't we a little smarter now? Aren't we a little more aware of our world?

"We now know that the Earth is round, but they didn't. We know about the solar system, and gravity, and bacteria, and all sorts of things that those ignoramuses did not. So why do we still follow them?"

Robby, responding to the fervor in Father Dunne's voice, smacked his hand on his desk.

"Is it the morals of the desert peoples that we so admire? I hope not, because they didn't have any. Even according to Jehovah, God the Father, they would rather worship a golden ass than Him."

It was the word *ass*, I suppose, that elicited the high five from the McCains.

"If you think all peoples were like that back then, you had better think again. In Europe, the Greeks were inventing democracy—and perfecting music, and art, and philosophy— while the desert peoples were slitting anybody's throat who didn't believe in their bloodthirsty god."

He took a moment to compose himself. I glanced around. Teresa looked really worried. Mr. Clark looked annoyed. All of us students, though, were entranced. Even the McCains.

Father Dunne pointed to Robby. "Have you ever heard the term *camel vengeance*?"

Robby shook his head. "No."

"It's something that camels do. They're stupid beasts, really. They kill each other over any slight insult, like if one camel sits down in another camel's spot. Well, Jesus came to tell us to reject camel vengeance. To trade it in for Christian love. Jesus came to tell us to leave the brutal, murderous desert religions behind. That's what Christian love was supposed to do."

He touched Robby's cheek kindly. "Do people ever say to you, 'What would Jesus do?'"

"All the time!"

Father Dunne laughed heartily. "Well, that's what Jesus would do. He would reject camel vengeance. He would forgive his enemies. That is something only human beings *can* do. Camels can't. Neither can any other animal. That one idea, Christian love, could have transformed the world over the last two thousand years, but alas, it did not."

Father Dunne was finished speaking, but we didn't know it yet. He placed a hand on Teresa Zorn's desk to steady himself. Then he stared at the floor, as he had at the beginning of his speech. After a moment, he wandered back to the seat behind Petra.

Teresa walked over and took his place at the front. "Well, thank you both. That was very informative."

I thought, *Informative? That's it? Were you listening at all?*

Apparently not. There was no question-and-answer period. Teresa clearly wanted nothing more to do with the topic. Instead, she pointed at her sixteen-millimeter projector and apologized, "Today's filmstrip, I am sorry to say, is not compatible with this projector. Unfortunately, I found that out right before class." She held her hands out and smiled a pure, Teresa Zorn-marketing smile. "Remember: This *is* a soft opening. Things will go wrong."

She gestured toward the accordion-pleated back wall. "What we will do instead is something very common in the 1950s—recess. We will have a fifteen-minute recess period, during which Douglas and I will serve some of the most delicious hot chocolate you have ever tasted." Teresa looked at Robby, hoping to get a big reaction, but he was busy whispering with his father.

The rest of us, though, obediently shuffled back, pulled down our coats from their hooks, and started out in twos and threes. I checked to see if Father Dunne needed any help with standing or walking, but he was now sitting comfortably and smiling. He seemed to have recovered okay.

Outside, the gray cloud cover from the morning had descended even further. The clouds looked low enough to touch, like they were about to burst open. Patrick and Rosemary paired off to my left. They started talking about what Mr. Clark and Father Dunne had said. I stopped to listen to them, but not for long.

I became aware of a commotion to my right, over by the gate. I turned and saw an ugly scene, a scene that was about to get a lot uglier. Matt McCain was looming over TJ. He shouted at him, "I hear they call you T-Gay. Is that right?"

TJ looked terrified, like that mouse in the snake box. He squeaked, "No."

"Are you calling me a liar?"

"No."

"You see, that's what I think you are—a gay little T-Gay homo. But I'm not one hundred percent sure. So you're going to have to prove it to me."

Dennis positioned himself directly behind TJ. He laughed evilly.

I saw Ray and the twins standing next to the building, watching nervously, unsure of what to do. I hurried over to join them. Rosemary followed me, but Patrick stayed back where he was.

Matt grabbed TJ by the hair violently. "Come on! We're going around the corner to find out." He looked at Dennis. "You watch the door."

Rosemary stepped up first. She yelled, "No! Let him go!"

When Matt ignored her, she went further. She forced herself into the space between them, causing Matt to relinquish his grip on TJ. Matt stared at the girl in front of him in disbelief. Then he pulled back his hand to slap her.

But Ray moved faster.

He reached Rosemary just as Matt's slapping hand connected, cracking Ray across the ear instead.

Ray winced. He called over to me, "Alice, come on! Everybody! This is what we do with a bully. We make a circle of friends around his victim and just walk away."

So I did what he said. I ran and threw myself into the pile, wedging between Rosemary and Ray, completing a tight little circle around TJ.

Matt kicked Ray in the buttocks with a painful snap of the foot. "Oh no! You ain't walking away from me!"

Ray winced again, but he kept us moving toward the door, muttering, "Yes I am," defiantly.

Dennis sneered, "Maybe it's Ray who's gay. Right? Ray-Gay. It even rhymes."

Matt struck at Ray with his fist this time, catching him in the back of the ribs. "Yeah, it even rhymes with gay, right?"

Matt aimed another punch at Ray's head, but Rosemary threw her arm up and blocked it enough to turn it into a glancing blow. I wanted to do something like that, too, something brave. But I was too scared to do anything but shuffle ahead, step by step, toward the door.

Matt screamed at Dennis. "Come on! Get on the other side of them. They ain't going nowhere."

But that wasn't true. Our little scrum kept moving steadily toward the door. Then Matt reached in and grabbed a hold of Ray around the throat, yanking him backwards. This split us apart enough to let Dennis grab TJ's hair. Dennis yelled, "I got him, I got T-Gay!"

Matt panted, "Take him around that corner. I'm gonna finish with Ray-Gay first." He held Ray at arm's length and threw a punch that Ray managed to duck under while slipping clean out of Matt's grip. Then Ray raised his hands in a boxing stance.

Matt looked very confused for a second; then he took a step back. He waved one hand at Ray dismissively and turned his attention to TJ, who was now cowering in Dennis's grasp.

Matt seized TJ by the back of the neck and tried to force-march him around the corner, but TJ wasn't going anywhere. He dropped to the ground, slamming down hard on his knees. Matt and Dennis both grabbed him and tried to pull him back up, but he had become dead weight.

The Nordstrom girls, who had not moved at all, now took off toward TJ like a shot. They dropped to their knees, just like he had, and draped themselves over him as a human shield. I looked at the three of them and thought, *Duck and cover.*

Matt and Dennis started pulling at them, but they hadn't gotten anywhere when we all heard a loud voice. "What in the name of God is going on out here? Matthew McCain? What are you doing?"

It was Father Dunne. He was standing in the doorway looking red-faced and angry. Behind him stood Teresa and Douglas, holding a pitcher and cups, looking confused and clueless.

Matt McCain threw his hands up in the air and protested, like he was the victim, "This kid! He disrespected my uncle!"

Father Dunne stepped outside, shaking his head. He told him slowly and deliberately, "You disrespect your uncle every time you use him as an excuse for your loutish behavior." He pointed at he double doors. "Get inside! I'm calling your mother right now." He made a grab at Dennis's arm. "You get inside, too, you little instigator!"

Dennis snarled, "Don't touch me! Don't you dare touch me!"

"Get inside!"

Dennis did as he was told; so did Matt. Father Dunne turned back to Teresa. "Get me Mary McCain on the phone. Right now." He stared at TJ and the girls, trying to understand what had just happened. Then he turned and followed the two McCains into the building.

Teresa called after him, "Yes, sir. Yes, Father. I will." But before she left, Teresa turned to us and made a hasty

198

announcement: "Class! Your attention please. I just talked to the park management. Because of the threat of snow, we're canceling the rest of the day's school activities. There will be no lunch. There will be no afternoon session. Rosemary Clark, your father will take Robby home with him. The rest of you are free to go right now."

I couldn't believe what I was hearing. Who did she think she was fooling? It might snow, yes, but we all lived one block from the school. She was punking out on us, that's all. She had had enough. She had had enough of being a certified teacher in New York State.

Teresa gestured for Douglas to follow her into the school building, which he did. I stood staring at the closed door, getting angrier and angrier. Just that quickly Miss Zorn, our teacher, was done with teaching? Forget that. I turned and called to Ray and Rosemary, "Can you stay with TJ a minute?"

They both nodded. Ray answered for them, "Yeah."

"I'll be right back. One minute." I ran into the schoolhouse, turned left, and looked into our classroom. Robby and Mr. Clark were now seated in the back, talking very seriously. Father Dunne was sitting at the teacher's desk. He was holding the receiver of a rotary phone in his hand, listening intently to whomever was on the other end. The McCain boys were standing in front of him, squirming.

I continued down the hallway, passing two empty classrooms, until I heard a voice. It was Teresa's voice, but it did not sound perky. She demanded to know, "So how did you research them, Douglas? Did you just write down whatever they told you? Do you think that's research?"

I heard Douglas whimper, "No."

"If they had told you that they were astronauts, or movie stars, or major league baseball players, would you have written that down on the form, too? With no research?"

"No."

"Dammit, I trusted you, Douglas! I trusted you to do your homework on these—" Suddenly, Teresa Zorn became aware of another person in the room. Me. I watched her struggle to get back into character, from a bitchy boss to a happy teacher. She did a remarkable job. "Alice! Can I help you?"

"Yes, you can. I need to talk to you."

"Right now?"

"Yes, right now."

"Sure. Douglas, please excuse us." Douglas was not as practiced at changing gears. He hurried past me with his eyes averted. His ears and neck were flushed red. Teresa smiled. "What did you want to talk about? Is it TJ? Does he need medical attention? I can call for the ambulance."

"No. TJ's in good hands. Now."

"Good."

"I want to talk to you about teaching."

"Teaching? In general?"

"Yes."

Teresa's smile receded. She took a step. "I see. Are you interested in teaching?"

"Yes, I am. I believe I have made that clear."

"Well . . . That's good. It's a great profession."

"No. It's not. Not really. It's a lot of work, and you don't get paid much, and you get attacked and abused by people, verbally and otherwise."

Teresa folded her arms. The smile was gone. "So, then, what did you want to talk to me about?"

I let her have it. "I want to talk to you about a teacher who lets one of her students get assaulted out on the playground."

"Look, I am very sorry about that. We did break up the fight before anybody got hurt."

"Did you? How do you know what this did to TJ? He might not need an ambulance, but he is really hurt."

"Again, I'm sorry."

"Did you even know that Matt McCain has been kicked out of every school he's ever attended because he's a complete nutcase? Because he's assaulted other students, just like he did here? Did you know that?"

Teresa's eyes flitted toward the door, the site of Douglas's recent retreat. She admitted, "No. There were problems with the research that Douglas did."

"The research? Douglas? No, here's the real problem." I told her, "The real problem is that you think anyone can do this job, don't you? Like anyone can be a roller-skating waitress, or a soda jerk."

Teresa started babbling something back to me, but I wasn't listening. I talked right over her. "Let me tell you something, Miss Zorn. You lost control of this class on day one, and every kid here paid the price; not just TJ. Don't you dare call yourself a teacher again, not in front of me! My mother was a teacher!"

I turned and stomped back through the empty hallway. I heard Father Dunne talking loudly into his phone receiver. I didn't catch any of his words, but I think he was telling somebody off, too.

I burst through the door, still full of righteous anger. TJ was where I had left him. Ray, Rosemary, Pia, and Petra were all positioned around him in a protective circle.

I hurried over to join them. I heard Pia saying, "Your pants are ripped, Tommy. And look at your knee. It's bleeding." She peeled back the fabric of his Gabardine pants to reveal a round, red abrasion.

TJ wasn't able to reply. He was still trembling, and he had tears in his eyes. The twins kissed each side of his cheek. Petra said, "Here's Alice. She'll take you home. You get that cut cleaned up right away. We'll see you tonight. We love you." As they took off, I thought to myself, *Tommy? Did they just call him Tommy?*

I turned and looked around the playground for Patrick. He was skulking by the fence with his head down. I wanted to scream at him, but he looked so pathetic that I controlled myself. I started screaming at Ray instead. "You! You told Dennis McCain!"

"What? What did I tell him?"

"That Patrick calls his brother T-Gay!"

Ray began rubbing his left side. He grimaced at me. "No, I didn't."

"Did you tell anybody?"

He fidgeted. "I might have. I might have told the twins."

"You might have?"

"Okay. I did. I did tell them."

"And where were the McCains?"

"I don't know. They were around, I guess."

"You guess?"

"I don't know!"

"Was Dennis McCain around or wasn't he?"

"He might have been."

"Really? And Lee Harvey Oswald *might* have been in Dallas?"

"What?"

"Are you the Warren Commission now? Are you covering this all up?"

Ray looked wounded to the core. "No. Okay, Dennis did hear me. Obviously. And I'm sorry. I never wanted to get TJ into this. I like you guys."

I looked down at TJ. Hot tears were still streaming down

his cheeks. I leaned over and whispered to him, "It's all over now. Let's go home and wash that cut."

TJ choked through the tears, "Why did they do that to me? Why? I've never done anything to them."

"It's not your problem. It's theirs. Guys like that—weak, cowardly guys—always have to prove themselves."

TJ shook his head miserably. He wiped his nose on his coat sleeve. "Maybe I'm not ready for public school."

"I think you're ready. Most kids aren't like the McCains; they're like you and me. And look at all the kids who helped you today." I gestured toward Rosemary and Ray. Then we both glanced sideways at Patrick.

TJ struggled to his feet. He took several deep breaths. Rosemary, Ray, and I re-formed our protective circle around him and moved out. We didn't actually touch him this time, though. Ray walked in front and Rosemary and I took the sides, like his bodyguards. Patrick trudged along behind us, still unable to make eye contact with anyone.

When we reached Ray's house. He turned and asked TJ, "You okay, buddy?" TJ gulped and nodded. Ray smiled sheepishly at me and then started up his walkway. He was limping, and holding his side.

Rosemary peered closely at TJ. "I'll leave you guys, too, if you're sure you're okay."

TJ waved at her and spoke, pretty firmly, "Thanks. I am okay."

But then Rosemary asked me, "What about Patrick? Is he okay?"

I turned and looked at Patrick. He had stopped still, about ten yards behind us, and was staring at the ground. I answered, "I don't know. I have to see about TJ's knee first. It's all cut up."

"Oh, sure. Well, I hope it's nothing worse than a cut." Rosemary then told me, "It's not something to write in the *Golden Memories* book, is it?"

I agreed, "No. They don't have a bullying sticker." I added, "Hey, thanks for your help today. You were great."

Rosemary blushed. "Oh sure. Glad to help." Then she spun on her heel and took off running.

I led TJ up to his door and opened it. Aunt Betty was on the couch reading *Look* magazine. Her eyes popped open. "Oh? School's over already?"

I answered, "They sent us home early. I guess it's a snow day."

"Really? Is it snowing?"

"No. But Teresa Zorn said it was going to. You can take that for what it's worth."

Then she spied TJ's pants. "What happened to your knee?"

She leaned forward, "Oh my God! You're bleeding." Aunt Betty rushed down the hall to the bathroom medicine cabinet.

TJ muttered to me, "Any excuse to panic."

Patrick trudged in behind us. I think he went straight upstairs. I didn't really watch.

Aunt Betty returned holding a pair of pants and a small bottle. The label on the bottle said *Mercurochrome,* and it actually had a skull and crossbones drawn on it. TJ, sounding like his old self, asked, "Is this intended to cure me, Mamà, or to kill me?"

"Don't be silly. This will disinfect the cut on your knee, that's all. What happened, anyway? Did you fall?"

TJ made strong eye contact with me, as if to say, *I'll handle this.* He told his mother, "Yes, I fell."

"Where?"

"The school playground. During recess. I was playing too roughly with the other children. I don't know what came over me."

Aunt Betty unscrewed the cap and pulled out a little dipstick. She used that to apply a few strokes of dark, violet liquid to TJ's bloodied knee. He winced in pain. "Ah! That stuff stings!"

"I'm sorry. It's what they used in 1957."

"What a barbaric age."

Aunt Betty said, "I had these pants drying in the bathroom." She handed them to TJ who kicked off his shoes and pulled his old pants off right then and there. He was wearing a pair of white *Jockey Jr.* briefs, with a rounded bulge in the front. Aunt Betty's eyes widened. "TJ! You can't do that in front of Alice."

He seemed genuinely surprised. "No?"

"No! You boys will need to remember that we have a young lady living with us."

TJ smiled contritely.

Once his knee was bandaged, and his pants were changed, TJ and I got out the Dominoes and played. I took the opportunity to ask him, "So . . . Do you want to be called Tommy now?"

He grinned. "That's something the twins came up with. I don't know. I'm trying it on."

"Yeah. Yeah, you should. TJ was your childhood name. You should be able to change it now."

"To Walter?"

"Or Ernest. Your call."

Uncle Jim walked in from the kitchen with a bottle of Schmidt's. He held it up to us and said, "It's the beer that made Milwaukee famous."

He stood over TJ and me and watched the game. "Look at that—The Domino Theory. That's what the government said would happen if Vietnam fell to the communists. They said all the countries around it would fall, too, like dominoes. Well, Vietnam fell to the communists, but that other stuff didn't happen."

TJ asked him, "What year are you talking about?"

"The Vietnam War? I'm not sure. Mid-sixties; early seventies."

"We can't talk about it then because it hasn't happened yet. It's a you-know-what."

"Okay. Sure. No problem."

I asked, "What year are you reliving today, Uncle Jim?"

"Today? It's 1966."

I had never been clear on all that. I asked him, "How does it work in your house? Is it a different year every day?"

"No. Just for the first three days. Then we join you in 1957 for the anniversary."

"I see."

Uncle Jim elaborated. "I asked for those three days for personal reasons. The first was November 8, 1952, the date of a great Notre Dame victory over Oklahoma, twenty-seven to twelve. Oklahoma was considered to be the greatest college football team *ever*, until Notre Dame knocked them off. On that day.

"The second day was November 16, 1957. That was one of the greatest college football games of all time. It was Notre Dame against Oklahoma again, but it was five years later. Oklahoma had bounced back, and had put together the longest winning streak in college football history, forty-eight games, but the streak would end on that day. Notre Dame beat them again, seven to nothing."

He didn't say anything else, so I asked, "What's happening today then? Day three? Is it another Oklahoma game?"

Uncle Jim's eyes blinked rapidly. I hadn't noticed before how red they were. Red and watery. "No. No, today is Michigan State. Number one Notre Dame versus number two Michigan State. A big game. Games didn't get any bigger than that one."

"What's the date?"

"November 19th, 1966."

TJ picked up on that. "Wait a minute. It's 1966? Shouldn't we be in the next section of the park wearing disco clothes? *1966 to 1976* is another section. Right?"

"Technically, yes. But since it was only for one day, and since I was handing Teresa Zorn a big check, she let it slide."

TJ and I exchanged a glance that said, *We're not surprised.* I asked. "So what happened in the game?"

Uncle Jim got suddenly shifty. "What do you mean?"

"Well, did Notre Dame win?"

Uncle Jim's eyes went out of focus, then they snapped back in. He answered in a husky voice, "No. They didn't. In fact, nobody won." He looked at each of us in turn, for about five seconds. It was kind of creepy. "Because the game ended in a tie. Notre Dame could have gone for the win, but they didn't." He looked over at the TV and whispered, "It wasn't one of their finest moments."

The phone jingled on the kitchen counter. TJ pointed to his leg like it was broken, and he could not possibly stand up, so I hurried in to answer it. I said, "Hello" and waited.

After a pause, I heard Teresa Zorn's voice. "Yes, hello? Alice?" She sounded really weird. Was she just puzzled that I was at the Blanchards? Or was she afraid to talk to me? "Alice? Is that you?"

"Yes." I wasn't about to say anything else.

After a few more seconds of dead air, Teresa Zorn switched smoothly into marketing mode, as if nothing had happened. "I'm just calling to remind you guys that there will be a really cool double feature at the Bijou Theater tonight starting at seven: *I Was a Teenage Werewolf* and *I Was a Teenage Frankenstein*."

I thought, *How lame,* but I said, "All right."

"I hope to see you there."

I hung up without replying and went back into the living room. I did not bother to pass along the message.

At 5:50, Francis delivered dinner all by himself. Aunt Betty let him in. I could hear the two of them talking about the food—spaghetti and meatballs. Francis told her, "I brought the

Coke bottles that Mr. Blanchard requested, too. The 1966 bottles. I have a whole case of them, ice cold."

My grandparents and Father Dunne arrived just after 6:00, and we were all seated in front of plates of spaghetti by 6:10. Father Dunne began the meal by telling us, "Tonight, I shall delegate the saying of grace to my sister Margaret."

My grandmother did not look pleased, but she did lead us through a grudging version of "Bless us O Lord and these Thy gifts." She did not add the Latin part.

Then Father Dunne got down to business. "I was talking to Margaret and John last night about their plans for the future, their plans to move into an ALF." He looked around the table. "I'm glad to hear they are leaving their house to all of you. I'm glad to hear that this family will have continuity." He looked at me. "Alice will benefit from her mother's inheritance now, when she really needs it, instead of at some time in the future."

He stated, "That was good news." Then he changed his tone. "I have some other news, but it's not good. If you believe in God, like I do, then it's not so bad, either." We had all stopped eating at this point and were waiting for his next words. "The doctors tell me that I do not have much longer to live, and I believe them. For those of you who may not know, I was diagnosed with Hodgkin's lymphoma." He looked at me again. "You're such a smart girl, Alice. Do you know what that is?"

I was taken aback by his question, but I did have an idea. "Lymphoma? Cancer of the lymph nodes?"

"That's exactly right. It's a curable cancer when it's caught early. Unfortunately, that was not the case with me, and that is entirely my fault. I have since been through radiation and chemotherapy, and the prognosis was promising for a while, but . . . " His voice trailed off. "You can't argue with the facts, and the facts are that my cancer is back, and there's nothing more that medical science can do about it."

I looked at Aunt Betty. Her eyes were filling up with tears. Hadn't she known? She replied, "Oh Father, I thought you had beaten it. I thought it was in remission."

"I thought so, too, Betty. For a while. But now that it's back, I need to face it and prepare for it. I need to set my lands in order, so to speak."

Uncle Jim asked quietly, "Are you sure you're up to all this Memory Lane stuff, Father? Talking at the school? Hearing confessions? Saying two masses?"

"Absolutely! I'm thankful for every opportunity I get. I'm thankful that I'm not sitting in a hospital bed, all alone, watching a liquid drip into an IV bag." He indicated the food on his plate. "Instead, I'm here, with all of you, enjoying this fine meal. No. This trip is a real blessing for me."

Aunt Betty dabbed at her eyes with a napkin. "And for us, Father. It always is, whenever you join us."

I looked at all the faces around the table. My grandmother, I must say, did not seem very upset by her brother's fatal news. I had seen her more upset by a plot turn on a soap opera. Patrick, TJ, and I were all feeling it—getting misty-eyed, swallowing hard. Uncle Jim, though, seemed more lost than upset. Like my grandfather, he seemed to be staring away into his own private world.

Father Dunne continued, "So anyway, when Teresa Zorn called and explained Memory Lane to me, she asked what *I* would like to relive from 1957. I told her that I would like to sit inside an old-fashioned confessional again, and forgive some old-fashioned sins. Do you know the type I'm talking about, Margaret? John? A confessional with a dark screen that you drag across, where you can't see the person, but you can hear their sins? And you assign them penance, and they make an Act of Contrition? Anyway, I'll be doing all that at the church tomorrow at ten. I hope you will join me."

Aunt Betty seemed genuinely enthused. "I'll be there."

But my grandmother snarled, "I won't be. What nonsense! Play-acting at the sacrament of confession."

My grandfather suddenly spoke up. "'Bless me, Father, for I have sinned!' That's what you're supposed to say. Right?"

"That's right, John. Confession of sins was a good thing for people—the penance, the absolution, the Act of Contrition. It helped them get on with their lives."

My grandmother added, "And there's the bond of the

confessional, too, so people won't have to fear they'll be betrayed for telling their sins."

Father Dunne looked at his sister. "Yes, there's that." He told her pointedly, "You know, the children were asking me last night about the McCains, and about Jack Gallahue. I didn't know what to tell them."

My grandmother glared at him; then answered, "Jack Gallahue? There's nothing to say about him after all these years. Let the man be."

"But they asked."

"We don't pry into other people's business, and we hope they don't pry into ours."

A long, uncomfortable silence followed. It was broken by a knock at the front door. Patrick opened it, looked out, and just walked back into the kitchen. I said, "Who was it?"

Patrick gestured toward the living room just as Ray Hoffman stuck his head in. I jumped up and snapped at Patrick, "I can't believe you just did that!"

"What?"

I hurried over, took Ray by the arm, and led him into the kitchen. "Ray, I am so sorry."

Aunt Betty echoed the sentiment. "Patrick! How dare you treat a guest that way?"

Patrick reddened. "Sorry."

Aunt Betty pointed at a chair. "You take off your coat and sit, Ray. We're happy you're here."

I'm not sure the feeling was mutual. Ray did sit down, but he kept his coat on, mumbling, "I can only stay for a minute."

Uncle Jim was not looking look well at all. He was listing slightly, and he had a weird expression on his face. Out of nowhere, he turned to Patrick and asked, "Patrick, what's your problem? Do you have B.O.? Body odor? If you do, use Ban Roll-on deodorant.

"What about you, TJ? Do you have halitosis? Bad breath in dogs? You should use Listerine.

"Alice, do you have the frizzies? You need Beautiful Hair Breck."

He smiled at Aunt Betty; she was not smiling back.

"Personally, I have ring around the collar, so my wife had better use Wisk. Wisk around the collar. Those dirty rings!" He looked at all of us. "Because if we do not use these products, we will never be happy in life."

Father Dunne sounded concerned. "Jim, what's going on here?"

"I'm thinking about all the ads I saw on TV today, Father. Ads from 1966. I'd like to buy the world a Coke and keep it company. I'd like to buy everybody a Coke, a Coke and a smile. It's the real thing. But I can't. So I worry about it. And worrying about it shoots up my blood pressure. Way up. Sometimes to one hundred eighty over one hundred twenty. Does anybody know what a normal blood pressure is? Alice? Come on, I bet you do."

I did know, approximately. I guessed, "One-ten over eighty?"

"Good. That's a good and healthy blood pressure reading. Anything over one-twenty for the first number is dangerous. Anything over one-forty is really dangerous."

He continued, "One hundred eighty is, well, let me explain what it is: I watched a *Twilight Zone* episode last night. It was about a guy with a bad heart who was having a nightmare. Every time he fell asleep, he had this nightmare that was so *terrifying* that it was about to make him die of a heart attack in his sleep.

"So this guy had to keep himself awake, at any cost, in order to stay alive. But soon, he had stayed awake for so long that his heart couldn't take it anymore, and he was going to die of a heart attack *anyway* because of lack of sleep. So there was nothing he could do! He was damned if he did, and he was damned if he didn't. I'm sorry. Can I say *damned*, Father?"

Father Dunne nodded warily.

"Maybe I'm damned, so I'm allowed to say damned." He lowered his head. His voice dropped along with it. "It's not like we could record games back then, or pause, or pop in a tape. We didn't have any of that. You either saw the game or you didn't. You were either there, at the moment, in front of the TV, or you weren't."

His head bowed all the way down to the table, so that strands of his hair touched the meat sauce. He stayed like that for so long that I thought he was really asleep.

Ray took advantage of the awkward pause to say, "Thanks for your hospitality, but I have to get back home now. This is the actual day of the assassination, you know. The three networks are scrambling to fill airtime. CBS anchorman Walter Cronkite is crying on camera."

He stood up and walked quickly out the front door. Aunt Betty and I started to wave goodbye to him, but he was too fast for us. The others at the table just continued to stare at Uncle Jim in horrid fascination, like at a car crash.

Finally, Uncle Jim's head snapped up. He pushed back his chair, squeaking on the linoleum, and struggled to a standing position. He walked unsteadily to the refrigerator and pulled it open. Then he selected a bottle of 1966 Coke, opened it, and staggered out of the kitchen. Ten seconds later, we heard a crash in the living room.

I ran in with Aunt Betty, a step ahead of the boys. Uncle Jim had collapsed on top of a TV dinner tray, spilling the contents of the Coke bottle and a can of Charles Chips. He lay face down in the mess, not moving, his flannel shirt soaking up the debris.

Aunt Betty touched his shoulder, and he lashed out, hitting her hand so hard that she let out a little cry and backed away.

Father Dunne came up behind him and said, "There's no reason to be hitting Betty, Jim. She's just trying to help you."

Uncle Jim moaned pitiably. He turned so that his face rose

six inches above the carpet. I could see tears and saliva running together as he sobbed out these words: "I wanted a Coke. And I wanted to see the end of the game. It was the biggest game ever."

He pulled himself up slowly so that he was on his knees, like a sinner at confession. He directed his words at Father Dunne, but he sometimes turned to include us. "Notre Dame versus Michigan State. November 19th, 1966. A Saturday afternoon. Michigan State took the early lead, but we all believed the Fighting Irish would come back. We kept cheering them on—my dad, my brother Dan, my brother Terry. We all believed. And we were right! Notre Dame came back to tie the game at ten.

"I was so thirsty, from all that screaming. So thirsty. But I was glued to that TV set. We all were.

"Mom wasn't in the room. She didn't follow football; never did. She'd spend the game in the kitchen—either making food or doing a crossword puzzle."

Uncle Jim sat back on his haunches. He talked down toward that wet stain in the carpet. "We were all going crazy, screaming and yelling at the coach to finish Michigan State off! To go for the win! Then, naturally, the commercials came on, in the middle of that incredible scene, and we were looking at ads for body odor and halitosis and everything. Ring around the collar.

"Then, I remember distinctly, a Coke ad came on. And I

knew I had to have one. Right away. Coke adds life. So I got up and rushed into the kitchen, to the refrigerator, and pulled it open. I saw that Mom's head was down on the table. The pencil from her crossword puzzle was lying on the floor at my feet. I just figured she had fallen asleep. I grabbed a bottle of Coke, slammed the door, and turned to go.

"That's when I saw her face.

"It was bright red.

"I should have stopped then and there. Any decent person would have, but we didn't have DVR or TiVO or tapes. If you missed the game, you missed it.

"I heard my brother Dan scream, so I ran back into the living room. It was a scream of anger; of outrage; of the most extreme disappointment. Ara Parseghian, the Notre Dame coach, wasn't going to finish Michigan State off after all. He was going to take the coward's way out. He was going to sit on the ball and settle for a tie.

"Dan was totally disgusted. We all were. But it was Dan who went stomping out of the room. Then he yelled, 'Dad! Quick! Come look at Mom!'

"They all ran into the kitchen. I ran in behind them. They all started yelling at once:

'Call an ambulance!'

'No, there's not enough time!'

'We need to take her to a hospital!'

"We drove to the emergency room with Mom laying in the

back seat of Terry's Buick, turning purple. They were still yelling:

'I don't know CPR!'

'Don't look at me. I don't know it!'

'Do you know it?'

"We carried her into the ER and started yelling for people to help us."

Uncle Jim exhaled loudly. It was nearly a minute before he spoke again. "As it turned out, she lived. They saved her. Her heart was strong. But her brain had been damaged. Damaged due to a lack of oxygen for too long.

"Dad and Dan and Terry always felt guilty that they didn't know CPR. I pretended I felt the same way, but that was a lie. I had seen her right when it happened, and I had ignored her. Just to get back to the game.

"She never spoke again, for the rest of her life, which was okay with me. She might have told my dad and my brothers the truth. She might have told *me* the truth—that she knew what I had done." He bent down, with his forehead in that wet spot, and started to cry uncontrollably.

Father Dunne looked at Aunt Betty, thought better of it, then looked at me. "Alice, get on the phone to that Teresa girl. Tell her we need an ambulance here. Right now."

I hurried to the kitchen and snatched up the black rotary phone. My grandmother and grandfather still had not moved from their places at the table. Their faces, as always, gave nothing away, but I could tell that they had heard it all.

The ambulance, a 1957 Ford Mainline, pulled up minutes later. Those low clouds had finally opened up, and it was snowing hard. Father Dunne, Patrick, TJ, and I stood outside in the wet flakes while two paramedics hurried in, loaded Uncle Jim onto a stretcher, and carried him out past us. Aunt Betty followed and climbed into the ambulance with him. They pulled away into the night, with their red lights flashing.

As they disappeared, I noticed Ray standing across the street, watching. I dawdled while Father Dunne and the boys went back inside.

Ray crossed over and asked, "What happened?"

"I think my uncle had a nervous breakdown."

"Yeah?"

"Yes. It was awful. He was talking crazy."

"I know. I was there for that Beautiful Hair Breck thing."

"Well, after that he started confessing. Like a deathbed confession."

Ray nodded knowingly. "Yeah. My dad talks about those. In the end, I guess, everybody has something to confess."

We stood in the snow for a moment. Then he pulled out a copy of an old *Life* magazine in clear, protective plastic. It had a picture of Lee Harvey Oswald on the cover. He held it up in the swirling flakes, "This is why I came over before. I was going to show you this. But if it's not cool right now, I completely understand."

I turned toward the Blanchards' house. The boys had left the front door open, apparently waiting for me to follow. I could see Patrick and TJ settling down to a game of Pick Up Sticks. If they were upset about their father, their faces didn't show it. Did this sort of thing happen at their house regularly? I sure hoped not.

I shrugged and told Ray, "I guess it's cool. I guess we're moving on. What's on your mind?"

Ray stepped closer with the magazine. I had seen the cover before. Lee Harvey Oswald was holding a rifle and some newspapers. Ray asked, "Has there ever been a murderer, in the whole history of murder, from Cain and Abel onward, who willingly posed for a picture holding the murder weapon in one hand and two newspapers in the other? Communist newspapers at that? Newspapers which established the date?"

I thought about that and answered, "No. I don't suppose there has."

"And the rifle, the murder weapon, was left behind on the sixth floor, to show the cops *exactly* where the murderer was when he committed the crime."

"I know."

"You do?"

"Yes. I've seen that photo. I've wondered about it, too."

"You have?"

"Yes."

Ray seemed genuinely touched. It was kind of sweet, under the circumstances. He started to back away. "That's great. Well, I just wanted to show you this. I'm sorry about your uncle."

"Thanks. Good night."

"Good night." He hurried back across the street, nearly slipping in the ice ruts left by the ambulance.

I walked inside and stood over the boys for a minute, trying to decide whether to stay or go. The room seemed a little less messy. I finally asked, "Did Grandmom just clean up in here?"

TJ replied, "Is the Pope Catholic?" He pointed absently toward me. "Pull up some floor."

"Why?"

"Why not? Don't you want to stay?"

"To play Pick Up Sticks? No thanks." I stared hard at the tops of their heads. "What's wrong with you two, anyway?"

"What do you mean?"

"I mean your *father*, TJ! He nearly died here. He might die still. Out of shame, or stress, or—"

Patrick interrupted me. "He gets upset sometimes."

"Like this?"

Patrick thought about that. "No. He's never gone completely nuts like this."

TJ offered, "He has blood pressure issues. He blows a gasket sometimes. It's no big deal."

I pointed to the spot on the carpet. The chips were gone, but the stain remained. "*That* was a big deal."

TJ looked at the spot. "Yes, I agree. But maybe he'll feel better now, you know? He's gotten it out of his system."

"Has he been depressed lately?"

TJ answered warily, "I don't know."

Patrick slid over the Charles Chips can, opened it, and plunged his hand in. He said, "Dad does get depressed."

"Oh? I didn't know that."

He added, with a shrug, "It's a family secret."

I held myself perfectly still, and I waited for their undivided attention. When they were both looking at me, I said, "I am supposed to be joining this family. Right? Isn't that the idea?"

TJ and Patrick were taken off guard by the question. They exchanged a confused, childlike look. TJ then answered emphatically. "Yes! Yes. That's the idea. Definitely."

Patrick confirmed that. "Yeah," and added, "Mom and Dad talk about it all the time. Like we have to be ready for you to join our family. And we are ready."

"You are?"

"Yeah."

"Well, let me tell you something. I don't think *I'm* ready."

They exchanged that look again.

"Let me tell you why." I deliberately placed my foot on the pile of Pick Up sticks. "The family that I want to join gets upset—really really upset—when someone has a nervous breakdown. They don't act like nothing happened!"

TJ looked down, ashamed.

I switched to Patrick. "And the family I want to join gets really really involved when someone is being attacked. By a psycho! On a playground!"

Patrick bowed his head, too.

I gave them both a minute to stew in their misery. Then I asked, "So, is that the kind of family I'm joining? The kind that gets upset, and involved, and that helps each other?"

The boys exchanged a final look. They nodded at each other and then at me, and said things like, "Yeah. Yes. Absolutely," over and over.

I let them babble for a few seconds. Then I said, "Okay. Let's remember those things. Those are important things."

On that hopeful note, I sat on the couch to watch them finish their game. When TJ finally picked up his last stick in triumph, he turned to me. "All right, Alice. Here's what I really want to know: Why me?"

"What?"

"Why did Matt McCain attack me?"

"Oh. Well, I have a theory about that. I think it goes back to Patrick calling you T-Gay."

Patrick sputtered through a mouth of potato chips, "What? It's my fault? Because I said one thing?"

"That's all it takes. One thing. One word can kill."

"Get out, I—"

"You used that word, Patrick, and it got back to Matt McCain, and he acted on it. He saw TJ as someone he could abuse; someone who was weak; someone who was different from him."

"I never talked to Matt McCain!"

"It didn't matter. You said the word, and the word reached his ears."

TJ tried to summarize. "So Matt McCain attacked me because he thought I was gay?"

"Yes."

"Is *he* gay?"

"I don't know."

TJ stared at the sticks in his hand for a long time.

I was thinking about what to say next when Father Dunne entered from the kitchen. He sat down and announced, "Your grandparents have gone home, Alice." Then he looked at the boys. "What are you talking about in here?"

Patrick answered, "Being . . . different."

TJ added, "Being different, like, being gay-different."

Father Dunne nodded like he had already known that answer. Then he told us, "There are all kinds of different. Different can be good. The French say, 'Vive la difference.'"

TJ arched his eyebrows at me. "Ooh la la."

Father Dunne smiled at him kindly. "I used to do prayer breakfasts with Rabbi Blankman, a truly lovely, truly spiritual man. And a great student of history.

"He said that back in Germany, even before the Nazis came to power, a Jewish person was given an extra suffix at the end of his name—Mr. Fisher's name became Fisher-Jew; Mr. Cohen's name became Cohen-Jew." He paused for emphasis. "By 'othering' them like that, it made it easier for people to think of them as inferior. Then it became easier to treat them as inferior. Soon it was conceivable to force them into gas chambers and kill them."

Father Dunne looked at me. "We could attach suffixes to people now. You could be Alice Lynch-Catholic."

"Or Alice Lynch-orphan."

"Yes."

TJ suggested, "Or Patrick Blanchard-fat."

To which Patrick retorted automatically, "Or TJ Blanchard-g—" and stopped himself.

TJ told him. "That's right! Say it: 'Blanchard-gay.' That's what you've been calling me for years."

I aimed one finger at Patrick. "He's right."

Patrick reddened deeply. He looked truly ashamed, like he actually got it. He told TJ, "I'm sorry. I really am. I won't do that anymore." He replaced the lid on the chips can and pushed it away.

Father Dunne smiled happily. "Good. That's good." But then he looked away, and his smile faded, as if he were seeing a difficult road ahead. He exhaled loudly. "In the end, TJ, you will have to live your life as best you can. You will have very little control over how the public sees you. People used to see me as a priest and think I was a holy man. Now some people see me as a priest and think I am a pedophile. How crazy is that? And I am exactly the same person. Are you following me?"

TJ squinted. "I think so."

"You have to know what you can control and what you can't. You will never be able to control what bigoted people think when they hear you speak, or watch you walk. So don't waste your time trying. Speak and walk as you will. Live your life as best you can."

TJ, Patrick, and I all sat silently and contemplated his words. At least that's what I was doing, and I'm pretty sure they were, too.

Father Dunne left shortly afterwards, and with him left all serious discussion. The boys had all they could take for one night. We wound up playing Sorry for the next three hours and squabbling constantly over the rules.

Aunt Betty returned at 11:00 pm. She announced to us, "Uncle Jim is at the hospital and resting comfortably."

I said, "Good."

The boys didn't say anything until I shot them a look. Then they both shouted, "Good!"

Aunt Betty relayed some quick orders to them, "TJ, you pick up the game pieces. Patrick, you see Alice home. It's very late."

I got up and led Patrick into the kitchen. We pulled our coats down and walked out the front door, zipping and buttoning. The snow had stopped; the temperature was dropping. I immediately assured him, "You don't have to 'see me home,' Patrick. There's nobody out here."

Patrick looked down the street. "Are you sure?"

"Yes."

He did start walking with me, though, from the doorway to the sidewalk. I took the opportunity to tell him, "Hey, I need you to remember something for me."

He answered dumbly, "Remember what?"

"An incident. I was three years old; you were five." I paused to make sure I had his attention.

He answered, "Okay."

"We were in the parking lot at St. Bernard's Church. Our moms were screaming and yelling at each other. I never understood why. Do you have any memory of that?"

He answered immediately, "No." And I knew he meant it.

I tried, "Come on, Patrick! You were five years old. You were in kindergarten. You were doing standardized testing already! You must remember something about it. It was a big deal. Obviously!"

"Uh uh. Sorry."

"This is really important!"

"I'm sorry."

"Will you try to remember—like try to travel back mentally to that place and time? Like a trip down memory lane? Maybe something will come back to you."

"Sure. Okay." He pressed his eyelids together.

"I don't mean right now! Tonight, and tomorrow, and whenever you can. Work on it. Okay?"

Patrick opened his eyes. "Okay." He hit himself on his hard head. "I'll try. But I don't think it's in there. Why do you want me to remember it?"

I explained to him as best I could, "I think about that scene a lot. I think about my mom in that scene. And . . . she's not like my mom. She's standing there and screaming at her sister, in public, like she just doesn't care who hears it. And that wasn't like her. She always cared what people thought. The public, you know? She thought of herself as a teacher. She was always *on* in public, if you know what I mean."

Patrick just stared at me. I thought, *He has no idea what I mean.* I exhaled sharply in the frigid night air, shooting a long dagger of white smoke in his face. Then I dismissed him with, "Fine. Okay. Go inside."

Patrick started back in. I watched him reach the door, enter, and close it behind him. I suddenly felt very alone, and very miserable. Why was I standing out here watching over Patrick? Who was watching over me? I set off slowly down the sidewalk, lost in my thoughts, oblivious, until a movement across the street startled me.

Was it the McCains?

No. It was Ray. He crossed over quickly, looking very concerned. "Alice? Are you okay? Is your family okay?"

I exhaled one of those white breath daggers at him. "The Blanchards are okay, I guess. If you don't count Uncle Jim." I told him, "My *real* family is dead, though, Ray. My real father dropped dead at the Blimpies on Hempstead Parkway. Do you know the one I mean?"

He squirmed uncomfortably. Then he answered, "Yeah."

"And my mom got killed by a drunk driver. On the same road."

He nodded. "I heard something about that."

"You did?"

"Yeah."

"From whom?"

"Teresa Zorn."

"Ah. Well, take that for what it's worth."

"Yeah."

"I can imagine what she said about it."

"Well, she—"

I held up one glove. "No. I don't want hear it." And I didn't. But then I had a sudden impulse. I asked Ray, "Do you want to know what *really* happened?"

He answered very sincerely, "Yes, I do."

"The whole thing?"

"Yes."

Okay. He had asked for it, so I told him. I told him the whole thing, standing out there in the dark and the freezing cold: "I was sitting in Miss Dwyer's class, near the end of the day, when I first found out that something was wrong. Mr. McWhorter came into the room, causing Miss Dwyer to stop her lesson. He just stood there, looking bald, until Miss Dwyer asked him, 'Yes, Mr. McWhorter? What can I do for you?'

"He whispered something. Miss Dwyer glanced at me and said, 'Alice, please accompany Mr. McWhorter to the office.' Then she added, 'You should bring your backpack.'

"Mr. McWhorter walked into the office ahead of me and just stood there again. When the principal came out, he muttered something like, 'Here she is, Mrs. Burnam. Do you want me to take her?'

"Mrs. Burnam answered, 'No, I will." She pulled out a set of car keys and said, 'Come with me, Alice. There has been an accident.'

"We drove to the ER in silence. I was totally clueless. An ER clerk led us into a room with a poster of the parts of the brain on the wall. I knew something was wrong, of course. I was hoping Mom would get there soon, you know? To explain it to me. I was surprised when my grandparents showed up. I remember thinking, *Well it's not one of them who died.*

"Then my Aunt Betty came in. She was red-faced and crying. She leaned close to me and started to choke out a frantic story. It went something like: 'God called your mother to Him. It happened one second before the car crash. She flew immediately to heaven.' I had this ridiculous image of someone getting sucked up to heaven through a giant pneumatic tube. But then it occurred to me that she was talking about my mom. And she was serious. I stared at her crestfallen face until the truth sank in: My mother had died in a car crash."

Ray was looking down. I added, "The next afternoon, at my grandparents' house, I picked up their copy of *Newsday*. There was a short article under Long Island News. A salesman from Massachusetts, in a rental car, had too many drinks at lunchtime. He was heading east on Hempstead while Mom was heading west. I read all the facts. But I didn't look at the picture." I backed away one step. I told him, "And that's the real story."

Ray gulped audibly. He finally spoke, "Okay. Thank you for telling me."

A picture of my real family popped into mind right then—Mom, Dad, baby me.

The kitchen. The cake. The candles.

I paused to look at every detail in it, like I was examining an old photograph. I actually forgot that Ray was standing there until he cleared his throat. Then I muttered, "Oh, sorry. I had better go back inside now."

"Yeah. It's cold out here."

"Yeah. Good night."

"Good night."

I retraced my steps up the path. I had gotten all the way to the door before it even occurred to me to wonder: *What was Ray doing outside anyway? By himself?* I turned back to ask him, but he was gone.

I trudged upstairs, entered my room, and reached into the dresser, pretty much by habit. I took hold of Blue Belle and flopped down on the bed, still in my coat. I started turning Blue Belle to and fro, to and fro, as if she were trotting. She never got to speak, though, because we both fell asleep like that.

Chapter 5

Saturday, November 23, 1957

When I woke up, I stashed Blue Belle away and changed into a sturdy pair of corduroy pants, a heavy wool sweater, and lined boots. It was going to be a really cold day.

Several breakfast items had been placed on the counter in the kitchen. I was appalled by the Aunt Jemima pancakes box. It showed an actual black slave woman, in house-slave attire, happily cooking pancakes for 1950s white children.

I decided to go to the Blanchards for breakfast instead. I bundled up quickly and pushed open the kitchen door. Someone from Memory Lane had already shoveled the snow off the stoop, the driveway, and the sidewalks.

Just as I passed the Hoffmans' house, Douglas came out carrying two finished breakfast trays. He called over to me, "Hey! We flooded the school playground for ice-skating. Pia and Petra are there now skating with their grandmother. Wouldn't that be cool? To skate with an Olympic athlete?"

I told him, "I don't skate."

"Neither does Ray, but he's heading up there as soon as he can."

"Yeah. I'll bet he is."

"Can you tell Patrick and TJ about the skating rink?"

"All right." I continued on my way without another look at him. I knocked on the Blanchards' front door and waited, just in case they didn't want to see any visitors yet.

TJ opened the door. And he seemed perfectly fine, as if yesterday's tragic events had never happened. I told him dutifully, "Douglas says there's ice skating at the school playground. The twins are there now. Do you want to go?"

"Sure!"

"Do you skate?"

"Heck yeah."

"How about Patrick?"

"No. Not so much. I don't think Patrick wants to leave the house today. He says it's because of Dad." He shot a glance toward the McCains' house. "But I think it's really because of *them*."

He stepped back to let me in. Aunt Betty was acting like her old perky self, but with a more manic edge. She announced, "Uncle Jim had something called the *delirium tremens*! That's what his doctor said. Stupidly, he drank all that beer without eating anything, just sitting watching football and drinking beer until he poisoned his liver. Delirium tremens. It means you get delirious, and you start saying crazy stuff. Just made-up stuff. Don't take anything he said last night seriously, Alice. The doctor said he was completely delirious."

I just smiled and nodded, but I thought to myself, *Aunt Betty has put together an acceptable version of events, like the Warren Commission.*

Patrick, without raising his eyes, announced, "I'm gonna

watch all three of Dad's football games today. With commercials. I'm gonna try to figure out what happened."

TJ replied disapprovingly, "Right. And eat Ring Dings and Tastykakes."

"What's that to you?"

"Not a thing. I wasn't the poster boy for childhood obesity."

"Shut up."

"I'm sorry. Was it juvenile diabetes?"

"Shut up!"

I asked TJ, "Do you remember a talk we had last night, about how we're going to treat each other from here on out?"

He pursed his lips together, and then nodded. He followed me sheepishly into the kitchen. Aunt Betty had an Aunt Jemima box, too, and she held up the cover. "Isn't this awful? They didn't have to be *this* authentic, did they?" She pulled out a mixing bowl, though, and a big wooden spoon. She told me, "I'm going up to the church after breakfast, to Father Dunne's confessions. Do you want to come?"

"Uh, yeah. Sure. Can I meet you at the playground?"

"Yes. That's a good idea. I hear there's ice skating up there!"

When TJ and I got close to the school, we saw that most of the playground had been flooded with water that had turned into a four-inch layer of ice. Sandbag barriers held the ice in a circle extending out to the fences. Mrs. Nordstrom was skating in the middle, doing figure eights, as Barney the photographer snapped away with his 1957 Hasselblad. The twins were circling the perimeter, slowly, holding Ray up between them.

TJ spotted a row of shoeboxes with ice skates inside. He said, "Come on, Alice. Show Ray what you can do."

"Fall on my butt?"

"Yes. Let's get him focused on that."

"No thank you. You go ahead."

He didn't ask again. He pulled off his Engineer Boots and pulled on a pair of black leather skates with gleaming silver blades. As soon as TJ stepped onto the makeshift rink, the twins let go of Ray and skated to him.

Ray struggled to make it to the green fence where he hung on for dear life. Then he hobbled, hand over hand, toward me. He sat down on a sandbag, pulled off his skates, and threw them toward the empty boxes, snarling, "Guess what. I can't skate."

"Guess what. Neither can I."

He pointed toward Pia and Petra. They were now doing long, gliding moves with TJ, like steps from a Viennese waltz. "They can, though."

"Yes, they can. They're talented, and smart, and beautiful. I'd totally hate them if they weren't such nice people." I placed one foot onto the ice. "I guess if I were you, I'd want to skate with them, too."

Ray looked up at me curiously. He pulled on a pair of Searolite Work Shoes and struggled back to his feet. We stood back by the fence in silence, watching the skating. Then he said, "Thanks for telling me that . . . true version of what happened. You know, with your mom."

"Oh. Yeah. Thanks for listening."

"Sure." Ray shook his head ruefully. "My God. Dealing with two deaths at your age. Your father *and* your mother. Horrible. I mean, look at how upset my dad and I get dealing with the death of somebody we didn't even know."

"JFK?"

"Yeah. "

I really didn't want to start talking about death again. Especially not JFK's. I switched to, "Hey, thanks for helping TJ yesterday."

"Oh yeah. Sure. It was the right thing to do."

"Yes, well, it was brave of you." I added, "It might not be over, you know."

He looked down the street. "With the McCains?"

"Yes. You never know with them. What else do they have to do except seek vengeance?"

Ray snorted. "I'm not worried about Dennis. He's a coward." He added, "And you know what? I realized yesterday that I'm as tall as Matt."

That surprised me, but I had to agree. "You're right. You are."

"He was always big for his age, but now everybody else has caught up."

"Yes."

"His little victims aren't so little anymore."

"No." Just then, a series of beautiful, melodic notes drifted across the park. The church bells were pealing. I pointed toward the steeple. "That reminds me. I have to get over there."

"To the church?" He extended his fingers toward the east, wove them together, and recited, "Here's the church and here's the steeple." I laughed appreciatively. More appreciatively than he could know. He asked, "What's happening over there?"

"Confessions." I added, "It's a Catholic thing."

"Yeah? What do you do?"

"Well, you go into a private box, and it's all dark and anonymous, and you confess your sins."

"To a priest?"

"Right."

"Then what happens?"

"Then he forgives you."

"Really? That's all you have to do? Say it, and he forgives you?"

"Yes. He might assign you a penance, like: *Say three Hail Marys*. But then you're forgiven."

"No matter what you did?"

"No matter what."

"So, you could have murdered the President of the United States. And all you have to do is go into this box, and tell a priest about it, and he forgives you?"

"That's the deal."

"But if a priest heard something like that—like, a crime against the whole nation—he'd have to tell the police, wouldn't he?"

"No. In fact, he'd be bound *not* to, by the bond of the confessional. He can never tell anyone anything that he hears in there."

Ray stared at the steeple. "So there could be a priest somewhere, or two priests, or three, who heard the confessions of the assassins?"

I nodded wearily. I knew I had lost him. He started inching along the fence toward the exit. "I need to tell my dad about this."

"Of course. See you later."

I watched Ray hurry off down the slippery street. Aunt Betty passed him at the corner, moving very surely in a pair of High-top Oxfords. She waved at Ray and then at me. Then she smiled with delight at the sight of TJ and the twins twirling around on the ice, chirping, "Oh! I wish I had my camera!"

We watched them for another two minutes. Then we set out together across the snowy park, staying on a narrow trail carved out by a Memory Lane snow blower. Aunt Betty observed, "This is all so beautiful."

I agreed. "It is."

"And how about that TJ and those girls!"

"Yes."

"I just wish I could get Patrick interested in girls."

"Yes."

"He'd just as soon sit in front of a football game, eating, like his father."

I looked up from the icy path long enough to make eye contact. "How is Uncle Jim?"

"Fine. He's doing fine. I just talked to him, and he said he couldn't be better. He just needed a rest. And to stop drinking beer."

We soon reached the front of the red-brick, high-steepled church. I followed Aunt Betty in through a wooden door and looked around. This church was much smaller than St. Bernard's. It only contained about twenty wooden pews, left and right, divided by a wide aisle.

The altar area was currently occupied by about a dozen McCains.

Aunt Betty pointed out a structure with three doors, like three old phone booths, set against the back wall. "That is Father Dunne's confessional. It's very authentic-looking."

"Is it? I wouldn't know."

"Oh yes." With that, Aunt Betty reached into her pocket and pulled out a black veil. "This is what the women used to wear to confession." She pulled it over her head and let it fall over her face.

"Wow, Aunt Betty. It makes you look really guilty of . . . something."

"It does?"

"Yes. Like a real, serious sinner."

"Really? Little old me?"

Up on the altar, the McCains, and the photographer, and Teresa and Douglas were all talking and pointing. I figured it was about their next round of marketing photos.

Father Dunne opened the middle door of the confessional and stepped out. He was wearing a thin purple sash that fell from his shoulders to his knees. He announced, "I will begin hearing confessions now. Come one, come all." Then he stepped back inside.

I heard Captain McCain reply to no one in particular, "No way! I don't believe in that crap." But a couple of the old women around him looked over with interest.

Aunt Betty whispered, "Wish me luck." She walked up to the left door, pulled it open, and entered.

I crept closer until I could hear Father Dunne say, "Bless you, my child."

Aunt Betty answered ritually, "Bless me, Father, for I have

sinned. It has been one month since my last confession. These are my sins." Then her voice dropped down, and I couldn't hear any more.

I turned back toward the front. The McCains' photo shoot was not going well. The McCain men had brought several bottles of wine with them, which they were pouring into paper cups and drinking like water. Teresa Zorn's phony smile was stretched as tight as it could go. It occasionally slipped when she locked eyes with Douglas. Even the normally happy-go-lucky Barney looked like he wanted to kill somebody.

They had set up three photo areas in the front of the church. Those were: (1) the altar itself, a high table in the center where they were posing Captain and Mrs. McCain; (2) an easel on the right side of the altar, which held an original photo of Captain and Mrs. McCain from fifty years before; and (3) a white unity candle mounted on a pewter pedestal, where they were posing the bride's family on one side and the groom's on the other.

While lining up a shot around the candle, Captain McCain shouted, "This candle's not even lit. What kind of half-ass operation is this?"

Teresa answered, "We thought it might be dangerous to have it lit for the rehearsal."

"Dangerous? Who the hell do you think you're talking to? I've been the fire chief for thirty years! Light the damn thing!"

Teresa answered, "Yes, sir. Yes, Captain."

I thought, *Have you no pride at all?* And I remembered that

Dear Abbey quote: "The best index to a person's character is how he treats people who can't fight back." If Teresa Zorn were not such a phony, I'd have shared that quote with her then and there.

Aunt Betty remained in the confessional for quite a while. I started to creep toward the door again, but I stopped when a trim, gray-haired man bounded into the church right in front of me. He wore a *Global Entertainment* windbreaker with the word *Manager* stitched over the pocket. He stared at the altar and frowned at what he saw.

The man gestured to Teresa and Barney to join him at the back, so I sat in a pew to listen. Teresa called the man "Mr. Bitner." So did the photographer. It was clear that Mr. Bitner was in charge; probably of the whole place. I couldn't hear too much of their conversation, but it was serious. As soon as it ended, and Mr. Bitner hurried back out, Barney started to pack up his equipment. He told the McCains, "That's it for today."

Captain McCain repeated, "That's it?"

"Yeah."

The captain shrugged. "Good."

Teresa immediately called Douglas to the back and started to whisper, but I could hear it all. "Mr. Bitner is very angry. He said you didn't do your research on these people."

"I told you I did."

"Well you missed a few things, didn't you? They are a disaster." Douglas hung his head. "But they're not *my* disaster,

Douglas, they're *your* disaster." Teresa then plastered her smile back on and returned to the altar area with Douglas trailing behind.

Aunt Betty finally emerged from the confessional, crossing herself and mumbling a prayer. She looked at me, smiled, and pointed toward the door in an encouraging way. "Your turn, Alice." I froze for a second, thinking, *No way!* But then I thought, *Well, why not?* I walked back to the door, slipped inside, and sat on a bench.

I hadn't gone to confession since I was eight, right before my First Communion. And I had never been in a real confessional. It *was* like a phone booth, but instead of a phone in front of me, there was a dark screen. Suddenly, the dark screen slid to the side, revealing the silhouette of Father Dunne. I thought: *How's this supposed to be secret? I can see him, and hear him, and he can see and hear me!*

I heard him say, "Bless you, my child."

I started in from memory, "Bless me, Father, for I—" but he cut me off.

"Let's not be so formal, Alice. You can just talk to me. Just talk about whatever you like."

I answered, "Okay." But then I couldn't think of anything to say.

Father Dunne suggested, "You don't have to waste time confessing to me how you've lusted after that Douglas boy." I could feel my face turn crimson in the dark. "That's not a sin because he's not even real. He's a theme park character. He walks around and poses for pictures, like Mickey Mouse. You need to find someone who is real. Someone like your father."

"My father?" I immediately thought about the light switch and the cake and the candles. I answered, "I don't remember much about him."

"No? I do. Your father was a good man, with a solid job, and a girlfriend he was very much in love with."

"My mother?"

"Yes, of course your mother. He loved her, and she loved him. And I should know. I officiated at their wedding."

I leaned back. "Their wedding! I thought they went to Atlantic City, with no church and no priest and no mass."

"Yes. That's the story the public knows. But I know another one. Right after you were born, Donna and Al drove down to my parish in South River. She asked me to marry them and to baptize you! So I did, one right after the other, with nobody else around. Just the four of us."

"But . . . Why? Why would she do that?"

"I'd say it was to cover her bets. She'd made a point of rejecting the church. That was her decision, and she had to live with it. But now she had you. So she asked me to perform the sacraments for you, just in case."

"In case what?"

"In case she was wrong, and I was right, and God does love you."

"Wow." After a pause I told him, "That's all news to me."

"I know. That's why I told you."

I stared at him through the dark screen. "I've been thinking about my mom a lot."

His silhouette leaned forward. "Yes? What have you been thinking about?"

"I remember one scene. It was with Mom and me, and Aunt Betty and Patrick. It was outside a church. Mom and Aunt Betty were angry and screaming at each other."

He interrupted, "It was outside a church. Which one?"

"St. Bernard's."

"Hmm. And did they usually fight like that? In public?"

"No. Never."

"I didn't think so. Was it Donna who was yelling at Betty? Or vice versa?"

"Donna was yelling at Betty. That's the way I remember it, anyway. Donna was yelling, which was not at all like my mom."

Father Dunne muttered, "No. She must have been very upset." Then he stopped speaking.

I finally prodded him, "Do you know why?"

Father Dunne remained very still. He finally answered, "Well, if I did, I couldn't say."

"Why not?"

"Do you remember what I was talking to your grandmother about the other night?"

I looked around me at the narrow walls of the box. "The bond of the confessional?"

"Yes. The bond of the confessional. I would never break that." He exhaled and sat back. "So here is your penance for today: You are to talk to the other people who were in that parking lot. You are to find out what they remember. I believe it is very important."

"All right. I will."

"For now, go in peace, Alice. Pax vobiscum."

"Yes. All right. Thank you, Father."

I got up quickly and pushed open the confessional door. Aunt Betty was gone. So were the McCains, and the photographer, and everybody. I felt suddenly frightened— alone and frightened. I hurried through the big door, and out into the cold sunlight. Then I half-walked, half-ran down the snow blower path back to the school playground.

TJ was still there, sitting on a pile of sandbags, waiting for me. The other kids were gone. He hopped up and joined me on a quick march to his house. Along the way, I told him what had just happened—with Father Dunne, and my confession, and that screaming scene in the parking lot.

All of it.

He listened attentively and then commented, "Well, if I had been there, I'd remember what happened."

"Yes. I wish you had been there."

"I'd remember a vicious catfight between two girls. That

Patrick is so hopeless."

When we opened the front door of the house, I saw that Aunt Betty had joined Patrick in the living room. They were both staring at their GE Self-Tuning TV. And they had both been crying. TJ stepped right in front of the tube, blocking their view. He raised his left foot and delivered a gentle kick to the on/off button. Then he turned and repeated my screaming-parking-lot-memory story to them, practically word for word.

Both listened politely.

When TJ finished, he stepped aside and I spoke up. "Please, Patrick! Think hard. Tell me everything you can remember about that scene."

Patrick shook his head emphatically. "No. There's nothing. I've been trying, but there's nothing."

"Come on! I remember *some* of it, and I was only three!"

"I'm sorry."

"Then Aunt Betty, it has to be you. Please!"

She stared at the blank TV screen. "I don't remember it, either, Alice. I'm not even sure it happened. Maybe you dreamed it."

"No, I didn't! Please!"

TJ scolded her, "Come on, Mamà. Patrick was too young, but you weren't. You should remember something about it. It sounds like you were having a screaming argument with your sister."

"I have no memory of it, TJ. To me, that means it never

happened."

I assured her, "Oh, it happened."

After a few tense seconds, TJ shook his head in disappointment. He reached back, pulled the on/off button, and the football game resumed.

TJ and I sat by the entertainment console, rooted through the board games, and pulled out Sorry. We played it for about half an hour as the Notre Dame-Michigan State game rolled on to its awful conclusion. (At one point, TJ went out to the kitchen and returned with four of those 1966 Coke bottles. None of the Blanchards saw any irony in that. That wasn't good.)

When the phone rang, Aunt Betty got up and answered it. She came back in and announced, "Teresa Zorn says there is a great double feature at the Bijou Theater at seven: *Gunfight at the O. K. Corral* and *Tammy and the Bachelor*."

TJ and I groaned. Patrick just kept staring at the TV.

Aunt Betty suggested, "You kids should go. I'll wait to hear from Dad." She added for my benefit, "From Uncle Jim."

I answered for TJ and me. "No. We're staying here with you."

She patted Patrick's arm. "What about you? Wouldn't you like to get out?"

Patrick shook his head slightly, indicating no. I saw that he was crying again.

Father Dunne, after spending most of the afternoon at the church, arrived at Aunt Betty's door at 5:30. My grandmother managed to get herself and my grandfather there just before 6:00.

As we took our seats around the table, Aunt Betty made a valiant effort to be chatty. "The ambulance driver said that Mr. Hardy left on a stretcher, too, earlier in the day." She looked at me, "Right before Uncle Jim left with his delirium tremens. Mr. Hardy was feeling chest pains."

I said, "Uh huh." No one else said anything. We stared at each other glumly. And we stared at Uncle Jim's empty seat.

Aunt Betty looked at Father Dunne, "I'd like to say the prayer tonight, Father, if you don't mind."

He replied, "Not at all."

Aunt Betty pulled out and unfolded a sheet of paper. "This is called The Serenity Prayer." She smiled weakly at TJ. "And it's not an anomaly. I found it in the *Readers Digest* in our magazine rack. It was first used by Alcoholics Anonymous in 1942." She inhaled and exhaled. "Here's what it says: 'God grant me the serenity to accept the things I cannot change, the courage to change the things I can, and the wisdom to know the difference.'"

This time, we all answered, "Amen."

After dinner, Patrick, TJ, and I adjourned to the living room and watched a bowling show on TV. That was followed by something called *Highway Patrol,* a cop show that made me think about drunk drivers and deadly accidents. No fun.

Near the end of that, there was a loud knock on the door. Aunt Betty answered it and practically shouted, "Ray! So nice to see you! Come in."

TJ whispered, "He is so in love with you."

I answered, "No way."

Aunt Betty took Ray's coat into the kitchen and pointed him to a place on the couch, next to me. Ray sat there uncomfortably for a minute. He finally asked, "How's your uncle?" Patrick half turned; so he added, "And your father?"

I said, "He has delirium tremens."

"Really?"

"So they say."

Patrick muttered, "Glad you could join us for his nervous breakdown, Hoffman."

Ray tried to be philosophical. "Hey, every family has its problems. And the problems come out sooner or later."

Patrick snarled, "You should know. Your family's obsessed."

Ray remained calm. If anything, he warmed to the topic. "We are obsessed. I am obsessed."

Patrick, apparently not listening, replied, "You're no better than anybody else."

"No. I'm not. I have a lot of faults." Surprisingly, he proceeded to name some: "I'm obsessive. I'm not very friendly. I'm not handsome in any acceptable sense of the word."

I marveled at his honesty. I felt compelled to join him. "I'm not a lot of things, either. I'm not small."

Ray looked puzzled. "Yeah. So?"

"So I wish I was."

"Really? You wish you were small?"

"Really. Every girl wants to be small."

"Do they?" He shook his head. "I don't think that's true." He rattled off, "Not basketball players; not policewomen; not women who need to lift things off high shelves."

TJ added, "And that covers just about everybody."

Ray continued, "You're watching too many ads. Like your uncle was saying last night."

I pointed out, "He wasn't exactly making sense."

"He was to me. Those ads will drive you insane. They tell you all the things that you are *not*, over and over, like you have some kind of disease. Then they sell you what you need to get better."

Patrick suddenly said, "I'm a fat blob. And I wish I wasn't."

TJ sighed. "Okay, my turn. I'm small, and slight, and

effeminate. And I wish I wasn't."

I summarized, "Okay. So we all have faults. I guess only the Nordstrom twins are perfect. They're beautiful, and brainy, and athletic."

I looked at TJ for confirmation. He didn't say anything at first. Then he asked, "Did you know that they're rich, too?"

Ray and I gasped together, "No!"

"Yes. They're paying for their grandmother's trip down Memory Lane. They've been professional models since they were two. And they've been making six figures a year since they were four." We all shook our heads in disbelief. Then TJ added, "But they would be very surprised to hear you say they're perfect. They think of themselves as losers."

"What?" I sputtered. "Why?"

"Because they have no friends. And I mean none. They were home-schooled so they could travel for modeling jobs. They grew up with no other kids around. They don't even have relatives their age. I talked to Petra this morning, and she actually started to cry."

I was astounded. "Why would she cry? Because of the McCains?"

"Because of us! Yesterday was the last day of school, and none of us had stopped by." He qualified that. "Except me for the kissing games. Once." He shook his head. "They set out snacks every afternoon and every night hoping we would all come watch the Olympics. They knew that we visited the

Hoffmans and the Clarks, but we never visited them. My God! We came closer to visiting the McCains!"

Ray said, "I'd have visited them. But I was afraid to."

Patrick agreed, "Me, too. I didn't think they'd let me in."

"Okay," I said. "I feel really awful now."

TJ smiled. "Then my work is done."

"Well, maybe we can make it up to them. Maybe they can visit us at our real house. Where do they really live?"

"Huntington Station."

"That's not far! They can come over." I ordered him, "You need to call and invite them. Now."

TJ struggled up onto one knee. "Yes, ma'am." Then he had a thought. "Should I tell them where the McCains really live?"

I looked at Ray and Patrick. They both nodded. "You had better. But say that they'll be safe, and that we really want them to visit, and that we're really sorry about what happened here."

TJ started toward the kitchen. "Okay, I will."

We then watched a complete episode of *Gunsmoke* in relative silence, except for Patrick's incessant crunching of Ritz crackers. He left a mess of crumbs on the carpet, prompting TJ to call him, "the poster boy for emotional eating." But he apologized immediately after.

At 11:00, Ray offered to walk me home, "In case the McCains are out."

I answered, "That sounds like: In case the mosquitoes are

out, or in case the horse flies are out."

"Yeah. Or the vampire bats."

"Or the rats. Or the snakes."

As we walked out the front door, we both looked left to see if Matt and Dennis were indeed lurking there. They were not, but that was small comfort. They were lurking somewhere. Ray commented, "The McCains! You know? All you have to do is say that name and people cringe in fear."

"Yeah. I know my cousins do."

"If I were a McCain, I'd change my name."

"Funny you should say that. When you were growing up, did you ever hear the story about the dead paperboy?"

"Jerusalem Avenue? Hit-and-run? Jack Gallahue?"

"Yes!"

"Nope. Never heard it."

"Ray!"

"Of course I did, every time I wanted to ride my bike somewhere allegedly dangerous."

"Well, Jack Gallahue was a real person. And, because of that hit-and-run, his wife really did change her name."

"I don't blame her."

"But do you know what she changed it to?"

"What?"

"McCain."

"No!"

"Yes! I should say she changed it *back* to McCain, her

maiden name." I pointed down the street. "And she's sitting in that house, right over there, right now."

Ray shook his head in wonder. "That is just incredible. She exchanged one infamous name for another."

"Yes. You're right. She did."

"Can you imagine being named Lee Harvey Oswald?"

"I bet some people are. I bet some people are named Adolf Hitler."

"Yeah. And Sirhan Sirhan. And James Earl Ray. And Mark David Chapman."

He had lost me. "Sorry. Who?"

"The assassins of Robert Kennedy, Martin Luther King, and John Lennon."

"Oh." I turned right and started walking up the sidewalk to my house. Then, out of nowhere, it suddenly occurred to me that Ray might want to kiss me goodnight. Then it un-occurred to me, and I kept walking. I turned back, with my hand on the doorknob, and he was still standing there. Watching. Waiting?

He waved and called, "Good night."

"Thanks! Good night."

I stepped inside and closed the door, still wondering if I was imagining things, or if I had missed an opportunity. If I had skipped right over a page in "The Book of Love."

I hung up my coat, wandered into the living room, and flopped down on the couch. I picked up the *TV Guide,* debating whether to turn something on, when I heard Father Dunne's door open.

He walked out dressed in gray sweats, like Mrs. Nordstrom's Olympics outfit. He was holding a DVD in his right hand. "The cleanup boy dropped this off. He said it was about Levittown, but nobody wanted to watch it. Do you?"

I took the DVD from him. "Sure. It beats watching bowling."

"Just give me a minute." He unfolded his left hand and showed me an array of different colored pills. "Let me get some water for these. I'll be right back."

I said, "Okay" and tossed *TV Guide* into the magazine rack. I slid the DVD into the back of the Admiral, turned it on, and sat back on the couch.

Father Dunne returned with a tall glass of water and sat next to me. He took a sip and commented, "They didn't get the water right. The water tasted different back then. It had more iron in it, and it didn't have fluoride."

The opening shot of this DVD said, "A film produced especially for John and Margaret Abel—*Levittown in 1957.*" The screen showed an aerial shot over New York City. Then it turned east and passed over the Brooklyn Bridge. Soon, the camera was gliding over potato fields on Long Island.

As it turned out, Father Dunne knew all about Levittown,

more even than the filmmakers. After about a minute, he instructed me, "Turn the sound down, will you, Alice? Let me tell you some things."

He started talking right over the narration. "Levittown was the Garden of Eden for all the GIs, the soldiers who had just come back from World War Two. Here they had just won a great war, conquered the world, and where were they? They were back home living with their parents because there was no housing to be had. They were ready to marry their girlfriends and start families." He stopped narrating and looked at me slyly. "But how could they do that if they were living with their parents in little apartments in Brooklyn, and little houses in Queens? It was like being a teenager again. Mom and dad were always listening in the next room."

I shivered. "That's sick."

"There never would have been a post-war baby boom under those circumstances, I can tell you that."

Father Dunne pointed at the screen as we watched a bald man in a suit pore over a set of blueprints. "Then Mr. Bill Levitt found a way to mass produce houses at prices the GIs could afford. It was a Godsend! Suddenly, hundreds of young couples were saying goodbye to their nosy in-laws and moving into their own homes. They were free. They were independent. They had shiny Fords and Chevrolets. And they did indeed have those babies, thousands of them. And the babies had their own bedrooms, and back yards, and baseball fields, and community swimming pools."

I commented, "It sounds perfect."

But Father Dunne shook his head knowingly. "Well, no. Nothing's ever perfect. Is it? Bill Levitt wouldn't let black people live in his Garden of Eden. He wouldn't even let them apply. And they had fought in World War Two, just like the whites. It was ironic, since Levitt was a Jew. Why would he discriminate against people who had fought against Hitler?"

"That's awful."

"Yes. That was Levittown's original sin."

"So is that where it all went wrong?"

He seemed puzzled. "What do you mean?"

"That's where the Garden of Eden thing fell apart?"

"Well, perhaps. For some people. For black people certainly. But for most people, it never went too far wrong. It never fell apart. Levittown kept its promise. Most people raised their families there quite happily, in that ideal environment."

Father Dunne pointed an old brown finger at me. He spoke gravely, "It's always about choices, Alice. You make your choices in life, and you live with them. For better or worse."

He redirected the brown finger at the TV screen. "Listen to me: There is no Garden of Eden. There is only Levittown. There is only the place that *we* built, by ourselves, for ourselves."

The screen showed a winding street of brand new houses. He explained, "Each house had a refrigerator and a stove, and a washer and dryer, and a television." His voice fell as he continued, "And the milk man delivered the milk. And the mail man delivered the mail." He was barely audible when he added, "And the paperboy delivered the paper."

With those words, Father Dunne stopped talking. A minute later, after a montage showing Levittown home models, the DVD ended. We sat for a few minutes in silence. Father Dunne seemed to be straining to breathe. He finally asked me, "How's Betty holding up?"

I answered, "Okay." Then I thought about that. "Okay, I guess. But I think she might be in denial."

He nodded somberly. "I don't think she knew about that . . . incident in Jim's life. Do you?"

"No. I don't think so." I felt brave enough to ask him, "Did she talk about that in confession?"

His old face crinkled into a smile. "You know I can't answer that."

"But can you tell me about the part where you're just talking together, informally, like we were?"

"No. If I heard it in the confessional, it's private."

"Okay. Sorry." Then I pointed out, "That was a really terrible thing that Uncle Jim did to his mother."

"I suppose it was. Yes."

"And he had to carry around the memory of it, reliving it every day, for all those years."

Father Dunne swigged down the last of his water.

"Everybody does terrible things, Alice. Terrible things that they don't want anybody to know about—not anybody—not family, or friends, or a husband or wife."

"So do they tell you about it in confession?"

"Some do, but many do not. They cannot. Imagine that: They cannot even tell a stranger in a darkened room."

"Why?"

"I'm not sure. Perhaps they think that terrible thing will just go away some day, on its own. But that's not true. It's always there, waiting."

"And it caught up to Uncle Jim last night?"

"Yes, it did. Or he let it catch up."

"What do you mean?"

"Consider: Jim planned this trip, and he spent a lot of money on it, just so he could relive that moment. He had to get back here. He had to do it all again. But this time, he had to get caught."

"Yes. Yes."

Father Dunne smiled kindly, and changed the subject. "Betty has invited me over next week for Thanksgiving dinner. For what will be, I believe, my last Thanksgiving dinner." I must have looked shocked, because he added soothingly, "It's all right, Alice. Truly. The fact is I've never liked turkey." He added, "I do like pumpkin pie, though. With Cool Whip."

I felt a shiver run up my back.

"Please, Alice. Don't be upset for me. This is the way life works. You only get so many times around the track, no matter who you are. So this Thanksgiving will be my last Thanksgiving. This Christmas will be my last Christmas." He raised his eyebrows comically. "I'll be glad to get away from that dreadful *Twelve Days of Christmas* song, I can tell you that. I could never abide it. And that supposedly funny movie about the boy with the air rifle?"

I provided the title. "*A Christmas Story.*"

"Yes. What's so funny about that? Can you tell me?"

I shook my head.

"And *The Nutcracker?* God spare me another version of that. Spare me the version on ice, please."

Father Dunne stopped smiling. He told me seriously, "This reunion has great . . . significance for me, Alice. I need to set my lands in order, to set some things straight."

I replied just as seriously. "You need to set some things straight here? At Memory Lane?"

"Yes, as it turns out." He stood up. "Therefore, I need to get my rest for tomorrow. For whatever lies ahead tomorrow. Okay?"

"Okay."

"Good night, Alice."

"Good night, Father."

Father Dunne headed back down the hall and into his room.

Two minutes later, I walked up the stairs, ready to change my clothes; ready to go to sleep. But that was not to be.

As soon as I reached the top of the landing, I heard loud voices outside. I heard the sound of running feet, followed by a series of *thuds*. I got to the window in time to see Matt and Dennis McCain running away from the Blanchards' house. They stopped on the sidewalk, as if waiting to see if anyone was going to come after them.

As I watched, they dug into the snow banks and made thick ice balls which they hurled high onto the roof of the house, right over Patrick's and TJ's bedrooms.

No one seemed to be stirring at the Blanchards, but they had to be awake in there. They had to know what was happening. And they had no Uncle Jim to protect them. I hated the thought of Aunt Betty and the boys cowering in the dark because of the McCains. I considered picking up the phone and calling *O* for the police.

But then I had another idea. And that idea grew, until I knew I was going to do it. I had to do it.

As I stood at the window, waiting for Matt and Dennis to tire of their idiotic sport, I pulled out TJ's drawing of the McCain family tree. I actually spoke aloud, "Let's settle this matter for good, Mom. Let's have another parent-teacher conference."

Once I was sure the McCains were back inside, I walked down to the kitchen, put on my coat, and slipped out into the cold night. I turned left at the street and retraced the walk we had made with Father Dunne, right up to the McCains' property.

Then I went a step further. I continued all the way to their front door, raised my gloved hand, and rapped on it loudly.

After a few seconds, I heard the Captain's voice. He did not open the door; he merely growled through it. "Who's there? Who is it?"

I answered with authority, "It's Alice Lynch."

"Who?"

"Alice Lynch!"

After a pause, he continued, just as rudely as before, "What do you want?"

"I want to tell you that Matt and Dennis are throwing snowballs at the roof of my family's house, keeping them awake. My uncle is not here to speak to you about it, so I am. You need to stop Matt and Dennis from terrorizing innocent people."

"Terrorizing?"

"That's right."

"They're throwing snowballs?"

"Yes."

"That's not terrorizing. Nine-eleven was terrorizing, and I know a little bit more about that than you do. So get out of here."

"Will you stop them from throwing snowballs at the

Blanchards' house?"

"I can't stop them. Boys will be boys. Now get out of here."

I could hear the sound of him walking away. I raised my hand again, and knocked even louder.

"I told you to get out of here!"

"I need to speak to Mrs. Ellen McCain?"

"Who?"

"Your sister. She's probably listening to us right now."

Sure enough, there was a scuffle behind the door, and it cracked open slightly. I could hear the Captain tell someone, "Fine. *You* talk to her then. Leave me out of this."

I saw an elderly woman's face appear in a crack. After sizing me up for a moment, she opened the door about twelve inches and waited for me to speak. I said, "Hello, ma'am. I am Alice Lynch. Matt and Dennis have been keeping my aunt and my cousins awake by throwing snowballs at their roof. Will you ask them to stop, please?"

She answered right away. "Yes, I will. I'm sorry they disturbed you."

Her voice sounded old, but it was not the harsh crone voice I was expecting. I felt encouraged enough to ask, "Is Mrs. Mary McCain in there, too?"

The woman nodded. "Yes. She's here. Did you want to speak to her?"

"Yes, please."

The woman left the door ajar and disappeared for half a minute. She returned with a younger woman who, like her mother, had a harsh face but a pleasant-enough voice. The younger woman asked me plainly, "What do you want?"

"My name is Alice Lynch, Mrs. McCain. My mother was Donna Lynch, a teacher at Jonas Salk Middle School." The two women exchanged a look. "You once had a school conference about Matt, a conference that included my mother." The woman turned to her mother again, puzzled. "If she had been allowed to," I went on, "my mother would have given you some advice at that conference. It was advice that really would have helped Matt." I paused; then I asked her right out, "Would you like to hear that advice now?"

The woman blinked several times. Then she said, quite nicely, "All right."

"My mother told me that Matt has a condition called Conduct Disorder. It's a syndrome found in young males that often causes antisocial behavior. She also thought Matt had a touch of ADHD. Do you know what that is?"

"That's the attention deficit one?"

"Yes. He probably should be taking medication to help him with his problems. He could become a productive person, Mrs. McCain. He could at least become a non-destructive person."

The woman certainly did not get mad. She looked at me with nothing but pain in her eyes—eyes that had watched her son fail day after day, year after year. She said, "Thank you.

I'll ask the doctor about those."

"But drugs are not enough. My mother was very clear about that. She said that Matt needs to talk to a professional about his feelings. The meds won't do him much good without having a therapist to talk to."

I stopped there. Mrs. McCain was looking down, but I knew she had really listened. She finally answered, like she was agreeing to a contract, "All right."

I answered the same way. "All right. I won't take up any more of your time. Good night."

"Good night. Thank you."

"You're welcome." I turned and walked away. In the short distance between the McCains' house and ours, large snowflakes started to swirl around me. They stuck to my hair, and my coat, and my gloves. They were a beautiful sight, sparkling in the streetlamps.

I stopped, looked up, and let the cold, white flakes fall onto my face. I stayed still for many minutes, with my head back, thinking about my mother. Thinking about everything that had just happened in the McCains' doorway.

Soon, I felt hot tears running down my cheeks. Just a few at first, but then my eyes filled up and overflowed. The tears started rolling down my face in a flood, like waters from a broken dam. I knew I had reached the end of something. I had closed some kind of circle. And that was good.

I think my stage now is *acceptance*.

—Alice

Chapter 6

Sunday, November 24, 1957

I woke up at 6:00, crept to the window, and looked out. Apparently, it had continued to snow, a lot, and for a long time. The moon was glowing in the west, illuminating our street like a 1950s Christmas card. I dressed quickly in my warmest clothes, crept downstairs, and picked up the phone.

TJ answered on one ring. I said, "Are you guys dressed?"

"Is this an obscene phone call?"

"TJ!"

"Yes, we are dressed. We're waiting like salivating dogs for someone to deliver breakfast."

"Breakfast can wait. It's a winter wonderland out there."

"Oh? Okay. What are you suggesting, Miss Alice?"

"That we be the first ones out in the snow, before anyone comes along to ruin it. Come on, I'll meet you guys halfway."

"I'll see if I can rouse Patrick."

"Tell him I said he *has* to do this!"

"I will try."

I was really pumped. I whispered out loud, "Here we go," as I pulled on my boots, coat, and gloves. Then I walked to the side kitchen door and pushed on it. It would not budge. It took all my strength to jam it open enough so I could squeeze out onto the stoop. I stepped down and found myself knee-deep in white powder, and in the most beautiful world I could imagine. It was pure white frost for as far as I could see. Not a soul had set foot on it.

I looked west toward the Blanchards' front door. It was sealed off by a five-foot-high snowdrift. I watched as an unseen force pushed against the door from within, again and again, until it had carved out a wedge wide enough for Patrick and TJ to slip through. I started wading toward them, struggling to move my legs through the hip-deep snow. I covered more ground than the boys, though, and we met on their front lawn.

The three of us turned slowly, taking in the panorama. Nothing stirred. No one else moved. The world was ours. In a burst of exuberance, we fell backward and made snow angels; we ate handfuls of the white powder; we rolled up big balls of snow and tossed them at each other. All without saying a word.

Finally, after about fifteen minutes, Patrick had had enough. He announced, "Okay. That's it. I really have to eat now."

TJ and I nodded in agreement. We followed the path I had made earlier, back to my grandparents' stoop, and entered the kitchen. We stomped our boots and peeled off our wet overclothes, dropping large puddles of icy water onto the linoleum floor.

I pulled out two pots, a quart bottle of milk, and some other ingredients. I then set to work like Harriet Nelson on a school day. Patrick and TJ sat at the kitchen table and watched me—like David and Ricky Nelson, or Wally and Beaver Cleaver, or Bud and Kitten Anderson—take your pick. In ten minutes, we were eating hot bowls of Quaker Oatmeal with brown sugar on top and drinking steaming cups of Ovaltine, fortified with eight essential vitamins. Then we all headed into the living room.

I picked up the *TV Guide*. I complained, "This *golden age of television* stuff is so bogus! We've got three channels, and here's what's on them: *Rural America, Faith for Today*, and *Mass for Shut-Ins*."

Patrick pointed dismissively at the *TV Guide*. "You still follow that thing?"

"Yes."

TJ explained, "We don't have to watch what's really on. Mamà called Teresa Zorn and said we wanted to watch what we wanted to watch, when we wanted to watch it, and of course she said okay. That craven coward. All we do is pick up the phone and call her."

"What about authenticity?"

"Authenticity is so over, sweetie. We have moved on."

"I see. Thanks for letting me know. So what do we want to watch?"

TJ marched back into the kitchen. We heard him pick up the phone and say, "Miss Zorn? It's TJ Blanchard calling from the Abels' residence. We would like to view the final episode of *Davy Crockett*, the one where he dies at the Alamo. Yes, right now, please. Thank you."

TJ returned, all smiles. "There. That wasn't so hard, was it?" He pulled the on/off button on the Admiral and the screen soon filled with *The Adventures of Davy Crockett*. I asked him, "How long have you been watching whatever you want?"

"Since we got here, basically."

"That's so bogus!"

"Welcome to Memory Lane."

We sat on the carpet, with our backs to the couch, and watched Davy Crockett fight Mexicans in Texas. Patrick seemed really fascinated by the show. Totally into it. His eyes started to tear up when Davy and his men turned down a chance to leave, choosing honor over survival. And he was crying openly when Davy got killed, fighting against overwhelming odds—fighting to the death—as hundreds of Mexicans overran the Alamo.

Then, right as the credits were rolling, we heard the rumble of a truck outside. TJ jumped up to look through the bay window. "I guess it's a snow plow. It's like a big shovel stuck on the front of a little truck." TJ leaned his face against the window. "And two men with snow shovels are digging a path to our front door. We're saved! We're saved!"

Aunt Betty arrived five minutes later, walking quickly up the cleared path. She opened the front door and told us, "They've almost finished plowing the roads, so breakfast will be here soon!"

TJ informed her, "We already ate."

"Oh? Well, good. I'm going to go get your father now. He called and said he's feeling much better."

Patrick pulled himself together enough to ask, "They're letting him out already?"

"Of course. Why not? He's completed his thirty-six hours of medical observation."

TJ asked her, "You're not driving in this snow, are you?"

"No. No. That nice boy is driving me, in one of those big, heavy cars."

TJ's lip curled up. "Douglas?"

"No. Not him. Francis."

As she was talking, Father Dunne passed through the living room and into the kitchen. As soon as Aunt Betty left, he came in and joined us, cradling a cup of Instant Maxwell House coffee. He seemed different in some way. Excited? Agitated? Anyway, he got right to the point. "I called the hospital myself last night, children. Here's what really happened: The first twelve hours of Jim's observation were in a medical ward, to dry him out. But the next twenty-four hours were in a psychiatric ward."

TJ sounded bewildered. "Why was Dad in a psychiatric ward?"

"Because there was nothing wrong with his body, TJ. Too much beer can hurt your liver, but that wasn't the problem with your dad, was it?"

"No."

"No. His soul was in torment." Father Dunne looked disapprovingly at the TV. "Can you turn that thing down? Or off?"

TJ reached out with the side of his foot and turned it off.

Patrick spoke up. "I don't think we should be talking about this."

Father Dunne told him kindly, "But you *must*, Patrick. Look at the result of not talking! Look at what it did to your father." He spoke with authority. "I have experience in this area. I am in the confession business; I have been for sixty years. I know the kinds of sins people carry around with them every day, like weights on their backs. And those weights always, always, crush them in the end."

Father Dunne waited to see if there were any comments or questions. When there were not, he eased himself down on the edge of the couch and began sipping coffee. TJ got up, marched into the kitchen again, and called Teresa Zorn. A minute later, we were watching the *Twilight Zone* episode "Perchance to Dream," the one about the man who couldn't fall asleep or he would die.

Just after nine o'clock, Aunt Betty returned with Uncle Jim.

Uncle Jim appeared pale and shaken. He headed straight to the couch and collapsed onto it. His haunted eyes found Patrick and TJ. He whispered these words, as if he had memorized them: "Patrick, TJ, I want you to know that I love you for who you are. I want you to be yourselves. To be true to yourselves."

They both nodded awkwardly. Patrick mumbled a reply for both of them, "Okay, Dad."

"In the end, all we have is the truth. I've made a mess of my life trying to hide from the truth."

Aunt Betty insisted, "You had delirium tremens, Jim. You didn't know what you were saying."

He corrected her, "Oh yes, I did."

"You were saying some crazy stuff. We don't believe a word—"

"Well, you need to believe it!" he cried. "Because it was true. Every word of it. I've spent my whole life replaying that scene, in the kitchen with my mother, trying to understand how I could do such a despicable thing." He paused, perhaps remembering the scene one more time. Then he continued, "But that's not important now. What's important now is that I have admitted it. It happened. I am the person who did that."

We all sat in silence for a moment, unable to think of anything comforting, or helpful, or even not-stupid to say to him. Father Dunne finally offered, "You're a lot more than that one action, Jim. You're the sum of thousands, millions of actions. And you've done many, many good things."

Uncle Jim just stared at him.

Father Dunne asked, "Did they assign you a counselor?"

"They did," he gulped. "I was in group therapy yesterday. Then I met with someone privately last night."

"Good. I've done counseling myself. It can help a great deal. Will you be seeing the counselor again?"

"Yeah. I think so. If my insurance will pay for it."

Father Dunne was emphatic. "Go even if they won't pay for it. In the end, money does not matter. Look how that money just fell into your lap, the money you used for Memory Lane."

Uncle Jim wiped his face with his coat sleeve. "I didn't want that money. That was my mother's money."

"I understand. But look how you used it. You found a good purpose for it here."

He looked at Father Dunne hopefully. "Yeah?"

"Definitely."

The room fell silent again. Then we heard sounds coming from the back bedroom. My grandparents were awake and moving around.

Aunt Betty said, "It'll be time to get ready soon, boys. Time to change into your good clothes for the mass and the wedding party."

More scuffling noises were followed by my grandmother's entry from the hall. She was wearing a matronly, off-white dress. She looked particularly old, and particularly angry. Still, Aunt Betty greeted her cheerily, "Good morning, Mom. And happy golden anniversary!"

We all said the same, except for Father Dunne. My grandmother just scowled back at Betty and asked, "Where's your father?"

"I thought he was in there with you. Getting ready."

"He hasn't been in there since I woke up."

We all looked at Uncle Jim, like it was his job to find my grandfather. But Uncle Jim was still reeling from everything that had happened to him, so I said, "He must be in the garage. I'll go get him."

My grandmother told me, "He doesn't need to go to that church if he's not feeling up to it. Some days, he's just not feeling up to things."

"Okay, Grandmom."

She then told the group, "I don't need to go, either. This is silly."

Aunt Betty admonished her, "Oh, Mom. You'll love it when you get there."

I slipped into the kitchen, grabbed my coat from the hook, and pulled it over my shoulders. I stepped out onto the stoop and saw that a path had been cleared all the way to the garage. Banks of snow were piled up on either side of the driveway.

When I reached the window, I fully expected to see my grandfather on his knees again, by the front bumper, polishing it with Turtle Wax.

But he was not.

It took me a few seconds to spot him. He was seated inside the car, behind the steering wheel, with his hands in a driving position. I thought, *This is a good sign*, until I heard the sound. A low rumbling sound was audible through the window, and I realized what it had to be: The engine was running!

I immediately panicked. I grabbed at the cold metal knob, turned it, and pulled the side door open. A wave of carbon monoxide fumes hit me in the face. I spun myself back toward the outside and took in a deep gulp of air. Then I rushed inside to the glass window, unlatched it, and yanked it open to release the fumes.

Next I hurried to the big front door. I reached down and grasped the handle near the floor. I pulled up with all my might and the door rose, sliding into a groove near the ceiling, letting a great blast of cold air rush in. I exhaled loudly and leaned into the fresh air, with my back to the car. Then I turned around, made eye contact with my grandfather, and mimicked the motion of turning a car key—once, twice, three times.

He was looking back at me, and he obviously understood, because he reached down and turned off the engine.

I studied his face through the glass. Was he with it today? Or was he out of it? I decided that he was with it when he opened the car door, stepped out with one foot, and asked, "What is it, Alice? Is something wrong?"

"Is something wrong? Yes! You're running the car engine in a closed garage. What are you trying to do, kill yourself?"

He shook his head rapidly. "No! No. I was just running it for a minute. I was just listening to the valves."

"Well, even *I* know you can't run a car in a closed garage!"

He protested, "But it's cold outside. And it was only for a minute." He sniffed the air. "Is the smell that strong?"

"Yes!"

I kept staring at him in disbelief. He finally said, "I'm sorry, Alice. I guess I made a mistake."

The fumes were starting to get to me. I told him curtly, "Come out here, Grandpop. It's time to get dressed for church."

He stepped all the way out of the Fairlane, keys in hand, and answered, "Okay." He waved at the air. "I guess we could leave this place open for a bit. Air it out a little. If you think it needs it."

"Yes. I think it needs it."

He hung the keys to the Fairlane on a metal hook by the big door. "Maybe we don't need to tell anybody about this, Alice. It was just a mistake. Okay? I made a mistake." He didn't wait for a reply before he started walking up the plowed driveway. I was too confused and upset to answer him anyway, but I thought to myself, *Like hell I won't tell anybody about this.*

The last thing I did was to lift the car keys back off their metal hook. Halfway between the garage and the house, I stopped and flung them as far as I could over the left side of the snow bank, deep into the Blanchards' back yard. I thought, *Let Teresa Zorn find them. In the spring.*

When I got inside, Aunt Betty was standing in the kitchen with my grandfather. She was joking with him! And he was smiling happily, like nothing was wrong. Aunt Betty teased, "You're not getting cold feet, are you?" She looked at me and winked. "Don't worry. We'll get you there, Pop. 'Get me to the church on time.' Right?"

I hung up my coat and walked past them, without comment. It was clearly not the best time to discuss carbon monoxide poisoning. Or suicide.

Aunt Betty moved into the living room where she helped Father Dunne put on his big coat. "This is the moment we've all been waiting for. Are you ready, Father?"

He shook his head decisively. "What old priest could turn down the chance to say a Latin mass again? *Dominus vobiscum.*"

Aunt Betty smiled wide. "What does that mean again?"

Father Dunne looked at me; then Patrick; then TJ. "Who wants to answer that?"

I shook my head no. Patrick froze in place. But TJ tried, "Dominoes?"

Father Dunne laughed. "Well, the words are from the same root. 'Dominus' means 'Lord.' 'Dominus vobiscum' means 'The Lord be with you.'"

I asked, "And what is 'Peace be with you?'"

"Pax vobiscum."

I repeated that phrase to myself three times, hoping to remember it.

Aunt Betty asked, "Are you sure I can't drive you, Father? I can get that old Ford in gear."

"No, Betty. Thank you. I'm looking forward to walking. I need the fresh air. And I need to think." He opened the door and looked out at the cold, clear morning. I stepped to the bay window and watched him set off at a brisk pace for the church. And for whatever lay ahead.

By 10:45, Patrick, TJ, and I were dressed in our best Sears Catalogue outfits and standing out on the street. There was a lot of big-car traffic going by, as if all the imaginary inhabitants of Memory Lane were off to all their imaginary churches.

The Hoffmans were outside, too. Mr. Hoffman was leaning on a snow shovel; Ray was sweeping off some remaining snow with a broom. We crossed the street, stopping for a minute to talk to them. Mr. Hoffman said, "I've actually missed doing this."

Ray grimaced. "I haven't missed it because I'm still doing it. It's still my job."

His father answered, as if it were the latest exchange in a long argument, "Well, we all have jobs. Don't we?" He waited for a reply from Ray, but none was forthcoming. After a few more uncomfortable seconds, Mr. Hoffman hoisted the broad metal shovel over his shoulder and walked back into the house.

Ray changed the subject quickly. "What have you guys been doing?"

"We watched a *Twilight Zone* episode."

"Oh? Which one?"

"The one about the guy who was damned if he went to sleep and damned if he didn't."

Ray suddenly pointed at Patrick, as if he had just remembered something. "Hey! That's right! There's no way your father could have seen that episode this week."

Patrick didn't respond. TJ asked, "What do you mean?"

"That episode was called 'Perchance to Dream.'"

"We know. We just watched it"

"Okay. But did you know that it was not broadcast until November 27, 1959? And you are living in the year 1957. So Memory Lane is lying. They played that episode on your TV even though it had not been broadcast on that date, or even in that year."

TJ gestured toward Patrick, who now had his back to them. "I believe I speak for my entire family, Ray, when I say, 'Get a life.'"

Ray looked offended. "I have a life."

I felt compelled to defend him. "You're not speaking for me, TJ. Come on, you've been pointing out anomalies since we got here."

TJ told him, with surprising maturity, "FYI, Ray, my dad is living in his own little time warp here at Memory Lane. A Notre Dame-football time warp. He can be anywhere between 1952 and 1966."

Ray leaned back and sniffed. "Well, okay. I didn't know that. It doesn't matter then."

As we started walking, I asked, "Hey, do you want to come to the church with us?"

Ray considered it for a moment. Then he explained, "No. Lee Harvey Oswald is about to get transferred from the Dallas Police station to a more secure prison."

"Ah. Okay, well, enjoy that."

"Enjoy?"

"Yup." I waved goodbye cavalierly. Just then, a white limo driven by Mr. Bitner rolled into our driveway. It was clanking from the sets of metal chains wrapped around its tires.

TJ asked, "What's that?"

"That's the limo for Grandmom and Grandpop."

He rolled his eyes. "I know! What are those clanking

things?"

"Oh. Tire chains. I saw them in the Levittown video."

"They've never heard of snow tires?"

"Not yet."

"Anomaly?"

"Yes." I pointed to the Clarks' house and asked Patrick, "Do you want to get Rosemary?"

He stared straight ahead. "What for?"

"As your guest."

He snarled, "She's not my guest." Then he took off alone, with his head thrust forward, heading east.

I held up my hands in surrender. I called after him, "Okay. Sorry." I watched him for a few puzzled seconds. What had happened since our early-morning romp in the snow? And since Davy Crockett? Now he was acting like Uncle Jim did before the nervous breakdown.

TJ and I made one more stop, to get the Nordstrom girls. They came bounding out wearing white faux-fur coats and hats and white Majorette Boots. Each twin latched onto one of TJ's arms. They let go of him briefly, though, to plant kisses on my cheeks. They smelled of Chanel Number Five.

I was pretty sure I knew them apart by now, so I gave it a shot. Looking from left to right, I said, "Petra, Pia, we are so sorry we didn't visit you after school or at night. That was terrible of us."

I could tell by their faces that I had gotten the names right. Petra held her hand at eye level and turned it over flat, like she was measuring a child's height. "Let's see. Terrible in our class would start up here, with the McCain boys." She dropped it down about a foot. "Followed by Oscar Mayer Sandwich Spread."

I laughed. "And then us?"

"No. Not even then."

Pia had her arm around TJ's shoulder and was leaning in hard, making him work at standing up straight. He loved it. She said, "We had to throw out some potato chips, but they were super-greasy. I don't know what kids did about zits back then. Everything was super-greasy."

Petra added, "There was no Proactiv; no Accutane."

"There must have been a national plague of acne," Pia continued, "because all the foods are full of grease, and salt, and sugar."

Petra claimed her place on the other side of TJ. She said, "A lot of those teenagers developed problems as adults—like heart attacks, and strokes, and diabetes."

By now, Patrick was far ahead of us on a solitary, determined march across the park. We followed at a leisurely pace. TJ smiled blissfully, looking from one twin to the other, as they took turns blasting the 'golden age' we were living in:

"Cigarettes were really cheap, and kids could buy them in machines."

"Kids had their own *candy* cigarettes, and they pretended to smoke them! And they had guns with plastic bullets, and they shot each other with them."

"Everybody drank super-hard liquor, like manhattans and martinis, and then drove around at a hundred miles per hour, with no seatbelts on."

"They used butter to cook things, or Crisco, which was just lard. Pure fat."

I saw Patrick reach the church. He never looked back. He yanked the door open and disappeared inside. The twins went on:

"They had lead paint on the walls, and babies ate it, and died."

"They had asbestos in the walls of the schools, so kids developed lung cancer."

"If they didn't have cancer already from living in a house with two smokers and no ventilation."

Soon, the four of us were at the church, too, pulling the wooden door open. We paused for a moment in the vestibule, wiping our boots on a thick rope rug. Apparently, Captain and Mrs. McCain had just finished reenacting their wedding vows. The mass was over, and Father Dunne was out of sight. But the

family members—and there must have been twenty of them—
were still gathered near the altar.

I drifted over to the side with TJ and the twins. I saw
Patrick standing alone, in the aisle between the pews, about ten
yards from the altar. He was staring at the McCains.

He was staring at one of them anyway.

At Matt.

Matt was dressed in a white tuxedo that looked way too
small for him. He stood directly in front of the high altar table,
looking out. The photo easel, with a framed glass portrait of the
wedding couple, was to his left. So was the white unity candle,
which was now lit and burning brightly. The rest of the
McCains were milling about by the front pew, swilling down
wine from paper cups.

Patrick took a step forward. I could see that his face was
flushed, dangerously so. I could see that his teeth were grinding
inside his jaws. Matt McCain saw him, too. He started
watching him curiously, as he might watch a sunrise.

Patrick bent down and assumed a football stance, with his
right fist on the floor and his rump in the air. Matt didn't even
flinched when Patrick burst out of the stance and sprinted
toward him as fast as he could. Only Matt's eyes moved,
opening very wide like a camera lens, as Patrick's skull
smashed straight into Matt's, blasting into his skin, bone, and
cartilage like a human cannonball.

Matt flew backward from the impact. He crashed into the altar table so hard that, even though he had absorbed a tremendous blow, he remained on his feet. He stared wide-eyed at Patrick, who was already pacing back up the aisle.

When Patrick reached his original spot, he turned and crouched into the football stance again. It was all so bizarre, and so incredibly out of place, that the rest of the McCains seemed unable to move. They stood there with their mouths open, as if posing for a picture of a family in shock. A deep gash, six inches across, opened over Matt's eyebrows and started dripping blood onto his cheeks and then his white lapels. Matt managed to take two steps forward, like a drunken man, right before Patrick charged again.

This time, the full force of Patrick's skull caught him a glancing blow by the right ear, but it was enough to whirl Matt completely around in a wild pirouette. Matt's flailing arms smacked against the photo easel, causing it to move like he was, whirling about until it smacked into the unity candle.

Matt fell face-first onto the marble floor and stayed there. The photo fell next, and the glass shattered into a hundred pieces. The unity candle then crashed to the floor trailing a plume of flame. I managed to whisper, "The Domino Theory," just before the candle flame reached the McCains' pile of wine bottles and paper cups, which all immediately burst into flame.

By now, some of the McCains were yelling and pointing. I expected them to charge at Patrick en masse, like a pack of angry gorillas, but that didn't happen. The McCains simply had no idea what to do in the face of such a random act of violence. Patrick had beaten them at their own game.

The Captain looked at Teresa and ordered, "The cups are on fire! Do something!" Teresa took off to find a fire extinguisher. She didn't do it fast enough for the Captain, though. He yelled after her, "Move it! Put this damn fire out!"

I had heard enough. I stepped up and shouted at him, "You've been the fire chief for thirty years! You put it out!"

He stared at me with those old lizard eyes. But the best he could manage to say was, "What?"

I told him, "You heard me." Then I added, "Or why don't you get your friend the mayor to put it out."

The weasel son snapped at me, "You better watch your mouth."

I recalled what he once said to my mother in the office of Jonas Salk Middle School. I pointed at Matt and declared, "He grabbed the wrong kid. Nobody touches our kid. End of story." The weasel just stared back at me stupidly, the irony completely lost on him, like most things.

Chief McCain started to stomp on the flames with his foot. Teresa Zorn arrived with a fire extinguisher and aimed it at the burning pile. A blast of white foam covered the flames, along with the Captain's shoes. He pointed angrily at his feet and started to protest, but Teresa Zorn was already gone, hurrying to crank open the church windows and clear out the smoke.

The weasel and the Captain finally got hold of Matt and helped him to his feet. The whole top of his tuxedo, as well as his shirt and tie, were now stained blood red. His nose was swelling rapidly. His eyes were open but dazed-looking, like he was going into shock.

TJ, the twins, and I formed a protective circle around Patrick. Then we moved as a group toward the back door, glancing over our shoulders in case the McCains suddenly reverted to charging-gorilla mode. I studied Patrick's face. He looked very calm, almost relaxed. And he didn't have so much as a bruise.

My grandparents' white limo was idling next to the curb. I leaned in to Aunt Betty and Uncle Jim and explained briefly what had happened in the church. They both nodded nervously.

Aunt Betty said, "Didn't they hit him back?"

I shook my head. "No."

The Clark family was standing outside, too, in the middle of a Sunday stroll. They had paused to see the anniversary couples, I suppose, but that's not what they were looking at now. They exchanged puzzled looks.

The McCain men led Matt through the church door. He looked very frightened, and very confused, and a bloody mess.

Rosemary Clark looked from Matt to Patrick to me. She asked, "What happened in there?"

I told her, "Patrick just kicked Matt McCain's ass."

"Oh! Why?"

"Because he hurt TJ." I threw in for good measure, "And because he tried to hurt you."

Robby Clark looked up at Patrick with undisguised awe. He started to speak, but his father suddenly reached down, took Robby's hand, and led him and the rest of the family away.

Teresa Zorn ran out of the church with some sort of window-cranking pole in her hand. She called after the McCain men, "Wait, Mr. McCain! I called the ambulance. They'll be right here."

The weasel turned and threatened her. "You're gonna need to call a lawyer, Zorn. That's who you're gonna need. You just let the wrong kid get injured on your property." He pointed at Patrick. "And you! Fat kid! You're gonna answer for this. Big time!"

Patrick stepped away from our group and walked toward him, his hands extended outward. "What do you mean?"

"You'll find out what I mean. You just wait."

"I don't want to wait. Tell me now. I'm gonna answer to who?" Patrick pointed past the weasel to the weasel's son. "To Dennis? He's here right now. We can settle this right now." Dennis ducked behind the other men in the group. Patrick raised his voice. "How about it, Dennis, you little wuss? How about settling it right here? Right now?"

The father clenched his fists like he himself might charge at Patrick, but he didn't. He turned back to his cowardly son, and the whole group of McCain men continued on their way.

The McCain women, however, were still with us. They hadn't gone anywhere. They emerged from the church as one and clustered together outside the door.

Aunt Betty and Uncle Jim finally got out of the limousine. They took hold of my grandparents' elbows, helped them out, and escorted them into the church. They took seats in the front row, to the left. Patrick, TJ, and I—followed by the twins— filed into the pew behind them. We all just sat there, staring straight ahead, in a mild state of shock.

Teresa Zorn was now back inside, cranking the windows closed in the ice-cold church. At ten minutes past eleven, Father Dunne walked out to start his second mass of the day. He looked beautiful in a suit of white and gold vestments. True to his jack-of-all-trades self, Douglas Zorn walked out behind him in the white-and-black vestments of an altar boy. He carried a gold incense burner in his right hand, and the burner's gold chain in his left.

Father Dunne began by spreading his arms out and telling us, "Dominus vobiscum." A couple of the old McCain women muttered something back. Then Father Dunne turned around and continued speaking in Latin. The mass went on that way, incomprehensible, for about five minutes.

Then my grandfather spotted Douglas.

He suddenly became very agitated. He started to talk to himself, something like, "The paperboy. That's the paperboy."

I leaned forward and assured him quietly, "It's Douglas, Grandpop. He's the boy who brings us our meals. He's also the altar boy."

He turned and looked at me, but nothing registered in his eyes. He just repeated, "That's the paperboy," louder than before.

Teresa Zorn, apparently, was watching our small commotion. She quickly appeared at the side of the altar and gestured to Douglas. He lay down the incense burner and walked, in a stooped manner, over to her. I don't know what she said to him, but he left right then and he didn't come back. Still, the damage had been done. My grandfather rose to his feet in his black wool coat and announced to the whole church, "That's the paperboy!"

My grandmother, who had been determinedly ignoring him, grabbed at his hand to pull him back down, but he yanked it away. He stepped over her and into the aisle. By now everyone, including Father Dunne, was looking at my grandfather and listening to him repeat, "The paperboy! That's the paperboy!"

My grandfather lurched toward the back of the church. He stopped in front of the three confessional doors and stared at them, as if he were trying to pick one to escape through. He opened the door on the right, sat on the bench, and leaned his head against the sliding black screen.

Father Dunne stopped the mass. He walked down from the altar with his eyes locked steadily onto my grandmother's. With a gesture of his hand, he instructed the rest of us to sit down and wait. He opened the middle door and took his seat in the confessional. Then, in a voice loud enough to be heard by the congregation, he said, "Bless you, my child."

My grandfather answered him in an equally loud, equally clear voice: "Bless me, Father, for I have sinned. It has been fifty years since my last confession. These are my sins." We all listened, very attentively, to what he said next. "I drank too much. I drove drunk. I hit a boy. A paperboy. He was on a bicycle, in the rain. I didn't stop to help him. I left him on the road to die."

He stopped there, so Father Dunne prodded him, "And are you sorry for these sins?"

"Yes. I am sorry. I am heartily sorry."

After a long pause, Father Dunne replied, "Very well. For your penance, continue to tell the truth about this crime. Use the time you have left on Earth to tell the truth about it. Now make a good Act of Contrition."

But my grandfather had said all that he was going to say. He sat, silent and immobile, until Father Dunne stood up. Without looking at any of us, Father Dunne went around, leaned into my grandfather's booth, and pulled him to his feet. Then he gestured for my grandmother. "Margaret, you'd better take him home."

My grandmother rose, stiff and stone-faced. She walked to the back and took hold of my grandfather's elbow. Father Dunne then pointed to my uncle, "You'd better help them, Jim."

He replied, "All right, Father," and hopped up. Uncle Jim took my grandfather's other arm, and the three of them started toward the door.

That's when I noticed something unusual: The door was wide open. It had been all along. White glare from the snow was pouring in from the outside. And in the middle of that glare, in the middle of the doorway, stood a solitary figure. The figure took one step forward, and I saw who it was—Mrs. Ellen McCain. The grandmother of Matt McCain. The widow of Jack Gallahue.

She told my grandfather, in a voice filled with scorn, "Yes, go home and say your Act of Contrition, John Abel! But I doubt it will do you any good. You destroyed my husband's life. You let my husband, the father of my children, go to jail for a crime he did not commit. A terrible crime that *you yourself* committed. And you lied about it all these years. I doubt any Act of Contrition will do you much good now."

My grandfather met her withering gaze with his own tired eyes, nodding in total agreement. But my grandmother looked down and away, as if none of it concerned her.

Once Mrs. McCain had finished speaking, she stepped aside and let them pass. As soon as they were gone, Father

Dunne raised his own voice. "I'll continue the mass, because it is Sunday. But it won't be to honor the marriage of John and Margaret Abel. It will be to pray for the soul of Jack Gallahue, a man falsely accused and sent to prison."

Mrs. McCain's eyes filled with tears, and I knew: This was why she had waved to Father Dunne on Thursday night. This was why she had stayed behind today. This had been Father Dunne's hope all along; his agenda. It was why he had come to Memory Lane.

The McCain women re-entered the church and took seats on the right side, away from us. Then Father Dunne walked up to the altar, his face devoid of any expression, and continued saying the Latin mass.

Just one minute into it, Patrick leaned over TJ's lap. He whispered, "What the hell was that? What just happened? Who was that old lady?"

TJ leaned back. He asked his brother, "Do you remember the sketch I did of the McCain family tree?"

"No."

"Yes, you do. That lady is on it. She's Captain McCain's sister."

I said, "He doesn't remember it, TJ. He never saw the sketch. You made it for me."

"Oh. Yeah."

Patrick whispered, "She's not Captain McCain's wife?"

I tried to explain. "No. Not the woman who spoke. She's his sister. She changed her name back to McCain because of the dead paperboy thing."

Patrick's face was getting red. I told him, "Don't blow a gasket over this, Patrick." Just then, I realized that everything had gotten quiet in the church. I looked up and saw why. Father Dunne had stopped saying the mass again. He was now standing still, in front of the altar, and looking directly at me. I felt like a three-year-old who was about to get spanked.

But when he spoke, Father Dunne sounded more curious than angry. "Alice? Is there something you three need to talk about?"

There was, so I told him, "Yes, Father."

"You and TJ and Patrick?"

"Yes."

He nodded. "All right." He pointed to his confessional. "I have a good place for that back there against the wall. You can sit in the middle seat, and the boys can sit on either side, and you can close the doors."

I looked at Patrick and TJ. They both seemed up for it, so I answered, "All right, Father." I slipped out of my seat and led the boys down the aisle. I stooped over as I walked, like Douglas had done, as if that made me less visible somehow. I opened the middle of the three confessional doors, sat inside, and waited. I could hear Patrick and TJ enter on either side of me. I could see the dark screens on my left and right, so I reached forward and slid them both open.

Patrick picked up the conversation right away. "What does the friggin paperboy have to do with anything? I thought you said they made that story up to keep us from drinking and having sex."

"You don't listen! I told you that the story was based on the truth, but parts of it got changed over time."

"So what part is true?"

"Jack Gallahue! He was a real person. He was a veteran, and a father, and a husband. But he wound up the villain, the monster, the bad guy in the paperboy story."

"Okay. Okay. And that old lady was his wife?"

"Yes."

"And his wife is here, at Memory Lane?"

"Yes! So is his son's wife, Mary. And guess who her son is."

I could see Patrick's big head shaking rapidly. "Who?"

"Matt McCain."

"Oh my God! So Matt McCain is, like, like the grandson of a monster?"

"No. He's like . . . the grandson of a guy who was called a monster, but who really wasn't one."

Patrick banged his head into the screen. "Why not?"

"Because he was innocent! He didn't do it!"

TJ couldn't control himself any longer. He hissed his words across me to Patrick, "Listen, numbskull! It was Grandpop! Didn't you hear what he just said? About himself? It was our grandfather all along. All these years. And he let Jack Gallahue take the blame, and go to prison, and die for a crime he did not commit."

"Yeah?"

"Yeah."

Patrick asked, "So everybody out there understands that? Everybody but me?"

I told him, "I think so. You never can tell with people, but I think everybody out there got it."

"Okay."

TJ's perfect profile turned toward me in the gloom. "This is really bad, Alice. This is really really really bad."

"I know."

"We've been sitting around here and watching all those sitcom families on TV, all those perfect families—the Nelsons, the Cleavers, the Andersons—and not once, not in one episode, did Ozzie Nelson or Ward Cleaver or Jim Anderson ever get drunk, and kill a kid, and drive away from the scene of the crime, and then cover it all up and let somebody else go to prison. And die. Never. Not once."

Patrick seemed tuned in now. I think he understood. He sounded less desperate when he asked, "So what does this mean for us?"

I saw TJ lean back in his seat, holding his face in his hands. I breathed deeply for several seconds, formulating my answer. "It means that . . . the horrible punishment that happened to Jack Gallahue, and his family, for all those years, should have happened to our family instead. The Abels. We are the drunken, hit-and-run, killer-of-the-kid family. Not them."

I could hear TJ muttering low, "Oh my God. Oh my God."

"All the bad stuff that happened to the McCains should have happened to our grandparents. Getting shunned by the neighbors, having to change their name in disgrace, facing suspicion wherever they went. It all should have happened to Grandmom and Grandpop. And to their daughters, Betty and Donna."

We sat in stunned silence for a while, until I heard footsteps and then a low rap on my door. This was followed immediately by the door opening and Aunt Betty's face appearing. She whispered angrily, "Alice! What do you think you are doing?"

I whispered back, "What Father Dunne said to do."

She shook her head. "No! Father Dunne was telling you, politely, to be quiet during the mass. He didn't mean for you three to get up, cause a further disturbance, and come back here to talk!"

I thought for a moment before I replied. "I think he did mean for us to do that."

Aunt Betty's whisper rose up a level. "No! He did not! You, and I mean all three of you, are disgracing this family! And in front of the McCains! Now get back to your seats. Patrick, TJ, come with me right now!"

First Patrick, then TJ, rose in the dim light and opened their doors. So I got up, too. We all followed Aunt Betty, stooping even lower this time, and returned to our seats.

The after-wedding party at our house had to be cancelled. Mr. Bitner and Francis were already there setting up when Aunt Betty arrived. She told them to take everything away except for some sandwiches and drinks.

Patrick and I wound up in the living room, sitting in front of the TV; staring at its dark screen. I finally asked him, "Where's TJ?" He managed a shrug. "Did he leave with the girls?"

"How am I supposed to know?"

"Okay, sorry."

My grandparents locked themselves in their bedroom. Aunt Betty and Uncle Jim spent about half an hour outside their door trying to talk to them, clearly alarmed at what they might do following that public humiliation.

I was picking a magazine from the rack when the phone rang in the kitchen. Patrick didn't move, so I went in and answered it. It turned out to be for him. I heard Rosemary's voice, "Hello. May I please speak to Patrick?"

I set the phone down, walked back in to Patrick, and mentioned casually, "It's for you. It's Rosemary Clark." Patrick looked totally stunned. As he hopped up and rushed into the kitchen, I added, "Why don't you invite her over?"

I listened hard to the conversation in the kitchen, but I couldn't make out a thing. Patrick mainly grunted into the phone. When he joined me again about ten minutes later, I asked, "What was the call about?"

"Nothing. She just wanted to talk to me."

"About what?"

"My life. She wanted to know where I was going with my life."

"Yeah? Well, okay, do you know where you're going with your life?"

"No. But I'm thinking about it now."

"You never did before?"

"No. Not really." Patrick stood up. "I think I'll go over to the Clarks."

"Oh? What's happening there?"

Patrick didn't look at me. "Some kind of prayer circle thing, I guess."

"Oh. Okay."

Patrick walked into the kitchen, pulled down his coat, and left. I followed him to the door and looked outside. The world looked the same, and yet . . . it seemed very different. Everything in it had suddenly changed. I sat down at the table and stared at the tray of sandwiches—ham and cheese and roast beef. There was a bucket full of ice next to them. It contained tiny bottles of Coke and Seven Up placed around a large bottle of Mumm champagne, vintage 1957.

After a few minutes, Aunt Betty came out and joined me. She popped open the bottle of Mumm like a veteran champagne drinker and poured herself a glass. I let her chug one down and pour another before I asked, "So, how are they?"

She hiccupped, then replied, "Excuse me. Do you mean Mom and Pop?"

"Yes."

"Your grandmother's as tough as nails. Nothing gets to her. Your grandfather, though . . . ."

We both pondered that thought silently. Then I changed the subject. "Uh, yesterday, Father Dunne gave me a penance at confession."

"Me, too. Three Our Fathers and three Hail Marys. What did you get?"

"Mine was more of an assignment."

"Oh?"

"It was to keep asking you about that memory. The one with you and my mom screaming at each other in the St. Bernard's parking lot."

Aunt Betty set her glass down. "The one that I don't remember."

"Yes. Well, here's my problem: I think you *do* remember."

I expected an angry reply to that. Instead, I got, "Did you kids eat any sandwiches?"

Before I could answer, the front door opened and Father Dunne walked in. He asked me right away, "What did you and your cousins talk about in the confessional?"

There wasn't a trace of anger in his voice. I looked at Aunt Betty and then back to him. "We talked about what happened—with Grandpop, and Ellen McCain, and how she was once named Ellen Gallahue."

"Yes? What did you make of all that?"

"We were confused. And upset."

"Of course." Father Dunne looked weary to the bone. He assured me, "We can talk more about this later, if you like." He dragged his feet as he left the room and disappeared down the hallway.

Right after that, Uncle Jim walked out in his overcoat and handed Aunt Betty hers. She spoke as if thinking aloud, "I don't expect that anybody will want a formal dinner tonight. Not after all the excitement at church, and the sandwiches here. Maybe we'll all just catch as catch can."

I agreed. "Sure. If we get hungry, we can call for something."

"Yes. Okay. See you later then." She added, "This is our last night here. It really went fast, didn't it?"

I wouldn't say that, but I did nod. After they left, I made myself eat a ham and cheese sandwich and drink a Seven Up. Then I went upstairs. I opened my top dresser drawer, felt under the days-of-the-week panties, and pulled out Blue Belle.

I sat on the bed, propped up a pillow against the headboard, and leaned back. I turned Blue Belle to and fro, to and fro, as if she were trotting. Then I had her stop and look up at someone who wasn't really there. She said, "Hi, Mom. Would you like to hear a story? It's about Grandpop." I did not wait for an answer. I supplied my own. "You would? Okay."

Blue Belle dropped her voice, as if to confide something. "Well, one rainy evening, Grandpop got drunk, and drove, and hit the paperboy with his car. Yeah. That's right. And he didn't stop to help him. He just kept driving home. He left him on the road to die."

Blue Belle paused. "And then what happened? Well, nothing! Everybody pretended Grandpop didn't do it. Jack Gallahue got blamed, and Jack Gallahue's family got blamed, and they all became outcasts for many, many years."

Blue Belle fell silent for a longer moment. "And then what happened? Well, Grandpop got old and crazy, and he forgot to keep lying about it, I guess. Or he got old and scared, and he asked to be forgiven for it, by Father Dunne. I don't really know. Take your pick. Pick your own ending, Mom."

Mom of course, did not answer. She never did. She never would.

After that, I lay my head down and fell deeply asleep. I took an afternoon nap. I don't think I have done that since I was three years old and in daycare. I woke up at 5:00 pm, feeling *anger*, and *denial*, and *depression* all at once. I forced myself to get out of bed and to trudge downstairs.

I was surprised when I entered the kitchen and saw two people. Father Dunne and my grandmother were sitting there stiff and silent. Each had a sandwich that had not been touched. Father Dunne had a glass of red wine.

My grandmother wore the same detached expression she had in church when she looked away from Ellen McCain. Had the enormity of all this sunk in with her? It didn't seem so. It seemed like she was still removed from it. Like it was just a scene in *The Secret Storm,* or *The Guiding Light*, or *As the World Turns.*

Grandpop wandered out of the hallway and into the kitchen. His shirttail was half out; his zipper was down; his hair was disheveled. He walked straight up to Father Dunne, genuflected next to him, and repeated his words from before, "Bless me, Father for I have sinned."

Father Dunne answered kindly, "Yes, John. I know."

My grandmother stood up quickly and berated him. "What are you doing out of bed? You're all out of sorts. Look at you! Listen to you! You don't know what you're saying." She practically dragged him to his feet and led him back to the bedroom.

Once I heard the bedroom door close, I decided to take Father Dunne up on his offer to talk. I took the seat across from him and asked, "Father, did you know Jack Gallahue personally?"

He nodded. "I did. I wouldn't say I knew him well, but I knew him."

"Did you think he was the hit-and-run killer?"

He answered cagily, "When?"

"When the hit-and-run happened."

"At first, yes. Yes, I did."

"But then . . . you didn't think that anymore?"

"Correct."

"Because something happened?"

My grandmother opened her door and, a few seconds later, returned to the kitchen. She looked very, very stressed. I asked, "Grandmom, are you all right?"

"Of course I'm all right. Why wouldn't I be?" She filled a glass with water from the tap and carried it back out.

I waited a moment to resume questioning Father Dunne. "Did you hear something that made you change your mind?"

"Yes."

"In confession?"

"That I cannot say."

"But you knew for sure that he was not guilty?"

"That's correct."

"Did anyone else know the truth?"

He refilled his wine glass from a bottle of Gallo Burgundy. "Yes. Other people knew."

Suddenly, my grandmother was back in the kitchen, still holding the water. She hadn't really left; she had been listening to us. She demanded to know, "Did you not take a sacred oath, as a priest, to uphold the bond of the confessional?"

Father Dunne answered tightly. "Yes, I did. And I *have* honored it."

"You're sitting here talking to this child about things that you were told, in confidence, in the confessional!"

"I am not. She heard—we all heard—the truth about this crime in church today. That's what we were talking about."

My grandmother stared him down angrily, but she didn't reply. She then left for real, slamming the bedroom door down the hallway. I went back to questioning him. "Can you tell me what you did that day, Father? On November 22nd, 1973? There's no bond of the confessional to protect that, is there?"

He considered my question. "I suppose not." He pursed his lips and thought back. "I remember that it was a rainy afternoon. Cold and rainy. Your grandfather was supposed to pick Betty up at a party. We had just gotten to the bar, though, and we were having a drink."

"Who was there?"

"Your grandfather and I, and some others. Some regulars at the bar."

"Jack Gallahue?"

"Jack Gallahue was there, but he wasn't sitting with us. He kept to himself. He always did. He was a real nasty drunk."

"And what about you?"

"What do you mean?"

"What were you doing there?"

He looked suddenly sheepish. "What were any of us doing there? Men stopped at bars and drank back then. They smoked cigarettes, too. I stopped in for one drink on my way back to New Jersey. But before I left, your grandfather used the bartender's phone to call the birthday party. He hung up and announced that Betty could stay at her friend's house until later, and the friend's parents would drive her home, so he didn't have to leave."

Father Dunne pushed away his sandwich, still uneaten. "But I *did* have to leave. Presumably, your grandfather had another drink or two. Or more. When he finally left for home at five, the odds are he was legally drunk. The bartender shouldn't have let him drive away, but he did."

"Was Jack Gallahue still there?"

Father Dunne shook his head. "I don't know." He explained, "When the police arrested Jack Gallahue for the crime, he didn't even remember what bar he'd been in that day. He said it was the VFW bar. He didn't remember driving home, either. He had several dents on his truck already, and he didn't know where any of them came from. He lived on Jerusalem Avenue, so he had to drive right past the scene of the crime to get home."

He cupped his hands as if he were holding sand. "All these separate pieces added up to 'prove' he was guilty. But of course he wasn't guilty. It's strange to think that maybe even Jack himself didn't know that."

Father Dunne took a long drink and stared far away, like he was sitting in that bar in 1973. "Anyway, I was hoping to do something for Jack Gallahue before I left this Earth. And for his family. And for myself. Because I needed absolution, too. I had sinned the sin of cowardice. I let my own conscience be overruled by the bond of the confessional. I let an innocent man go to prison, and a guilty man walk free, over a . . . technicality. I could have broken the bond and faced the consequences, but I didn't."

He smiled the most unhappy smile I have ever seen. "Over the years, I rationalized it by saying that Jesus Himself was falsely accused, like Jack was. I guess you can use the Bible to rationalize anything."

I waited to be sure he was finished before asking, "Did Betty know what happened?"

"You'd have to ask her."

I took a deep breath. Then I asked the question that had really been gnawing at me: "What about Donna? Did she know?"

Father Dunne grimaced and pushed the wine glass away. He gestured toward the back bedroom. "I can't say anything else. Perhaps I *have* said too much. I don't know. I'm trying to do what's right. Sometimes that doesn't please everybody." He stood up. "There's a Ricky Nelson song about that, Alice. 'You can't please everyone, so you have to please yourself.' I need to go in and rest now." Almost as an afterthought, he asked, "Oh, did Betty or Patrick have anything to add to that scene? The one at St. Bernard's?"

I muttered, "No."

He muttered back, "That's too bad." He steadied himself against the table for a moment. Then he walked out of the kitchen.

I relocated to the living room and sat in front of the Admiral. I watched something called *You Asked for It* from 7:00 until 8:00. Then I turned on *The Ed Sullivan Show*. I was fully expecting Ray to show up, and he did not disappoint me.

He knocked on the door during a performance by the West Point Glee Club.

As soon as I let him in, he announced breathlessly, "I was standing outside about an hour ago—"

"You were standing outside? By yourself?"

"Yeah."

"Why?"

"It doesn't matter. Listen: I saw an ambulance turn into our street. It stopped at the McCains' driveway, so I walked over there."

"Wow. Really?"

"Yeah."

"The McCains didn't yell at you to get out?"

"No. There were hardly any McCains around. None of the women; just those two firefighter guys who came to our class. And they were too busy yelling at Teresa Zorn and that manager guy."

"Mr. Bitner?"

"Is that his name?" He went on, "So the ambulance guys came out of the house with Matt McCain walking between them. Matt looked really bad, like Lee Harvey Oswald after the Dallas police got through beating him with clubs."

I interrupted him. "For the shooting of Officer Tippet?"

Ray stared at me with such awe that I continued, "The Dallas police officer who Oswald shot while he was on the run?"

"Yes," he whispered. "Yes, allegedly. Yes."

I steered him back on track. "So they took Matt McCain away?"

"Oh. Yeah. They were threatening lawsuits, and threatening to call the mayor, and stuff. But get this: Neither of them wanted to go with him! So Matt's standing there with his eyes practically shut because they're so swollen, and he's crying and carrying on, and nobody's stepping up. So the manager guy tells Teresa Zorn, 'All right then, you go with him! You're his facilitator. You take him.'

"The last thing I saw was the back of the ambulance pulling away, and Teresa Zorn's face up against the window, terrified, like she'd just fallen into the gorilla cage at the Bronx Zoo."

I sputtered a laugh.

"Can you imagine," he continued, "being locked in a box with a freaked-out Matt McCain?"

I shook my head. "Well, too bad. You know? Miss Zorn is responsible for what happens to Miss Zorn." Ray finally unbuttoned his coat. I took it and draped it over the arm of the couch. I said, "Matt's face is that messed up?"

"Oh yeah."

We both sat down, pretty close. I added, "Patrick's face doesn't even have a bruise."

"No? That's cool. Yeah. I heard what the big guy did at church."

"What did you hear?"

"I heard that Patrick put some camel vengeance on Matt McCain."

"Yeah? Who told you that?"

"Robby Clark."

"Oh?"

"That's so great. I wish I had seen it. I wish I had *done* it. Those McCain boys were out of control."

"Yeah."

"And you and I know why."

I knew why. But I didn't think he did, so I asked dumbly, "Why?"

He answered as if it were obvious, "Miss Zorn! Miss phony, friggin Zorn! She calls herself a teacher? She was a joke! But it wasn't a funny joke, was it?"

"No."

"She let the McCains run wild. She let them get worse and worse and worse. Things never should have gone that far; never anywhere near that far."

I stared at Ray, and I started to feel something inside. Something really strong. Something right out of a 1950s love song. I had this thought, *Maybe Ray is the one.* I touched my throat, as if it were parched. I looked at him and asked, "Would you mind getting me a Seven Up from the refrigerator?"

His eyes registered surprise. But he did stand up, right

away, and head into the kitchen. I thought to myself, *Here we go.* I followed and caught him at the door of the GE fridge. I tapped him on the back and, when he turned around, I leaned forward and kissed him softly on the lips.

He just stared at me for several seconds. Then I leaned in and kissed him again, for a long time, like for a mile on the bus with Richard Hess. When I pulled back, he practically sputtered, "You're . . . what? Making out with me?"

"Yes," I whispered. "Is that all right?"

"Yes! Yes. I'm just surprised. What about Douglas?"

"Douglas? What about him? He's not even real."

"No?"

"No. He's a theme park character." I kissed Ray one more time, and he kissed me back. He was even better than Richard Hess, and I told him so. "You're a great kisser."

He sounded shocked, "I am?"

"Yes."

"Thank you. So are you. Great."

"Yeah?"

"Yeah." He added, "And, you're really beautiful."

"No. No, I'm not."

"Yes! You are. You know I don't make stuff up."

It was my turn to be shocked. "Okay." We suddenly heard the sound of a door opening in the house. It was either Father Dunne or my grandparents. We listened silently as whoever it was entered the bathroom and urinated, totally killing the mood. I whispered, "Come on, let's go outside."

We pulled on our coats and slipped out the front door. Ray crooked his arm inside mine and guided me up the slippery walkway, muttering, "They need more rock salt here."

His arm felt wonderful. I asked, "Are you surprised that I kissed you?"

"Yes! God yes."

"You didn't know we were coming closer together, like, every day? Step by step? Like in a love song?"

"I thought we might be. I hoped we were, but I figured I was just imagining it. That's how it usually turns out."

"Oh? Well, not this time. It was true."

"Yeah. That's great. Great, great, great." He sounded totally happy, but he soon reverted. I guess he couldn't help himself. "This is, like, the one good thing that's happened at Memory Lane. The rest of it is all bogus, you know. All that happy memories crap."

I had to disagree. "Oh, no. Memories are important, especially the happy ones. They're the most important things we have."

He asked, very cautiously, "Are you talking about your mother now?"

We stopped at the curb. "Yes. And my father. I'm already starting to lose some memories of him. I'm too young to be forgetting stuff; but I do."

Ray pressed his thumb against my forehead. "There's only so much room in here, you know? In your amygdala and hippocampus. You can't blame yourself."

I turned to point at the house. "Our grandparents thought that nobody would ever forget Pearl Harbor. *Remember Pearl Harbor!* But people did forget it. They forgot it so they could make room in their heads for Marilyn Monroe, and Elvis, and the Ford Fairlane, and 'Wake Up Little Suzie.'"

Ray nodded in agreement.

"And then our parents thought that nobody would ever forget the JFK Assassination."

He cautioned me, "Be very careful there."

"I'm serious. How many kids—outside of your family— even know what happened to JFK, and where it happened, and who was involved?"

"Even *in* my family, there's some major disinterest."

"There you go. One generation's story ends, somewhere, somehow. That's it; it's over; close the book. Then the next generation takes over. The story goes on, but the characters have all changed."

We stopped at the curb. It was lined with banks of white snow and silver ice gleaming in the moonlight. Another beautiful postcard. We didn't let this opportunity get away. We shared a long kiss goodnight in that wonderland setting. Then I broke away and took off, stepping quickly, not slipping once on my way to the door. I waved over my shoulder at Ray, but I didn't turn back. I didn't need to; I knew he was watching me. I knew that we were falling for each other, just like they did in "The Book of Love."

And, after I climbed into my bed upstairs, just before I fell asleep, I realized this: I was not feeling any stage of grief at all. —Alice

Chapter 7

Monday, November 25, 1957

I woke up early, or so I thought, until I got dressed and walked down to the Blanchards' house. When Patrick answered the door, I asked him, "Have you had breakfast?"

He informed me, "Yeah, at the Clarks. We had a prayer breakfast." He then disappeared up to his room.

TJ informed me that he had eaten breakfast, too. He was getting ready to go, as he called it, "vogueing on ice" with the Nordstrom twins. He told me breathlessly, "Petra called last night! Mr. Bitner and Barney have asked the twins if they'll be in the new print campaign for Memory Lane. They'll be replacing the McCains and that whole look-at-me-I'm-a-fireman vibe. Anyway, get this: The twins said they'll only do it if *I* can be in it, too. Moi. So I am!"

"Go TJ!"

"And I'll get paid!"

"That is so awesome."

If TJ had given any further thought to the family disaster at the church, it did not show. As he slipped on his coat, he inclined his head toward me and whispered, "Guess what? I played *Truth or Duck* with the twins yesterday."

I stared back at him, expectantly.

"Would you like to guess how many sex partners they have had between them? Remember: They are supermodels."

I had a feeling that I knew. I answered, "Zero?"

"Yes! Can you believe it? They'll do stuff, like the kissing games, but they're just playing, like little kids."

"Yeah. I believe it."

"They're sex symbols, but they don't have sex."

"Good for them."

"That means that, in the I-don't-have-sex department, Miss Rosemary Clark is, at best, in a *tie* with the Nordstrom girls. Can you believe that? In a tie at best!"

"Good for Rosemary, too."

"And do you know what else that means?"

"No."

"It means that you, Alice Lynch, are officially the sluttiest girl here."

I sputtered and laughed out loud, for a long time, until I almost fell down. I finally managed to choke out, "Oh! Mom would be so proud."

TJ's face showed a flash of discomfort, but then he added, "Yes, she'd be proud." He laughed with me for a little while longer, but he soon continued his exit, dashing out the front door trailing a wool scarf behind.

I sat in the kitchen, still giggling to myself, until Aunt Betty appeared. She was dressed like a happy 1950s mom, but she looked completely miserable. She exhaled loudly, like she had been holding her breath for a long time. "Jim's still asleep. They have him taking a strong sedative. It really knocked him out."

She sat down hard on a kitchen chair and faced me. Then, she told me flat out, like she was in confession, "I am so ashamed of myself, Alice. I have been married to this man for twenty years, yet I didn't know this . . . *fundamental* thing about him."

I did my best to console her. "Father Dunne says that people keep the deepest, most painful secrets inside of them. They are afraid to let them out, even to their wives, or their husbands, or their selves."

Aunt Betty shook her head ruefully. "Is that right?"

"They refuse to even think about it." When it looked like she wasn't going to reply, I prodded her with, "Why? Do you have a secret that you can't bear to think about?"

"No."

"What about the argument you had with my mother, outside of the church, with Patrick and me standing there?"

"Oh, Alice. Please. Are we back to that again?"

We were back to that, and I wasn't going to let her slip away this time. "Yes. You two were screaming at each other."

"Okay. If you say so."

"But you don't remember it?"

Suddenly, Patrick walked in. He came around and stood beside me at the very moment when she insisted again, "No."

Then Patrick told her, "I remember it."

Aunt Betty shook her head at him as if he had said something really dumb. "You don't remember it, Patrick. You remember Alice telling you about it over and over."

"No. I remember it." Patrick stuck up his thumb. "I remembered part of it yesterday, outside the church." Then he stuck up his forefinger. "And I remembered more today, praying with the Clarks."

I asked him, very carefully, "You remembered what?"

"Aunt Donna was yelling, like I had never heard before. She called Grandmom a weird name. She called her *Mrs. Clean.*" Aunt Betty's head snapped up. Patrick told his mother, "Aunt Donna said that you knew what really happened, and you had to tell. You yelled back, 'No! It's too late now!'

"Then you grabbed my arm and pushed me into the car. We pealed out of there so fast that we skidded on the ice. You stayed real mad for about a mile, and then you started to cry. You had to pull over, right on Jerusalem Avenue, because you couldn't drive anymore."

Aunt Betty's eyes flitted around the kitchen as if trying to find a way out, but Patrick and I had her trapped. We both kept staring at her. When she spoke, it was directed at Patrick first. "Your father kept a deep secret buried inside him." Then she turned to include me. "It's a bad thing to keep a secret inside you, isn't it?"

I assured her, "Yes."

"It can drive you crazy."

"Yes. It can."

"So what, exactly, should I do, Alice?"

I leaned toward her. "Just talk to me, like you should have talked to my mom that day."

Aunt Betty started tracing a figure on the table with her finger, slowly. (I think it was a figure eight.) She said, "Donna wanted us, both of us, to stop covering up. To admit the truth, the whole truth, about that night. That night when . . . that boy got killed."

"Timothy Strop."

"Yes. So here it is." She closed her eyes. When she spoke again, it was even-toned, factual, like a news reporter on TV. "I had gone to a birthday party at my friend Christina's house. Christina and her father drove me home at nine o'clock. Grandpop was asleep, passed out on the couch downstairs.

"I heard the kitchen door open. Grandmom entered from the garage. She was wearing a black raincoat over her blue nightgown. She was carrying a bucket of Mr. Clean, and a wire brush, and some rags. I asked her what she was doing. She snapped at me, 'Get upstairs!' Then she accused me, 'You should *not* have stayed at that party. None of this would have happened if you had come home when you were supposed to.'

"I got scared then and ran upstairs.

"Donna stuck her head out of her bedroom. She had heard the whole thing. She asked me, 'What's going on?'

"I was frightened. I said, 'Nothing's going on. Go to sleep.'

"But Donna wouldn't go. She came into my room carrying one of her Barbies. She said, 'Pop is really drunk. He's passed out downstairs. Mom is acting crazy. She's got her cleaning stuff out in the middle of the night. What's going on?'

"I said, 'Nothing. I just saw them both. They're fine. Go back to your room.'

"She didn't believe me, but she did go back to her room. The next day, we heard what happened to that boy out on Jerusalem Avenue."

Aunt Betty's voice dropped to a whisper. "And we knew." She shook her head slowly, "We all knew. But we never talked about it again." Her voice trailed off completely. Her finger stopped moving. All of her stopped moving, like she had run out of batteries.

Patrick made a puffing sound through his lips. Then he shook his head and walked away. I reached up and grabbed my coat. I said, "Well, thank you for telling me," and started out, leaving her immobilized at the table.

I took my time going back to my grandparents' house. I kept running the details of Aunt Betty's story through my mind. I finally stopped, looked up at the sky, and spoke directly to my mother. "How could you do that? That was a *really horrible* thing to do. How could you do it?"

Then, all of a sudden, I had an insight. I shouted, "Wait! Is that why you ditched your Barbies? Did they talk to you, like Blue Belle talks to me? Did they ask you about the paperboy and Grandpop? Did they ask you about it every day, so you had to ditch them?"

Of course. Of course they did. Of course that was why.

When I approached the side door, I heard two voices inside. Father Dunne and my grandmother were talking at the kitchen table. I crept up onto the stoop and leaned my ear close to the glass. I heard Father Dunne accuse his sister, "Why did you have to drive all the way to New Jersey, to my parish, to go to confession?"

My grandmother answered matter-of-factly. "John was troubled. He needed absolution."

Father Dunne replied sarcastically, "But not from any priest in New York?" She did not respond. "So you took him to New Jersey, and you figured that was the end of it?"

"It *was* the end of it."

"What about when Jack Gallahue went on trial? What about when he was convicted? When he went to jail? When he killed himself after? Did none of that matter because you'd driven across the river and confessed to me? Did you think I had that kind of almighty power?"

"God has the power! And you gave him God's absolution. Didn't you?"

"Yes, I did."

"You forgave him for his sin, and that was the end of it."

"No it was not! I gave him a penance that day. His penance was to go back and to tell the truth."

"He did tell the truth. To you."

"That doesn't count! I was bound not to repeat it."

"That's right. You were bound not to repeat it. That is the law of the church."

I waited by the kitchen door, with my ear starting to freeze, but they didn't say anything else. That's how their conversation ended: He gave her no penance. He gave her no absolution. She made no Act of Contrition. That was her story, and she was sticking with it. After a long pause, she said wearily, "I have to get ready to go. It's time to end all this foolishness. John needs attending to right away."

I stepped carefully off the stoop, crunched my way to the front door, and opened it. By then, Father Dunne had moved into the living room and was standing over the TV. He growled, "Is there no news on this infernal appliance?"

I told him, "Probably not. It's 1957. There wasn't much news."

He backed up and sat on the couch. "That's where you're wrong. They had their news—all that camel vengeance—and it really terrified them."

"Duck and cover?"

"Yes."

"And the Red Menace?"

"Sure."

I pulled off my coat and boots and left them to drip onto the carpet. I joined him on the couch.

"The frightening news in 1957 is exactly the same as the frightening news now," he said. "The only difference is that we know how the 1957 news is going to end. It ends just fine. We did all that agonizing for nothing. The Soviets never did bomb us. The Red Menace never did destroy us from within. The dominoes in Southeast Asia never did fall.

"It's all about control. Control through fear, just like Jim said. The corporations try to control you through fear of body odor, or bad breath, or frizzy hair. The church tries to control you through fear of hell; the government through fear of the communists."

I suggested, "And parents try to control you through fear of the dead paperboy."

He looked at me knowingly. Had he heard me outside the door? I asked him directly, "So, was Grandmom as guilty as Grandpop?"

He raised his eyes up and down one time. "I'll let God sort that out. Anyone can make a mistake, Alice. The paperboy's death was a tragic mistake. A criminal mistake if you will, but there was no malice in it. No *malice aforethought*. The cover-up, though . . . " His voice faded. He didn't speak for a long time. Then he pointed weakly at the TV screen. It was showing a test pattern, another test of the Emergency Broadcast System.

"When you get to my age, and you look back, you realize that you don't need to fear the news—the local, the national, or the international. It's just another TV show. What you really need to fear are your own sins. They are the things that can really damage you. What you need to find in life is forgiveness for your sins—for every evil, cowardly, hurtful thing you have done.

"So I wanted to forgive some more sins. Humans are the only creatures with the capacity to do that—to forgive someone who has wronged them. It's a beautiful thing to see. It's a way to rise above the rest of the animals; to be fully human."

I asked him, "If my mom had confessed her sin, would she have been forgiven?"

"Of course, but she did not really commit a sin, Alice. Her parents did. Donna and Betty were only children, and their parents forbade them to ever speak about it. Obeying your parents is not a sin, not for a child. You can blame the adults here, but not the children."

We sat in silence after that, staring at the test pattern.

Then things started to happen.

I heard the sound of a car on the snowy street. When I peeked out the bay window, a white limo was pulling into our driveway. Francis was at the wheel, with Mr. Bitner beside him. A moment later, I opened the door to Mr. Bitner, and he gave me a hearty, "Good morning, Alice!" (These guys are all good with names.) Then he added, "We're here to pick up Mr. and Mrs. Abel and Father Dunne." He inclined his head toward the couch. "Good morning, Father Dunne!"

Uncle Jim walked out a few seconds later. Mr. Bitner greeted him. "How are you feeling today, Mr. Blanchard?"

Aunt Betty appeared behind him and started to answer, "He's—"

But then she stopped herself. She looked at Uncle Jim. He answered, "Fine. But I'll be letting Betty drive the SUV today. I just hope the roads are clear."

"I hear they are! They've been plowing the 495 continually, and the traffic's moving on the side roads now."

"Good."

"How is TJ, by the way?"

Uncle Jim looked at Aunt Betty. I don't think he knew that TJ had been injured. She replied, "He's fine. He's out skating now, and posing for your photographer!"

"Oh yes. We're real pleased to have him as part of the ad campaign."

"He's pleased, too."

"Good. And let me say that I'm really sorry for his troubles at the school."

It was Aunt Betty's turn to look clueless. "Troubles?"

"Father Dunne told me that those two McCain boys were behind some bullying at the school. I'm really sorry."

Aunt Betty looked at me for confirmation, so I nodded.

"Nobody should have to put up with that. We bear full responsibility for it. As a result, Mr. and Mrs. Blanchard, I'd like to offer you a check for one thousand dollars, as compensation, to cover the emotional stress that you had to endure."

Aunt Betty rocked backward, bumping the kitchen door. "You would?"

"Yes. We appreciate you bearing with us during our soft opening. We hope you will tell your Levittown neighbors that we treated you well here, and that Memory Lane might be the best vacation destination for them."

Uncle Jim cocked one eyebrow. I don't think he had any intention of recommending Memory Lane to anyone, but Aunt Betty answered delightedly, "We certainly will!"

Mr. Bitner pointed toward the driveway. "Okay, folks. You take your time. Francis is ready to drive Mr. and Mrs. Abel and Father Dunne whenever they are ready."

After he exited, Aunt Betty could barely contain her excitement. She led Uncle Jim down the hall, eyeballing him furiously every step of the way. Father Dunne rose and stood by the bay window. He stared out at the snow with his mouth slightly open, as if transfixed by its beauty. Was he thinking about his life? About his death? I didn't dare disturb him.

After a minute, I heard some commotion from the bedroom area. Aunt Betty was moving Grandmom along the hallway, and Uncle Jim was doing the same for Grandpop. I stepped back to let them pass. I asked Aunt Betty quietly, "How are they?"

She smiled sadly. "They just don't know what to do next. So we're going to take them out to the car, and then home, and then maybe straight to the ALF." She looked past my grandparents to Uncle Jim. "We can pack their clothes ourselves, Jim, and maybe get movers to come for the big stuff."

Uncle Jim told me, "This is a medical situation now."

Father Dunne moved away from the bay window to confirm that. "You're right, Jim. They should have supervised care tonight. Alice should stay at your house."

Neither of my grandparents was making eye contact with me, or with anyone else. But they were not looking away, either. My grandfather was pretty much in another world—a world where, from here on out, people would be telling him what to do, and where to do it, and when. My grandmother's face was blank, like a dark TV screen. She stood next to my grandfather, and yet she stood alone—a woman, and her problems, and her decisions.

They shuffled through the living room and started out the front door. Uncle Jim told me, "We'll get them situated in the car. Then we'll head back to our place for a last look around."

I answered as kindly as I could, "Okay. Well, let me know if you need any help." As soon as the door closed behind them, though, I turned to Father Dunne. And I was not feeling kindly. I held out my hands, pleading, "This can't be it, can it? Is this all that happens? Is this how it ends for them?"

He shrugged. "Yes. I suppose so."

That wasn't good enough for me. I asked him, "But is this justice?"

He shook his head. "No. Certainly not. 'Justice delayed is justice denied,' as the saying goes. You can't undo all that's been done in fifty years." He took a last, wistful glance out the window. "But there is still the truth, Alice." He pulled on his big black overcoat. "'Veritas vos liberabit.' The truth shall set you free."

"But what about the Gallahues? What about the McCains? What's going to set them free?"

He exhaled loudly. "I talked to Ellen McCain for a good while after mass yesterday. I asked her if she wanted to reopen the court case. You can do that, you know. I said I'd submit a sworn affidavit to help clear Jack's name. But she said no. She said Jack's name had been cleared, in church, in public. Everyone on both sides of the aisle had heard it." He added softly, "And she said God had heard it." He shrugged and then pointed toward the driveway. "I suppose they're waiting for me outside."

"Are you going home tonight?"

"Yes, I am. Back to the desert." I must have looked perplexed. He explained, "Or at least to the Jersey Pines."

"Oh."

He asked me, "Have you forgiven Donna yet?" When I didn't answer right away, he added, "God has forgiven her. Will you?"

I looked at him curiously. "How do you know that God has forgiven her?"

He shrugged again. I stepped forward and challenged him, "She confessed to you. Didn't she? When she brought me over to New Jersey to get baptized?"

He allowed, "She did go to confession on that trip, as I recall."

"Uh huh. Did you assign her a penance?"

"I did."

"Did she perform it?"

"I don't know." Father Dunne reached out and touched my shoulder. "But I do know this: Donna Abel Lynch spent all of her adult life doing good works—teaching children, setting high standards for them, going above and beyond to help them. I can't think of a better way to spend a life than that." When I didn't answer again, he prodded me, "Can you?"

I admitted, "No."

"So? Will you forgive her?"

I nodded silently for a moment; then I managed to whisper, "Yes."

Father Dunne leaned in and gave me a light hug. He smelled faintly of incense. "Good. You're not a camel. Welcome to the human race."

"Thank you."

"And while you're at it, how about forgiving your father?"

"Why? What did he do?"

"He died on you."

"That wasn't his fault."

"No, but still, it hurt you. It made your life harder."

"Yes. Okay. I forgive him, too."

"Good. Great." He winked at me. "Now you can start to work on the Blanchards." I smiled as he buttoned up his big coat. He said, "I'll see you at Thanksgiving."

"Yes." I blurted out, "I'll bring the Cool Whip." He smiled back, so I added, "And we'll watch *The Nutcracker on Ice*." He laughed aloud at that. I told him, "Peace be with you, Father. Pax vobiscum."

He used his right hand to trace the shape of a cross in the air. "Pax vobiscum."

I stayed in the house alone for about twenty minutes puttering around, thinking about what to do next. I spotted a card from the Sorry game under the couch. A crew would be in to clean up at two o'clock, but I felt compelled to pull out the box and put it back inside. After the game, you have to pick up the pieces.

I pulled my wet snow gear on and went outside. I crossed the yard and continued around the Blanchards' house to their side door. As I peered inside, I saw Aunt Betty. She was seated at the Formica table with a totally blank expression on her face, like a mannequin in a 1950s kitchen.

I stamped my boots on the stoop, clearing off wet chunks of snow. When I opened the door, Aunt Betty turned to me slowly, and I got right to the point. "Father Dunne told me he spoke to Ellen Gallahue McCain at the church. He offered to write a letter to a judge telling everything he knows about Grandpop and the hit-and-run killing. We need to offer to do that, too. You need to offer for yourself; I need to offer for my mom." I added, "It's part of her penance."

Aunt Betty answered like a child, a clueless child. "We do?"

"Yes. So get your coat. We need to catch Ellen Gallahue McCain before she leaves the house."

Aunt Betty stood up obediently, but she still sounded confused. "What are we going to do?"

"Father Dunne has spoken to Mrs. McCain for *his* generation, for the old people. We need to speak to her for your generation, for you and Mom."

"Speak to her?"

"Yes! Aren't you listening?"

"Speak to who?"

"To Jack Gallahue's wife! We owe her that!"

"We do?"

I pressed my palms together, like I was going to pray. I said, "God grant me the courage to change the things I can. Remember that?"

Aunt Betty nodded. Then she slipped into a pair of boots and pulled her Sears All-Weather off the hook. She didn't say anything else as we plunged into the cold, taking the driveway–sidewalk route to the McCains' house.

I pounded on the door with my gloved hand, checking Aunt Betty out of the corner of my eye. It seemed like she could go either way: Either she would handle this well, or she'd break down completely.

The Captain again shouted through the door, like a big, scary dog. "Who's there?"

Aunt Betty took a half step back, ready to run, but I leaned my face closer to the door. "It's Alice Lynch again. I want to speak to Mrs. Ellen McCain."

This time, there was no argument, and no delay. Mrs. McCain appeared in the doorway and opened it wide. I reminded her, "I'm Alice Lynch, ma'am, Donna Abel's daughter." She nodded slightly in recognition. "And this is my aunt, Betty Blanchard. She's the former Betty Abel."

Aunt Betty received the same short nod. I gave Aunt Betty

a few seconds to speak for herself. When she did not, I started. "Mrs. McCain, Father Dunne told me that he offered to write a letter to the court, or to a judge, explaining what really happened in the hit-and-run death of Timothy Strop."

The old muscles in her face and neck stiffened. I turned and looked at Aunt Betty. She held up her right hand, as if asking permission; then she spoke. "Mrs. McCain, I knew the truth about what happened to that boy. I knew it that night. And I've known it for all these years."

I blurted out, "And so did my mother."

Aunt Betty continued. "Yes. Donna knew, too. We both knew that our father had hit that boy with his car, and left him for dead. We knew it wasn't a stranger named Jack Gallahue." Aunt Betty clenched both gloved fists. "Still, somehow, we let that stranger get sent to prison for the crime. We let that happen. We never spoke up."

Aunt Betty's voice grew louder. "We continued to go to St. Bernard's every Sunday, and to sit in the front pew, and to act like we knew nothing. We went to confession every Saturday, too, and never mentioned it. So, Mrs. McCain, I want you to know that I will write a letter, too, to a judge or to the police, or to the news, whatever you want. And in that letter, I will tell the truth, finally, about that crime."

I added, "And I'll write a letter, in my mother's name. She was just as guilty."

Aunt Betty added, "I'll stand on Jerusalem Avenue with a

sign, if you'll let me. I really will. I'll do whatever it takes to get the true story told."

Aunt Betty stopped and waited. Mrs. McCain had shown no emotion during all of this, and she showed none now. But she did reply, "The true story is out there. John Abel finally told it, out loud, in church, in public." She added, though, "But the false story has spread so far, and so wide, and for so long, that there's no undoing it. It's way too late for that. It can't be taken back."

Mrs. McCain looked into her living room. "Our family has no wish to see John Abel arrested. He doesn't even know where he is half the time. Does he? What good would it do to put him in a witness stand in court? Or to put him in a jail cell? None."

She took a step back like she was going to leave, but then she stopped. She looked at Aunt Betty, "For what it's worth, I forgive you. You were just children, after all." Then Mrs. McCain closed the door.

Aunt Betty and I stood still, taking in deep breaths of cold air. Finally, she looked at me with shining eyes. "Was that it? Did we do it right? Did we say the right things?"

I assured her. "Yes, I think we did."

"Good."

"How do you feel about it?"

"I feel better. I feel like I need to get to confession, though, at St. Bernard's, to *really* confess this."

I shrugged, "I'd say you just did that, but do what you have to do." I crooked my arm inside her elbow. "Come on, I'll walk you back."

Aunt Betty took my arm gratefully and we started up the path. After a moment, she asked, "Are you all ready to check out?"

"Yes. There's nothing left to do at my house. How about you?"

"I still have some clothes to pick up. From the boys. You know how that goes."

"No. Not really."

"No? Well, you will. We'll try to keep the mess away from your room."

We walked quietly down the sidewalk and back up to her door where she told me, "Thank you, Alice. You knew just what to do. Like Donna." She admitted, "I don't always know what to do."

We stood in silence for a few seconds. Then I just came out with, "For what it's worth, *I* forgive you, too, Aunt Betty."

She blinked rapidly, "You do?"

"Yes. I do. And I forgive my mom. I forgive Donna."

"Good. Good." Tears welled up in her eyes. Aunt Betty covered her mouth with a gloved hand and slipped inside.

I turned around and glanced both ways down the street. I saw some crewmembers working their way up the sidewalk with bags of rock salt. Then I saw Ray open his front door and walk out, followed by his dad wheeling the Western Flyer. His dad was dressed in dark blue thermal sweatpants and top, with a black bicycle helmet. (Anomaly?) I shoved my hands into my pockets and crossed over to join them.

When he saw me, Mr. Hoffman said, "Hello, Alice." (I was surprised he knew my name.) He asked, "How's your uncle?"

"He's doing better. Thanks."

"Good." He looked at the house next door and asked, "Did you hear what happened to Mr. Hardy?"

"I heard that an ambulance took him away."

"Yeah. You could say that." He and Ray exchanged a knowing look.

"What?" I asked, "What happened?"

Mr. Hoffman hunched up his shoulders. "They took him away because was dead."

"What?"

"Dead of a heart attack in his sleep. Dead when they took him away. Dead on arrival at the hospital."

"Poor Mr. Hardy! That's so sad."

He answered, "This is a sad day. This is the day that the nation buried President John F. Kennedy. It was also John Kennedy, Junior's, third birthday."

Ray looked at me intensely. He shifted from foot to foot, like he was about to plunge into something. And he was. He told his father, "You know, Dad, I've been thinking."

"Yeah? About what?"

"About something serious."

Mr. Hoffman steadied the bike in front of him. "Okay."

"I think that I probably know all I need to know about the assassination of President John F. Kennedy."

His dad's eyes narrowed. He answered tightly, "Oh? Really?"

"Really."

"Okay." He looked up and down the street; then back at Ray. "So, what are you saying? You don't want to be a CT anymore?"

"Right. I don't think I do."

Ray's father gave me a nasty, sideways look, as if to say, *This is your doing, isn't it?* He told Ray. "Okay. That's your choice. It always has been. So, you won't be taking over the family quest after all?"

Ray must have seen that look, too. He replied, very firmly, "It's not really the family quest, Dad. It's your quest. Honestly, the rest of the family isn't all that interested."

Mr. Hoffman didn't like that comment, but he managed to answer evenly, "Okay. If you say so."

We stood around for a few awkward seconds until he pushed off on his bike. Ray watched him go. Then he put his arm around my shoulder and said, "I hear they're skating again at the playground. Want to check it out?"

"I'd love to."

He didn't say anything else about his father, so neither did I. We set off walking. Before we had gone five feet, though, I dragged us to a stop. I had seen something off to the side, and it gave me another idea. I told Ray, "Wait here a minute. This is important. I have something really important to do." I slipped from under his arm and hurried back to the Blanchards' as fast as I could.

Ray called after me, "Be careful!"

I banged on the front door, and Patrick answered it. His eyes widened. "What? What's wrong?"

"Look behind me, Patrick. What do you see?"

Patrick's red face squinted. "Ray Hoffman?"

"No. Look to the left."

The Clarks had emerged from their house, wearing full snow-day regalia. As Patrick and I watched, Mr. Clark plunged his gloved hands down and rolled up a long, fat cylinder of snow. I said, "What's it look like they're doing?"

Patrick squinted harder. He answered, "Making a snow man?"

"That's right. And I'll bet they could use some help."

He stared across the street wistfully. Then he shook his head. "No. No, I can't just walk over there for no reason. It's not like the prayer circle. I was invited to that."

"Don't you like her?"

He admitted, "Yeah. I do."

"Does she know that?" He shrugged. "Have you told her that?"

His mouth drooped, and he told me, "I'm just no good at this stuff, Alice. I'm not what girls want."

I agreed with him. "Maybe not." He winced. "But you could *become* what girls want. Here's your new list, Patrick: You're thoughtful, and you're serious, and you're brave! You could become what that girl over there wants."

We both watched Rosemary laughing and playing with her family. Her cheeks glowed; her eyes sparkled. She really did look lovely. I told him, "Do it now, Patrick! You're a hero now. You're the guy who took on Matt McCain to defend Rosemary's honor."

He shook his head. "Not really. It was to defend my honor. And then TJ's. Rosemary was, maybe, third."

"Still, you did it! You showed real courage." I clapped him on his meaty shoulder. "Show that same courage now. Walk over there and help her make that goddamn snowman."

Patrick gulped. I knew I had him. I turned and hurried back over to Ray. I replaced his arm on my shoulder.

"What was that about?" he asked.

"Just watch."

Patrick burst through the front door with his Reversible Three-Season Coat still undone, tugging on his Leather Palm Gloves. He lumbered across the street steadily, in an unwavering line, like a man on a mission. The Clarks all stopped working to watch his advance.

Rosemary stepped forward. She smiled in delight, in excitement, in welcome: "Patrick! Are you coming to help us?"

Patrick smiled back so wide, and with such relief, that I could feel it from where I stood. He shouted, "Yeah!"

Robby jumped up and down. "Yeah! Yeah!"

I turned Ray to the left. "Okay. That's it. Let's go. My work is done."

"Your work? That?"

"Yep."

"Matchmaking?"

"Yep."

Ray shook his head. "No. No way. It'll never last."

"Why not?"

"Because Rosemary will disappear some day. Some day soon. She'll be sucked up into heaven, and Patrick will be alone again."

"Maybe Patrick will go with her."

He gave me an *are-you-kidding?* look, but he didn't say anything else.

When we reached the schoolyard, Ray and I staked out a spot along the green fence to watch. The Nordstroms, and their grandmother, and TJ, and Douglas were all gliding around the rink as Barney the photographer shadowed them. He aimed his

Hasselblad and called out encouragements like, "Big smile, TJ! That's it, girls. You love Memory Lane!"

During a break, TJ called over, "Come out here, you two!"

I answered, "No way! We can't skate!"

Ray added, "And we don't like people who can skate."

I chided him, "I wouldn't go that far."

"Oh no?" Ray pointed at Douglas. He was trying to get one twin to skate on each arm, like they do with TJ, but they weren't having it. "You told me you don't like that guy, and he skates."

I thought about Douglas's phony smiles, and his phony winks, and his expressions of sympathy about my mother. Phony, too?

Ray continued, "What did you ever see in him anyway?"

"Well, he was taller than me."

"I am, too."

"And older."

"Me, too. What else?"

"He has blonde hair."

"Ah. So I should dye my hair blonde?"

I elbowed him in the ribs. "No. Should I dye *my* hair blonde? Do you want me to be the third Nordstrom twin?"

He seemed shocked. "What?"

"What? You've spent half your time here drooling over them."

"I have?"

"Yeah, Mr. Truth, Justice, and the American Way."

"Sorry. You're right, I have. But that wasn't real, either." He pointed at Douglas again. "Just like the altar boy, paperboy, boy-next-door isn't real."

Douglas heard him, apparently, and skated over. He wasn't smiling. He asked Ray, "What did you say?"

"I said you were an altar boy, a paperboy, and the boy next door, and that none of them were real. Is there a problem?"

Douglas managed a tight smile. "No. No problem. I just didn't hear you."

I asked him, "Do you have another group coming in today? After we leave?"

Douglas stood still on his skates, shifting back and forth. "Yeah. There's a big group coming in, but I won't be their guide."

"No? What will you be doing?"

"I'll be doing field marketing again."

Ray interrupted. "You mean, riding a bike and tossing out fliers?"

Douglas didn't look at either of us when he replied, "Yeah. Something like that."

Ray persisted, "They don't even let you wear a helmet, do they?" Douglas was clearly tired of being nice to Ray, but Ray was relentless. "That's because helmets won't be worn until the 1980s." (It was an anomaly!) "Until then, I guess, paperboys just have to take their chances."

Douglas turned his back on us and skated away.

At two o'clock (check-out time), we all returned to the Town Hall. The scene inside was like before, but with one conspicuous difference—Teresa Zorn was missing. Instead, Mr. Bitner was greeting people and directing them to their changing rooms.

I mentioned this to Ray. "Look. No Miss Zorn."

"Right. I'll bet he fired her."

That seemed extreme to me. "Fired her! Why?"

"Why? The week was a disaster. Mr. Hardy actually died!"

I repeated, "Poor Mr. Hardy."

"And they took your uncle away in an ambulance, after sending him God-knows-how-many cases of beer. Then Matt McCain got his face re-arranged, perhaps permanently. And TJ got injured. He should have had medical attention, too. It was like vacationing in a war zone." Ray nodded toward Mr. Bitner. "That guy's looking at some serious medical bills; maybe even some lawsuits."

"But would he fire Teresa for one bad week? After she's been with the company for five years?"

"I don't know. Maybe he just busted her back to roller-skating waitress, or whatever she was."

"Yeah. That was it. In Effingham, Illinois." I saw my name pop up in blue lights over a door; then Ray's popped up, too. Mr. Bitner was walking past all the doors, using that clicker thing to unlock them.

I said, "I'll see you back in 2007," as we split up and headed toward our changing rooms.

I pulled the brass knob toward me and stepped inside. Everything was as I had left it—untouched, undisturbed—like I had traveled back in time, and I was returning at the exact moment I'd left. I quickly changed out of all my 1957 duds and re-dressed in my modern clothes. It felt weird to pick up my cell phone, still charged, and slip it into my pocket (next to Blue Belle).

When I opened the door again, everybody looked different. I suppose I did, too. The twins looked fabulous in their designer jeans. Ray looked much less nerdy in a pair of Levis, basketball shoes, and a Hofstra sweatshirt. Patrick and TJ had reverted to their old looks (but, I hoped, not to their old attitudes).

I saw Captain McCain and his weasel son off to my right. None of the McCain women were around, though, just the two men staring impatiently at the 'Dennis McCain' door.

Robby Clark emerged, without Rosemary. He had changed back into his *Armageddon Karate* gi. His eyes seemed to scan the waiting area with a burning purpose. I soon found out why. When Dennis McCain's door opened, Robby started toward him like an avenging angel. The older McCains didn't see him coming, but Dennis did. His eyes shifted around, looking for a way to escape. Dennis held up both hands and started backpedaling, like the coward he was, as Robby quickly closed the distance between them.

In a blindingly fast move, Robby grabbed Dennis's right wrist and turned it up and out, in a way that a wrist cannot be turned. Dennis's whole body locked up and twisted. He dropped to one knee, with his head sticking out sideways, and his imprisoned wrist straight up in the air. Still holding the wrist in one hand, Robby switched his legs into a karate stance. The older McCains finally reacted; the Captain shouted out something incoherent, as usual.

I moved over to a spot directly behind Dennis, where Robby could see me. He looked up briefly and then back down. Dennis's nose was there before him, like a wooden board waiting to be shattered. Both the Captain and his son were now yelling for help. But, as it turned out, they didn't need to. Robby suddenly released Dennis's wrist, executed a swift turn, and walked away. Dennis's body fell to the floor like a discarded overcoat. He immediately started to yell and cry and kick his legs so that he twirled around in a circle.

Mr. and Mrs. Clark and Rosemary came out of their changing rooms dressed in their *R4R* shirts. Patrick joined them immediately. Mr. Clark dropped to one knee, and they all gathered around him. Rosemary took Patrick's right hand, and Robby his left, as they started to pray.

A minute later, the three remaining McCains approached the group. The Captain and the weasel had Dennis propped up between them. Dennis's face was all contorted, like he was in great pain. What a wuss. The weasel stopped just outside the prayer circle and pointed a finger at Mr. Clark, but Mr. Clark was praying too intensely to even notice. Undeterred, the weasel started his usual routine. "You're gonna answer to us for—"

I stepped in front of the group, cutting him off. "Be quiet! Can't you see they're praying?"

The weasel let go of Dennis, who slumped toward his grandfather. "That's good. They're gonna need to pray. We're gonna sue them for assault on the nephew of a—"

I said, "Assault on a high school kid by a third grader? A third grader who, by the way, could have totally kicked his ass? Is that what you're going to sue them for?"

Spit was starting to ooze out of the corners of his mouth as I passed on one last piece of advice. "You need to take responsibility for your life, McCain! That's what my mother always told me. *You* are responsible for you."

By this time, the Captain had heard enough. He slouched off toward the exit with Dennis's sniveling face buried in his side. With a final gnashing of his teeth, the weasel took off after them.

Ray chose that moment to walk over, bend forward slightly, and kiss me on the lips. It was a short kiss, but a real one. Right there, in front of everybody. He said, "Way to go."

I thought, *Wow*. I whispered, "Thanks."

He reached into a pocket. "Tell me, Alice Lynch, what is your phone number?" I told him, and he entered it into his phone. He said, "I'll call you tonight. Okay?"

"Okay."

"I'm sorry to rush off now, but my dad's pissed off." I followed Ray's eyes and saw his father standing by his changing room door. He was haranguing Mr. Bitner—shaking his head, turning red, pointing.

"I'm thinking . . . your dad is usually pissed off, Ray."

"Yeah. True."

"You don't want to end up like that, do you?"

"No."

"Good. You are responsible for you."

"Yeah. So I've heard."

Mr. Bitner was trying very hard to placate Mr. Hoffman, but it wasn't working. I asked Ray, "What did your father get out of all this?"

"Not much. He got a new topic for his CT blog. I guess he'll post a review of his trip." Mr. Bitner held out his hand to shake, but Mr. Hoffman dissed him and stalked angrily away. "His bad trip. Who knows? Maybe he'll post that his son has given up the CT cause."

"Good again."

Ray gave me one last hug and an awkward kiss on my ear. Then he took off, half running, and caught up with his father at the exit.

I walked back over to Patrick and Rosemary. The prayer circle was over. TJ and the twins had now joined them. TJ pursed his lips and cooed softly, "Ooh, Miss Alice! Kissy-facing in public! Divulging her private phone number!"

Patrick held up a hand to preempt me. Then he explained to his brother, very maturely, "TJ, we're not doing that to each other anymore. That was the old way. Now we're treating each other as we would like to be treated."

TJ protested, "I was just kidding."

"It's called the golden rule."

"Yes, yes, okay," TJ sighed. "I've heard of it."

The twins leaned over and gave me another one of those double-cheek kisses. This time, I smelled Coco Mademoiselle. I reminded them, "We really hope you'll come and see us. We can all watch the next Olympics together. Your grandmom, too."

Petra replied, "Yes! That's a date. And Tommy will be working on this shoot, and on other shoots, so I know we'll get together."

TJ smiled slyly. "I am so looking forward to earning more money than my parents."

Pia interrupted, like it was unfinished business, "Wait! We have to decide on your name for the contract. Will it be TJ or Tommy?"

Petra told him, with authority, "It has to be Tommy—Tommy Bahama, Tommy Hilfiger, Tommy Blanchard." She looked at us and added, "Professionally anyway. He can still be TJ to friends and family."

TJ nodded thoughtfully. "Okay. I'll give it a try."

Mrs. Nordstrom came out of her changing room, still smiling. The girls started to walk back to her. But suddenly, Petra turned and held out her hands, like a photographer lining up a shot. She moved them inward to include both of the boys. She said, "Tommy and Patrick—" She stopped, scrunched up her face, and added, "Or are you Patrick and Tommy? I can never tell you two apart."

Patrick's jaw opened in astonishment. Then he got the joke, sputtered, and burst out laughing.

I heard Uncle Jim's voice behind us. He and Aunt Betty were just now exiting their changing rooms. He said, "Sorry we're late. We had to walk up here. We couldn't find the keys to the Fairlane."

Aunt Betty added, "We've been wandering around all this time looking for them, like Grandmom and Grandpop."

That gave me a sudden chill. At that moment, I could have told them about my grandfather, and the car engine, and the exhaust fumes. Perhaps I should have, but I didn't. I didn't see the point. Grandpop was over the edge now, in full dementia, or whatever they would call it at the Assisted Living Facility. I decided to let it go.

Barney popped up next to us holding a digital camera and a notebook-thin printer. "Can you line up like you did on the day you arrived? Here, I have the photo if you want to see it." He held out the black-and-white print of us taken last week. It seemed like a year ago.

We all did our best to replicate that pose, minus my grandparents. Barney clicked off three rapid shots. He turned the back of the camera to Aunt Betty and said, "Pick one, Mrs. Blanchard." Aunt Betty surprised us all by pointing to one right away, with no agonizing.

Barney pressed a button on the printer and a photo slid out. He placed it into a souvenir picture frame and handed it to Aunt Betty. We all crowded around her to see: The outside of the frame had the words *Memory Lane—Golden Memories* and a montage of images—the Town Hall, the shops, the school. The inside had the *before* and *after* photos of our family.

Grandmom and Grandpop had disappeared somewhere between the two photos. Into the past. Into the twilight zone. I concentrated on the *after* side, thinking, *Okay. Here we go. This is my new family.*

I looked for little details in the photo: Patrick had his hand cupped around a bible that Rosemary had just given him. TJ held a brochure from a modeling agency tight against his chest.

Aunt Betty, although smiling like a maniac in the *before* photo, looked very calm in the *after*. Uncle Jim stood forlornly in the middle, as if we had circled the wagons around him, and I guess we had. That's what you do when you're a family—you form a protective circle around someone, no matter what he has done.

And me in the *after* photo? My hair now looked too long for my face, and for my age. And—I had to admit—braids required too much work. I decided it was time to let it all go; to have it cut off; to donate it to kids with cancer.

That's what Mom would want me to do.

Mr. Bitner stepped forward. He swept his clicker in a dramatic arc, locking all the changing room doors and turning off their light fixtures. Then he indicated to everyone that they should gather around him in the center of the hall.

Only about half of our original group remained. Still, Mr. Bitner had not become the manager of the most successful vacation destination in the Midwest by looking at the down side of things. He smiled brightly as he arranged us into a semicircle.

TJ eased in beside me. He showed me the title of his agency brochure, 'STARZ Modeling.' I smiled my approval.

Mr. Bitner announced, "There is one last thing to do. We have a tradition here at Memory Lane."

TJ whispered to me, "A tradition that goes back almost a full week."

"As you know, Memory Lane is all about creating an authentic environment. We help you relive a wonderful time in the past."

TJ whispered, "Like the JFK Assassination."

I slapped at his arm. "Stop that!"

Mr. Bitner held up his clicker. "Before you leave us, I am going to ask you to think about all the memories that came back to you while you were here." He paused. "Then I am going to ask you to pick one of them—just one, the best one, as your golden memory."

I stole a glance at Patrick. What was he thinking about? Was his golden memory the one that I just gave him? Crossing the street, smiling a mile wide, into the arms of Rosemary?

And TJ? Was his golden memory from today as well? Gliding on the ice between the Nordstrom girls as the photographer snapped their perfect smiles? I'll bet it was.

But mine wasn't from today, or yesterday, although the kiss with Ray was really nice. Mine went way back. And I didn't need some theme park to provide it to me.

Mr. Bitner pressed the clicker ceremonially. Suddenly, the room went dark. Then golden light poured out from the fixtures above the changing rooms, casting a warm glow over everyone.

He said, "Memories are precious to us because they gleam, like bars of gold. I ask you now to close your eyes. Let the one memory that you selected gleam inside your mind right now, like a bright bar of gold. Everybody do that with me. Right here. Right now."

So we did.

So I did.

Like everyone else there, I closed my eyes, in that cavernous hall, in that golden glow. And I beheld this scene, in fine detail, with crystal clarity:

A chocolate birthday cake with yellow candles.

A plastic light switch in the candles' glow.

My father and mother standing there smiling in delight at me, just because I am me.

A golden moment. The three of us starring in a scene that will never end as long as I am alive. We will always be together in that kitchen, singing that song, eating that cake—a moment so real that it brings tears to my eyes every time I replay it.

That perfect little family, my first circle, will be there whenever I want to step into it, and that's a great comfort to me.

But now it's time to take another step. It's time to join the people in my second circle. And my third. And I mean *really* join them.

Really forgive them. Really accept them.

And maybe, really love them.

Here we go.

—Alice